The
Baobab Beach
Retreat

by

KATE FROST

LEMON TREE PRESS

Paperback Edition 2018

ISBN 978-0-9954780-8-4

Cover design by Jessica Bell.

The

Baobab Beach Retreat

by

KATE FROST

LEMON
TREE
PRESS

Praise for *The Baobab Beach Retreat*

"I enjoyed this book for all kinds of reasons and it is just as good as other romance novels I have read that grace the booksellers' tables." TripFicton.

"This is a truly beautiful story, expertly crafted and written. There's plenty of action and twists, especially when Connie discovers a dark, family secret. The romance is there in abundance and there's plenty of 'will they, won't they' moments to keep the reader guessing... An absolute must read." AnnMarie Wyncoll, author of *When Foundations Crumble*.

"This book has everything good in women's fiction. It deals with serious issues, family drama, adventure and romance." Elizabeth, Chick Lit Chickadees.

"I would recommend this novel to anyone who enjoys a complex, compelling book that is a romance, but so much more – a tale about the frailty of human nature, how we can all make mistakes but learn from them as Connie does." Elaine Jeremiah, author of *Love Without Time*.

"This is an intelligent, enjoyable and uplifting story told in steady, thoughtful detail, both regarding Connie's inner struggle and the daily life in the luxury beach resort around her." Debbie Young, author of *Sophie Sayers Village Mysteries*.

"I love Kate Frost's voice, she is a wonderful storyteller... A lovely read!" Tracey Rogers, author.

For Nik
This one's just for you

Chapter One

The heat of late morning dissipated the moment Connie walked into the light and airy entrance hall of Bella's hotel, The House of Stone. Ceiling fans whirred, stirring the air just enough for it to feel pleasant inside. The place hadn't changed in the sixteen years since she'd last been there, except many of the faces of the staff were different and *she'd* changed – that was the biggest difference. The last time she'd been to Tanzania and Zanzibar she was a carefree twenty-one year-old. She'd just finished her fine art degree and was eager to spend her second summer away from the UK with her aunt, travelling between the hotel in Stone Town and Bella's beach retreat on the Tanzanian coast. How things had changed over the years. Was it wasted time? Bella had offered her a job at the end of her final summer and despite being tempted, Connie had eventually said no, opting instead for the excitement of a shared flat in London with friends from university and a career in art. Fast forward sixteen years and she wondered if she'd made the wrong choice. Yes, she had her career as a jewellery designer but she was also childless, divorcing and unhappy. If she'd stayed in Tanzania the chances were she'd never have met Felix. That in itself would have saved her a whole lot of heartache.

Connie headed up the stairs to the top of the hotel and its rooftop terrace. It was one of the best spots in Stone Town and a tourist magnet, always busy, always buzzing whatever time of day. She was lucky there was a free table on the edge of the terrace. She ordered a coconut water and sat down in

1

the wicker chair and looked out over the jumbled rooftops, across to the blue expanse of the Indian Ocean. She'd never tire of this view, so exotic and full of life. The noise of the town drifted up: the tinkle of bicycle bells, shouts from the street below, the revving of a motorbike, but that was part of Stone Town's charm. She'd spent the morning exploring Darajani Market, with its mountains of colourful spices, before heading back into the old town, losing herself in a warren of lanes lined with whitewashed buildings now stained grey with dirt, and grand mansions with gaping cracks snaking down their sides, large flaps of paint curling away. But the roof terrace was high enough to feel disconnected from the humidity, the noise and the intoxicating smells of petrol fumes, salt-air, decay and spicy street food. Early morning was particularly magical before the sun had risen and the bells called people to prayer.

A hand on her shoulder jolted Connie from her thoughts.

'Asante said he'd seen you head up here.' Bella pulled up a chair and sat down next to Connie. 'Sorry I've been so busy and haven't had time to talk to you properly.' She leant back in her chair and grinned. 'It's so good to have you here.'

'It's good to be here. I'm just sorry I left it so long and it had to be under these circumstances that I've come back.'

Bella ran her hand through her short grey hair. 'That unfortunately is life – don't go beating yourself up about something you can't change and was out of your control to begin with.'

'I was just thinking what direction my life would have taken if I'd stayed here when you offered me that job. Do you remember?'

Bella nodded. 'It was asking a lot to tear you away from your friends and the possibilities you had in the UK. I didn't want to lose you. Selfish, I know. That and you'd have made a wonderful addition to the team here.'

Connie took a sip of her coconut water and was transported back to her twenty-one year-old self having a late night drink with the younger staff members once they'd finished work. A couple of them still worked here, also in their late thirties now with families to support and a good job in one of the best hotels in the city. Some of the others had moved on, to where she didn't know, but she felt like the last sixteen years of her life had been erased and nothing had really changed for her apart from being older and disappointed by life.

Connie placed her drink on the table and turned to Bella. 'It would have been my due date today.'

'Oh Connie.' Bella reached for Connie's hand and squeezed it. 'I don't know what to say, except I don't think there is anything to say. It's beyond awful.'

'It is what it is. I can't change it but at least I have the chance to try and put it behind me now. This day has been on my mind ever since the seven week scan. After the miscarriage, a week didn't go by when I didn't think about how many weeks pregnant I should have been. But it wasn't meant to be.'

'No, it wasn't, but that doesn't change the feeling of loss, does it?'

Connie shook her head and gazed out towards the sea glinting in the distance. The whitewashed buildings gleamed in the sunshine and she loved the different shaped rooftops spreading in every direction.

'It's a grieving process you're going through,' Bella said. 'And that takes time, whether it's a marriage breakdown or a loss of a baby, or for you, both. You'll come out the other side but that might not be anytime soon. Being here will help though, I can promise you that.'

'I know it will.' Connie smiled. 'I have the next few months stretching ahead knowing I don't have to go back to my old life. I spent eight years being Mrs Connie Vaughn; I need to rediscover Connie Stone.'

Bella leant towards her, cupped her face and kissed her forehead. 'I'm just thankful you're here and I can look after you. Ever since you arrived I've been pinching myself that you're not a figment of my imagination. By the way, it's only a short stop in Stone Town as we're going to Mchanga in the morning.'

'It really will feel like going back in time being back there.'

'There is no better therapy than time spent at Mchanga na Mawe. Or a lifetime in my case. At least the whole of my adult life.' She stood up. 'I have lots to do before leaving tomorrow, so I'll see you at dinner.' She smoothed down the creases in her knee-length cream linen skirt and retraced her steps past the tables and sofas of the rooftop bar, stopping to shake hands or briefly chat with a guest.

Therapy was exactly what Connie needed but not the kind of talking therapy she was offered when she was discharged from hospital earlier in the year. She played with the large silver bangles on her wrist. Her scar had begun to heal, turning from an angry red to a healthier pink, but it was a daily reminder about everything she'd lost and how close she'd come to destroying her own life. She craved the freedom to be herself and rediscover who she was sixteen years ago.

The sun was high in the clear blue sky and beat down on the canopy that covered the rooftop bar. There was little breeze and the heat from the streets seemed to permeate upwards hugging Connie tight. She downed the remainder of her juice and headed back downstairs for a siesta in her room at the front of the hotel.

The jeep bounced along the dirt road leaving behind Dar es Salaam and heading south along the coast. Connie couldn't see the ocean, but through the open window she glimpsed trees and the occasional makeshift home at the side of the road with chickens scrabbling in the dirt, children playing and men sitting in the shade. Even those thinned out the further they went until they passed only an occasional shack selling fruit, vegetables and bottles of Coke.

Bella was in the front talking to the driver, Mohammed, in Swahili. They'd left The House of Stone early that morning and had taken the ferry across to Dar es Salaam where Mohammed had met them. After a good start on dual carriageway through the outskirts of the city, they'd come to a halt waiting for the car ferry to take them across to Kigamboni and the road that eventually led to Mchanga na

Mawe. Without the breeze through the open windows Connie had sweltered in the back. The wait to board the ferry, while watching two boatloads of people disembark, had transported her back to the first time she'd done the journey to Bella's beach retreat. A young man with a bag of pineapples slung over his shoulder smiled at her as he passed, followed by women carrying buckets of fish. An older man with greying hair, skinny legs but strong muscular shoulders pushed a wheelbarrow with two swordfish.

Connie rested her head back and gazed out at the landscape whizzing past as the breeze buffeted her face. Would she have had a tiny newborn by now? Maybe if the baby had arrived on or before her due date. She forced the image of a wrinkled pink-faced newborn from her head. She couldn't keep enduring these thoughts – thinking she would have been twenty, thirty or forty weeks pregnant was one thing, thinking she should have a day-old baby was quite another. When would it end? Would she forever be thinking she should have a ten-month-old? A toddler? An eight-year-old? A teenager?

The jolting up and down of the jeep on the pot-holed road snapped her from her thoughts, and the promise of what was waiting at the end of their journey kept her mind focused on the present rather than the past. She had to keep reminding herself that this was the reason she was here, to move forward and not step back into the car crash that was her life back home.

Mchanga na Mawe was exactly as she remembered it. Screened by trees, the welcome building was open on two sides to make the most of the breeze coming off the ocean. Connie's first impression sixteen years earlier had been of understated beauty, the reception built from local stone and wood with the glimpse of blue ocean through the trees that surrounded it. She loved the fact that Mchanga's charms were hidden and each step that new guests took revealed a little more of the rustic, open-air luxury that Bella had created over the years.

A tall and handsomely rugged man, in his late thirties with dark hair, tanned skin and a beard, jogged down the steps from the building to greet them.

'Welcome home, Bella,' he said with a hint of an Australian accent.

Her aunt grasped his hands. 'I trust you've taken good care of the place while I've been away?'

'You know I have.'

Bella released his hands and stepped back. She took hold of Connie's elbow and manoeuvred her forward. 'This is my niece, Connie. Connie, this is my wonderful new manager, Theo.'

Connie met his blue eyes as he shook her hand. His hand was rough and dry, unlike her hot sticky one.

He smiled. 'It's good to meet you.'

'You too.'

He released her hand and she wiped it down the side of her olive green maxi skirt, immediately wishing she hadn't and that he'd think she was wiping her hand because it was his that was sweaty. She took a deep breath; she needed to relax.

A slim local woman in staff uniform offered Connie a cold towel. She wiped away the sweat and grime of travel from her face and hands before following Bella and Theo through the main entrance building and back outside. The path curved through the trees and then opened out at the bar and restaurant. The bar was shaded by a large thatched roof with a decked area dotted with tables. Wooden rails surrounded the edge of the bar and looked out over powdery white sand. Two couples, both in their forties, were sat on the low sofas beneath the covered part of the bar and Connie could only see one other person sauntering along the beach. This was the appeal of Mchanga, the absolute peace. Even in peak season when every villa was occupied, the place managed to retain its feel of exclusivity and remoteness from the rest of the world.

Theo led them to a table on the deck that jutted over the beach below, where waves foamed on to the sand.

'What can I get you to drink, Connie?' he asked, pulling

out a chair for Bella.

Connie sat opposite, in the wicker chair that faced down the beach. 'Whatever Bella's having, please.'

'My usual,' Bella said.

'I won't be long.' He sauntered over to the bar, his shoulders broad beneath his white linen shirt, his legs muscular in shorts.

Bella reached across the table and took Connie's hands in hers. Bella's nails were short and neat, her fingers loaded with chunky silver rings, the majority made by Connie. Her skin was tanned and her face make-up free. She was ageing gracefully and looked wonderful on forty-plus years of fresh air, sunshine and the laid back Tanzanian lifestyle. 'I can't tell you how much I've longed to see you back here. This place is home for me and I've missed you every day.'

'Oh Bella, don't set me off.' Connie wiped away a tear.

'I know, I'm sorry, I'm getting sentimental in my old age.'

'I'm glad you're cutting back on the workload and have finally let someone else take over.'

'Theo's fabulous and could run this place with his eyes closed if he wanted to. He's not afraid of hard work, which is just as well when he works from six in the morning until the last guest goes to bed for weeks at a time. He's been travelling most of his adult life and was running a safari camp in Kenya.'

'Why did he leave Kenya?'

Bella swept her grey fringe back off her forehead. 'Relationship problems. I won't go into it but let's just say his loss was my gain.'

Bella had always been forthright and Connie was pleased to see that the years hadn't mellowed her in that respect.

Theo returned with a pitcher topped with pineapple, cherries and fresh coconut slices and placed three glasses on the table.

'My homecoming drink,' Bella said, pouring the thick creamy liquid into the glasses.

'Cheers.' Theo picked up a glass and handed Connie one. They clinked glasses.

Connie took a sip and relaxed back into her chair as the

smooth coconut drink slid down her throat.

'The hilltop villas are all booked out so I hope you don't mind having one of the beachside ones.'

It took Connie a moment to realise Theo was talking to her. 'I'm not staying with you, Bella?'

'We're doing maintenance work on one of the beach villas, so as it's not currently booked I thought you deserved a lovely place to stay. Theo has my old cottage as I've built myself a new place but I only have one bedroom. I'll show you it this evening once you've had a chance to settle in.'

The beach villa was as lovely as Connie remembered. It combined the comfort of a villa with the rustic nature of a beach hut, being open at the front with a thatched roof and a large deck complete with hammocks, daybeds, and a plunge pool, leading directly on to the beach. And those ocean views. Connie left her rucksack on the floor, kicked off her canvas shoes and scrambled on to the double bed and sat cross-legged in the middle, looking out at the waves curling on to the pale sand.

It was far removed from everything back home and such a positive place with happy memories, yet Connie felt so very alone. She played with the frayed edge of her top and wished that Felix was with her. Despite them being married for eight years and together for twelve, she'd never brought him here. Maybe in hindsight that was a good thing, to not have memories of him to taint the place. He would have loved it though: the proximity to the beach; good sized waves for body boarding; miles of untouched sand in both directions; a short walk up the beach to the shipwreck where they could have gone snorkelling together.

She hated him and yet her heart ached for him. He had been the person she would talk to about everything – her best friend as well as her husband.

They would have brought their children here – something that her parents never did with her and her brother. Her father hated heat, humidity and anything the least bit exotic, but most of all he resented Bella. Maybe because she was living a life he never dared live.

Their children would have been able to play in the sand, digging with spades and filling buckets, their bronzed skin protected with factor fifty and a sun hat. They would have loved splashing in the shallows, and Felix would sweep them off their feet and pretend to throw them in the water.

Connie wiped away a tear with the back of her hand and stared past the beach to the horizon. There were hundreds, if not thousands of miles of ocean between her and the next piece of land. A couple, the man in shorts and the woman in a bikini with a sarong tied around her waist, walked along the edge of the ocean. Connie's dream of what could have been faded. The couple, younger than her and perhaps not even in their thirties yet, held hands and laughed together. She missed Felix's touch; she missed the way his stubble would rub her skin when he kissed her; she missed his deep voice and the way certain words sounded with his lilting Welsh accent. She missed him. He had been her soulmate and his betrayal hurt more than anything she'd ever known – apart from losing her babies in early pregnancy.

Unable to stop her tears, she lay back and sobbed into a pillow. A ceiling fan whizzed above, wafting a slight breeze over her. This was Tanzania – a place to be happy, to sleep uncovered, the sound of waves crashing on to the sand, the squawk of a bird overhead, and the smell of the ocean, of hot skin and sunscreen. But for the time being, it was a place to heal.

Chapter Two

'I'm here to help, Bella,' Connie said, joining her aunt on the restaurant deck where she'd enjoyed the welcome drink only a few hours earlier, the tables now candlelit and filled with couples eating.

'Of course,' Bella said, hooking her arm in Connie's. 'There's plenty to do but I want you to have time to relax, recharge and get over that good-for-nothing husband of yours while you're here.'

Even the mention of Felix sent a shiver through her but she tried to shrug off the feeling of panic tightening across her chest. After a good cry, a sleep and a shower, Connie felt refreshed in harem-style trousers and a vest top, her long chocolate-brown hair falling in waves around her shoulders. A dark and cooling breeze swept in from the ocean. She was a world away from home and she was determined to leave her worries behind her, far away in the UK with her 'good-for-nothing' ex.

'Tonight's our barbeque night.' Bella led her to the far side of the deck where half an oil drum had been turned into a grill. Behind it, one of the chefs was flipping marinated pieces of chicken and sizzling prawns. Spices and smoke filled the air, and next to the barbeque, the sight of salads, grilled sweet potatoes and rice dishes, made her mouth water.

Bella steered her away from the food and, as they passed the bar, Connie caught sight of Theo chatting to guests. With dark blue shorts and a white linen short-sleeved shirt that accentuated his tan, he looked relaxed and at ease. Being a manager of a beach resort like this was a way of life, and a good one, but it wasn't for everyone and Connie wondered about his story.

Almost without exception, everyone who stayed at Mchanga was a couple. It wasn't the type of place people came to on their own – unless of course you were the soon-to-be divorced niece of the owner. Honeymooners and retirees made up the majority of the bookings. It was the kind of place she and Felix would have considered when they planned their honeymoon all those years ago. How easily he hijacked her thoughts. Even on another continent and twelve hours away from him by plane, he was taking over her life.

'Let me introduce you to some people,' Bella said as they reached the comfy seating area of the bar, where a handful of couples were enjoying pre-dinner drinks.

'Bella!' A man in his late sixties with white hair and leathery brown skin waved them over. 'We were just saying how jealous we are of you living out here all year round.'

'It's a nice life.' Bella kissed him on both cheeks and hugged his wife.

'That's the understatement of the year,' the man said and laughed.

'This is my niece, Connie, over from the UK for a few months. Connie, this is David and Hilary, long-standing guests of mine – I think you've been here almost every year since we opened.'

'This is our twenty-second year,' David said. 'Ever since our children left home.'

'Wow,' Connie said, sitting down on the seat Hilary was patting. 'You must really like it.'

'A home from home,' David said. 'But with glorious sunshine, ocean views, fabulous food and a private plunge pool.'

'What's not to like?' Hilary laughed. 'We've heard lots about you, even if we've not had the pleasure of meeting you until now. I'm glad you've got the chance to spend some time with Bella. We've always loved the relaxed pace of life here.' She sipped her cocktail and waved her free hand towards the beach. 'I know there are many beautiful places in the world but this is definitely one of the best. I mean, the view of the ocean, particularly from the hillside suites, is out of this world. Bella's the most gracious host, and like my husband said, the food is sublime – I just love everything about the place. In fact, Bella, I should write the brochure for you.'

Connie relaxed into the evening, a stomach-full of barbeque food and a few cocktails doing their bit to help. She watched David and Hilary, the perfect couple, together for decades, finishing each other's sentences and encouraging each other with a nod, a smile, a hand gently placed on an arm. It was how she'd imagined her and Felix would have been if they'd grown old together.

Connie walked to the edge of the decking and leant on the wooden rail that overlooked the beach down to the dark ocean, where the foaming surf gleamed white in the moonlight. She was still thinking about him. How different would her life have been if she'd never met him? Would she be with someone else? Would she be married? Have kids? Would she have been happy instead of separated, childless and pining over a man who'd broken her heart?

Fingers tapped her shoulder. She swung around and came face to face with Theo, the first couple of buttons of his linen shirt undone, revealing tanned skin.

'Sorry,' he said. 'I didn't mean to make you jump.'

'Oh, that's okay, I was miles away.'

Theo leant on the rail next to her.

'It is the most incredible view,' he said. 'And I've travelled a lot.'

'Where were you before coming here?'

'A safari camp in Kenya.'

'What made you leave?' Connie asked, gesturing towards the ocean. 'A beach retreat is a bit different to the excitement of a safari camp.'

'Let's just say I needed a change.'

Connie didn't question further – she understood that tone of voice; it was one she'd used many times over the past few months. So, Theo had swapped safari and Kenya for Tanzania and the ocean, and she'd replaced Cardiff and a sticky British summer for the heat of Tanzania and the peacefulness of Mchanga.

'You've got a job for me, I presume?' Connie asked, turning away from the darkness and resting her elbows on the rail behind her. 'Bella's insisting I'm here to relax but I plan to be here for a while. I need to do something or else I'll go stir-crazy, even in a place like this.'

'Don't worry, I'll keep you busy. How does Guest Advisor sound?'

'It sounds like you've just made it up.'

Theo laughed. 'Not exactly. Normally a couple would manage a place like this but as it's just me, Bella pitches in and I'm trying to take stuff off her shoulders. Not only does she oversee things in Stone Town, she ends up trying to do everything when she's here too. We're a luxury resort and I want to offer our guests the best of everything – food, accommodation, the location – and personalised itineraries will add to that. If you're up for it, then you'll be employed properly. Paid and everything.'

'Bella knows about this, doesn't she? She's plucked this job out of thin air.'

'We need someone, it's not out of charity if that's what you're worried about.'

'I'm not. I'm pleased, really, I want to be of use.'

Theo turned to face the same way as Connie, looking across the restaurant to where guests were tucking into plates of barbeque food. The smell of smoky meat mixed with salt spray was intoxicating.

'When can I start?'

'Well, Bella's insisted you have the first week or so to relax and enjoy the place.'

Connie laughed. 'I can live with that.'

Chapter Three

'Morning, Bella.' Connie knocked on the wooden door, pushed it open and stepped into her aunt's villa.

'In the bathroom!' Bella called out. 'Won't be a minute; make yourself at home.'

Like the villas on the edge of the beach, Bella's place was open to the elements but higher up on the hillside, overlooking the whole of Mchanga. Connie sank down on the sofa. All she could see was the turquoise ocean merging with the deep blue sky. Nothing else. No wonder Bella had vowed to never return to the UK.

Bella emerged through the bathroom door at the rear of the living area with her hair wrapped in a towel, wearing a pair of cropped trousers and a fitted T-shirt. 'Did you sleep well?'

'Once I managed to nod off. The peacefulness takes some getting used to.'

'Theo told you about the job?'

'Yes, thanks, Bella, you know how much it means to me.'

'It's nothing, I know how good you're going to be at it – I benefit too, you know.'

'I can't just lounge on the beach for the next week though…'

'You can.' Bella smiled and sat down next to Connie. 'But there is an alternative, if you fancy it.'

'What's that?'

'A three-day safari at Mtazamo. Geoff offered as soon as he knew you were coming out here. In fact, he insisted you go visit. It is up to you though.'

'And you don't mind me going?'

Bella sighed. 'It's up to you, love, but of course I don't mind you going. It's generous of him, but then we all know what a charmer he is.'

'It feels wrong taking off when I've barely spent any time with you yet.'

'Oh don't be silly. My suggestion of you coming here was for your benefit after all, and anyway you'll see plenty of me when you get back. Remember, I've got you here for months – take the opportunity while you can. I know how much you love Selous.'

'Okay, if you don't mind.'

'That's decided then.' Bella kissed Connie's cheek. 'David and Hilary are leaving tomorrow morning for Mtazamo and there's an extra seat on their plane so you can travel with them. Then I'll see you in a few days.'

'You didn't have to do this, Geoff,' Connie said, taking hold of Bella's ex-husband's hand. She stepped down from the four-seater Cessna after David and Hilary, and on to the dry and dusty earth of the airstrip in Selous Game Reserve.

'It's my pleasure,' Geoff said, in his gruff voice, which still had a London twang. He reminded her of a cross between Ray Winstone and Sean Connery. Winstone's gritty no messing about attitude and London vibe, crossed with Connery's suave sophistication and good looks. A troubling combination and one that had unfortunately proved true for Bella. 'It's scandalous you've only been here once and a good few years ago too. Me and Bella have our differences but I still think of her as family. That extends to you too.'

'Well, I appreciate it.' Connie slung her rucksack on to her back and they followed Geoff to the jeep waiting for them by the side of the airstrip. 'My two weeks here were amazing. Seriously, Geoff, you have the best job in the world.'

Geoff guffawed. 'Bella might have something to say about that. Pretty certain she'd say hers is the best – the laid back vibe of the coast.' He turned to Hilary and David, took their bags from them and heaved them in to the back of the jeep.

'Now, I don't want to put you two on the spot, but you've stayed here enough times to compare it to Mchanga.'

'Well, they're both such wonderful and charming places and so very different, I don't think it would be fair to compare the two,' Hilary said, taking her husband's hand as he helped her up on to the back seat of the open-sided jeep.

Geoff laughed and clambered up into the driver's seat. He patted the seat next to him. 'Sling your bag in the back, Connie, and sit up front with me.'

They bumped their way to the camp along tracks obvious only to someone who had travelled them countless times before. Selous was vast, the largest game reserve in Africa, with the mighty Rufiji River snaking across the northern part. Connie kept a look out but only caught sight of an impala disappearing into the bush before they reached the camp, the communal guest area suddenly appearing through the trees.

A tall man, with black hair, a muscular build and dark skin accentuated by his cream T-shirt and khaki shorts, strolled over as they parked. The man grinned, and Connie realised why he looked familiar. His boyish features had morphed into those of a handsome young man. She grinned back.

'Jamil?' She jumped down from the jeep.

'Hey, Connie,' he said, reaching her and folding her into a bear hug. 'It's been forever.'

'You were what, eleven or twelve the last time I saw you?'

It was strange looking up at him instead of down at the skinny kid who had trailed her everywhere during the two weeks she'd been here when she was twenty-one. He was the image of his father in many ways, tall and domineering but with the deep brown eyes, dark hair and skin tone of his Tanzanian mother.

Geoff helped Hilary and David with their bags and slung Connie's rucksack over his shoulder. Ushering David and Hilary towards the open-air seating area next to the bar, he called back, 'Jamil pined for you for weeks after you left. Quite the crush he had.'

Connie's already hot cheeks flushed even more.

'I was twelve and you were the first good looking girl –

woman – who'd been here. Unless you count the female half of honeymooning couples but they were most definitely taken.'

'Well,' Connie said, at a loss of how to respond, knowing full well how much of a crush he'd had on her sixteen years ago, but thrown by how handsome and very much an adult he now was. Of course he would be – she was in her late thirties. Plenty of time had passed since she was a carefree twenty-one-year-old having the time of her life in Tanzania. 'I'm glad I was a distraction for you all those years ago.'

Jamil smiled. 'I'm about to head off on a walking safari with some guests so I'll catch up with you this evening.'

'Great,' Connie said, watching him saunter off to the tables around the pool where two couples sat chatting.

Memories of her unforgettable couple of weeks came flooding back as she followed Geoff to the main lodge, set back from the guest camp that looked out over the river. The lodge was separated into two parts – the staff quarters on the ground floor and Geoff and Jamil's home on the first floor where Connie had been given a guest bedroom. It was as she remembered it: cool stone floors, a large bed facing the doors that opened out on to a veranda that wrapped itself around the lodge with views over the bush and glimpses of the river through the trees.

Connie unpacked her rucksack and put her clothes away, thumbed through the books on the shelf and put her camera on the low table by the sofa at the end of the bed. She went out on to the veranda, leant on the railing and looked past the treetops, down to the wide expanse of river the camp was located on. She'd loved the view back home from their Cardiff waterside apartment but this was something else. Hippos bobbed up and down in the water and she could see crocodiles basking in the sun on the dry earth at the edge of the river. Jamil was out there somewhere in the bush, on a walking tour with a few guests and one of the camp's knowledgeable armed trackers – armed in case they got into trouble with a herd of elephants or a pack of wild dogs. Connie smiled and stretched her arms up to the sky. She was about as far from her old life back in Cardiff as she could be.

Lit by candlelight, flaming torches and fairy lights, the open-air bar and living area next to the pool oozed romance for all the honeymooning and wedding anniversary-celebrating couples. Pre-dinner drinks were already well under way with a dozen or so guests mingling by the bar. Dinner was served on tables on the deck next to the pool. Beyond the flickering torches surrounding the camp, it was dark. Only the stars and moon cast any light, but not enough to make out anything apart from an occasional shimmer on the fast flowing river.

Hilary touched Connie's arm as she brushed past her to the bar. 'They've set another place for you at our table,' she said. 'I hope you'll join us.'

'That's very kind of you, thank you.'

Connie ordered a glass of white wine and turned to see Hilary and David being seated at their table by the pool. Taking hold of her glass she squeezed past the guests at the bar and sat down in the spare chair between them.

'So, you really have been here many times before,' she asked, taking her white cloth napkin and smoothing it across her lap. 'Everyone seems to know you.'

'Not as often as we've been to Mchanga, but yes, you could say we're regulars. We can't get enough of Tanzania – everything about it, the people, animals, places to stay, the views, the food. Exceptional.'

Connie remembered the food being good when she'd last stayed here but now… Three small bowls filled with pumpkin soup were brought to their table for starters, followed by grilled red snapper with pineapple salsa for mains. Connie tucked in, content to listen to Hilary and David tell her about the boat safari they'd been on earlier where they'd seen crocodiles, hippos and giraffe on the shore.

'I'm stuffed,' Connie said, when their waiter placed cardamom crème brûlée in front of them.

'Me too.' Hilary winked. 'But I'm on holiday so I'm going to eat it anyway.'

Jamil walked by, pausing to squeeze Connie's shoulder.

'Have a drink with me after you've finished.' He was gone before she could reply, past the other diners to the bar.

Hilary leant towards Connie. 'He has quite the reputation, if you know what I mean.' She took a sip of her wine and watched Connie over the top of the glass.

'Jamil?'

She nodded. 'He flirts with everyone, quite blatantly mind, in front of their husbands.'

'Hilary's just jealous that he doesn't flirt with her.' David erupted into a throaty laugh.

'Really, David, I'm old enough to be his grandmother.'

Connie laughed. 'I remember him as a twelve-year-old trailing around after me – apparently I was his first crush.'

'Well, he certainly isn't a twelve-year-old any longer,' Hilary said with raised eyebrows. 'He has the temperament, smooth-talking and charm of his father and the best of both his mother and father looks-wise. A dangerous combination if you ask me, but you can't help but like him.'

Unlike Mchanga where the dominant sound was the rhythmic surf breaking on the beach, Mtazamo was filled with the noise of insects in the undergrowth, the rush of the river and the animals on its banks. At night hippos made their way closer to the camp, grunting and snuffling, often right next to the raised tents. Even from a distance the bush sounded alive.

'I've missed this place,' Connie said, relaxing in the armchair and taking a sip of cocktail number… she had no idea. She'd lost count after Hilary and David had headed back to their luxury tent and Connie had joined Jamil in the bar.

'What took you so long to come back?' Jamil asked.

'A lot of things…' The reasons were too complex to explain – getting married and her job; trying for a baby had meant travel to a country with malaria was a no-go, and fertility treatment had complicated things further. Jamil didn't need to know all that. 'Life, pretty much.'

Jamil took a sip of his beer and wiped away the foam from his lips with the back of his hand. 'I heard you're getting divorced.'

Connie looked at him sharply. 'You did?'

'Baba has a way of getting information out of Bella. Sorry.'

Connie sipped her mai tai cocktail. 'No need to apologise; it's not a secret.'

The bar staff were wiping down the tables and clearing away the last of the glasses. All the guests, apart from an older couple talking to Geoff on the deck by the pool, had headed back to their tents earlier in the evening.

'Bella threw me a lifeline inviting me out here. I don't know what I would have done if I'd stayed in the UK.'

'Well, it's his loss and our gain.' Jamil caught her eye and held her gaze.

Alcohol made the confusion in Connie's head even worse. She remembered Jamil the boy, and yet now he was an insanely attractive man paying her attention and compliments.

'By the sounds of it you're well shot of him – you deserve better.'

Connie leant forward and placed the dregs of her mai tai on the wooden chest in front of her. She stood up. 'I need to call it a night before I can't walk back to my room.'

'I'll call it a night too.' Jamil went over to the bar, reached behind it, picked up a rifle and slung it across his shoulder. Connie had heard the stories of hippos wandering through the camp at night and an elephant rampaging through. With a wave to Geoff she followed Jamil down the steps and on to the dusty path that wound through the camp past the luxury guest tents that looked down over the river. They continued along the lamp-lit path to the staff lodge.

Jamil held open the door and she went through, exchanging the outside humidity for the coolness of the dark hallway. She followed Jamil up the stairs. At the top he paused and kissed her cheek. 'See you in the morning,' he said.

'Night,' she said, watching him saunter down the landing. She opened the door to her room, closed it behind her and leant against it with a sigh.

Chapter Four

Connie woke to the ceiling fan whizzing above her. She sat up, resting on her elbows and groaned as her head throbbed. Sinking back on to the pillow she cursed herself for overdoing it on the cocktails. She kept forgetting she was well into her thirties and not a student any longer. Glancing at her watch on the bedside table she knew she wouldn't be able to get back to sleep with so many thoughts swirling around her head.

Jamil felt like a complication – the way he flirted with her, the same as he'd done the last time she was here, except then he was barely in his teens and easy to ignore. This time he was most definitely a man. Connie tried to shift him from her thoughts. She didn't want life to be any more complicated; she didn't want another smooth-talking, charismatic man around. Part of her longed for the boy she'd gotten to know and like sixteen years before.

She rolled on deodorant, pulled on khaki-coloured cropped trousers and a T-shirt, splashed water over her face, added a brush of mascara and walked to the end of the hallway.

'You fancy heading out on safari today?' Geoff asked, the moment Connie appeared in the kitchen-come-living area doorway.

'There's space?'

'Uh huh. Two couples were going but one has pulled out. The husband has a bit of a dodgy tummy, so they've decided to play it safe and stick close to camp.'

'I won't be a bit of a gooseberry?'

Geoff sipped his coffee and looked at her over the top of the mug from where he sat at the large wooden table in the middle of the room. 'When have you ever been a gooseberry? You're far too nice and accommodating.'

Connie grabbed a mug from the cupboard, poured herself a coffee and sat down opposite Geoff.

'Leonard's driving. He'll be pleased to see you.'

'He's still here?'

'Never going to let him retire.'

Connie laughed, took a sip of the strong coffee and stirred in two heaped teaspoons of sugar. The spacious kitchen-breakfast room had shuttered doors that opened on to a veranda that, like her bedroom, looked out over the bush and down to the Rufiji River. The slightest breeze wafted in through the open doors, mixing with the air being created by the two large ceiling fans.

Geoff drained the rest of his coffee and stood up. 'Relax and enjoy yourself, Connie, you deserve to. I'll see you this evening.'

Connie smiled at Geoff. He left the room, his footsteps clomping along the landing to the stairs. She closed her eyes, relishing the gentle kiss of the breeze on her face. The peacefulness of chattering birds and insects, the smell of heat, mud and river, was all oddly familiar and soothing despite it being years since she'd set foot in the place.

'Connie Stone, you haven't changed a bit.' Leonard gripped her shoulder and smiled his infectious smile, straight white teeth gleaming against his dark skin.

'Neither have you, Leonard.' She patted him on the back and grinned at him. Leonard had never known her as Connie Vaughn, and after eight years of marriage it felt strange yet comforting to be referred to again as Connie Stone.

'Ah, a little greyer, a few more wrinkles and a little less energy than I had all those years ago,' he replied.

'Well, that's the same for us all.' Connie wedged her sunglasses in her hair. 'You okay with me joining you?'

'Of course, would love to have you.'

Connie swung her rucksack on to the front seat. Memories of bouncing across rough ground in the back of a jeep, driving miles into Selous because a pride of lions had been spotted, came flooding back.

'It's strange being back, Leonard. It's changed but it hasn't changed, do you know what I mean?'

'Of course, I've seen many changes in thirty years here. It's gone upmarket, don't you think?'

'Just a bit, really posh now.'

'So many people have worked here over the years. Still some of the same people mind, like me. I miss your Aunt Bella being around.'

'I'm sure she misses coming here too.'

'A shame what happened between her and Geoff – I just can't believe how long ago that was now.'

'Life isn't fair at times.'

Leonard tapped Connie on the shoulder and stepped forward. 'Alice, Oscar, good morning.'

A couple walked towards them hand in hand, with one of the armed camp guards leading the way. He gave them a nod and headed back along the path between the trees and past the tents. Leonard took hold of the bag Oscar carried and swung it up on to the jeep.

'Oscar, Alice, this is Connie, an old friend of Camp Mtazamo.'

'I hope you don't mind me joining you?' Connie asked, shaking their hands.

'Of course not,' Oscar replied with a smile. 'You've been here before then?'

'Yes, many years ago now but it's good to be back. Is this your first time here?'

Alice nodded. 'We wanted to do something really special for our honeymoon.'

'Well, congratulations, this place is certainly that.'

They headed along the bumpy track that led from the camp. The Rufiji River cut through the landscape, a wild beast of a river as wide as a lake in places and used as a watering hole by hippos, elephants, wildebeest, giraffes and the crocodiles that lived on its banks. Connie had been to the Ngorongoro Crater in the north the first time she'd stayed with Bella in-between her second and third year at university, when Bella had taken her to a safari camp run by friends of hers. The crater had been spectacular and each jeep safari they'd been on they'd been swamped by animals – prides of lions, herds of zebra and wildebeest throwing up dust as they charged across the landscape. Connie would swap the guarantee of seeing the animals for the wild emptiness of Selous though. Four jeeps surrounding a pride of lions was not appealing, when in Selous – if you could actually find the lions to begin with, often after a hot and bumpy drive for miles – you'd be the only jeep and humans for miles around, watching lions in their natural surroundings who really were wild.

Leonard was the perfect guide, knowing when to stay quiet and let his guests soak up the sights, yet giving them enough information about the birds and animals they spotted as they drove. Connie was well aware that in Selous it was possible to see very few animals due to its vastness, but they'd barely left camp when Leonard urged them to look right. Through the trees were three giraffes, majestic as they disappeared into the treetops to pull off leaves from the highest branches.

They continued on, rocking against the sides as the jeep powered across rough, dry ground, a blissful breeze keeping them cool. Leonard slowed down, stopping in the shade of an acacia tree. He pointed straight ahead and amongst the green bushes was the grey wrinkled skin of an elephant, slow and steady as it disappeared into the bush.

Leonard's radio crackled into life. He listened to someone speaking in Swahili before turning to Alice and Oscar. 'A pride of lions has been spotted about an hour's drive from here. We can go and see if we can find them but it means we can't stop if we spot anything else as there won't be time to get back to camp. What do you want to do?'

Alice looked at Oscar and grinned. 'We've got to go and see the lions, haven't we?'

Oscar nodded. 'Definitely.'

'Hopefully they'll still be there,' Leonard said. He attached the radio back on to his belt. 'The other guides will keep us informed.' He released the brake, put his foot down on the accelerator and they shot off across the grassland, dust spiralling into the air behind them.

They skidded across open plains, the sun pounding down. They spotted zebra in the distance and caught sight of elephants emerging from the cover of trees, but they kept going, updates from other guides crackling to life via the radio that the pride of lions were still in the same location. After an hour of bumping up and down, rocking from side to side in the jeep, Leonard slowed as they reached an open area of grassland dotted with low hanging trees. Lying in the shade beneath one were four adult lions.

'Oh my goodness, they are amazing,' Alice said as Leonard pulled to a halt at a safe distance, yet close enough to see the lions perfectly – an uninterrupted view with not another jeep or person in sight.

Hot and dusty when they arrived back in camp, Leonard walked Alice and Oscar back to their tent and Connie back to the staff lodge. She said goodbye, climbed the stairs up to Geoff and Jamil's floor and headed to her room. She showered, changed into a knee-length linen skirt and a strapless top, and sat outside on the balcony to rub her hair dry with a towel. Away from the breeze created by the jeep, the late afternoon heat warmed every inch of her. Connie poured herself a glass of cold water from the bottle in the fridge, took it back out on to the balcony and sat in the wicker armchair. Moments like this stilled time for Connie – right then there was nothing more complicated than sitting and looking at the view. She took a sip of water and dabbed a tissue across her forehead.

There was a knock on her bedroom door.

'Come in!' Connie shouted.

Geoff popped his head around the door. 'I'm heading down to the bar if you want to walk with me?'

'Yeah, great.' Connie put her glass down next to her chair and got up. She followed him along the landing, down the stairs and out of the door on to the main path.

'Leonard said you saw lions on the game drive today.'

'Yeah, they were incredible. I didn't get to see any last time – just wasn't lucky I guess or always in the wrong place at the wrong time.'

They strolled along the path past the luxury guest tents. Geoff raised his hand in greeting to a couple sitting out on the veranda at the entrance to their tent.

'I remember you were always eager to go on either a walking or boat safari. Spent quite a bit of time in the pool too. Don't blame you mind, the easiest way to cool off around here.'

'I had the best time – a second summer in Tanzania with Bella and staying here was one of the highlights.'

'It was a highlight for Bella too, you being over here. It's a shame you never made it back until now.'

'Considering what's happened over the past twelve months or so, not coming back sooner is one of my biggest regrets.' They walked past the last tent and the path widened as they turned the corner to see the guest lodge with its open sides, thatched roof and view over the river appear in front of them. 'I should have made the effort – fitted it in, in-between work, getting married, buying our apartment and all the other things that took up time. It's not like Bella's got any family over here.'

Geoff turned sharply towards her. 'She's got plenty of friends out here who are like family.'

'Sorry, Geoff, I didn't mean it like that…' She hadn't intended her comment to be a dig at him but as soon as the words were out she realised it sounded like one. 'Of course she's got friends out here, I just meant…'

'I know what you meant,' he grunted, making her wonder if it was too close to home, the fact that he *had* once been family. 'Dinner will be served soon. I'm going to mingle.' He shot ahead of her towards the bar, a wave and a smile for each guest he passed.

~

After a drink and chat with David and Hilary by the bar and with her stomach rumbling, Connie stepped up on to the decked dining area with her glass of wine. She was about to head over to the table set for one when Alice waved across from a table that looked down towards the river.

'Connie, come and join us.'

'Oh no really, I'm fine, I don't want to impose.'

'Really, you're not, we'd love you to join us.'

Connie walked over and one of the waiters pulled up a spare chair for her. She sat down between Oscar and Alice.

'Cheers,' she said, as the three of them tapped their glasses together.

'How much did you enjoy the jeep safari today?' Connie asked, taking a sip of white wine.

Alice placed her glass of wine on the table and looked at Connie. 'Seriously, I've never done anything like it. I mean getting that close to lions in the wild and being able to see how they behave in their own habitat just blew my mind.'

'It was pretty special, wasn't it?' Connie said.

'I remember thinking how crazy expensive this place was when we booked it, but now I completely understand why. Worth every penny.'

Connie leant back in her chair as one of the waiters placed a seafood salad in front of her. 'What are you doing tomorrow?'

'I think the plan is to go on a walking safari in the morning,' Oscar said. 'Not sure about the afternoon, we might just stay around here, go for a swim, read our books on the veranda of our tent.'

'It's amazing what you can spot from camp. I remember sitting up on the deck at the main lodge the last time I was here and watching an elephant and her calf walk down to the river. Even the birds are incredible.'

'You should come on the walking safari with us, Connie,' Oscar said. 'I think we're going with another couple, plus guides anyway – in case you're worried about imposing on us.' He laughed. 'You're really not.'

Connie smiled. 'You're kind, thank you. And yes, I will join you. The walking safari was the best thing I did the last time I was here. An incredible experience.'

'I don't mean to pry,' Alice said, pushing a forkful of salad around her plate. 'Are you single? I'm assuming so because you're here on your own, but…'

'Alice.' Oscar frowned. 'You are prying.'

'That's okay, I don't mind,' Connie laughed. 'And yes, I am single. I'm actually staying out in Tanzania for a while – at least six months, maybe longer. You could call it a belated gap year. My aunt owns Mchanga, a luxury camp on the coast.'

'Mchanga na Mawe?'

'Yep, that's the one.'

'That's where we're going for the last three nights of our honeymoon, after we've been to Zanzibar.'

'Really? Well that's fantastic, I'm going to be working there when I get back.'

'How come you're here at Selous?'

'My aunt insisted I have a bit of a holiday – unnecessary really because trust me, even working at Mchanga will be like being on holiday. My aunt co-owns this place with Geoff, although she rarely comes here any more.'

'How come?' Oscar asked.

'Geoff's her ex-husband, and she's busy with her own projects.'

Alice frowned. 'Jamil's Geoff's son, right?' she asked, putting the last forkful of food in her mouth.

'Yep, and the result of a long-term affair he had with a local woman who worked here while he was still married to my aunt.' Connie swirled her wine around her glass and gazed out into the darkness beyond the camp, the river gleaming in the moonlight as it rushed past. 'I bet you didn't come on honeymoon thinking you'd find out so much gossip.'

Alice laughed. 'No, not really, but it's kind of fascinating.'

'A place like this is certainly inspiring in more ways than one.'

'Are you staying in one of the tents?' Oscar asked.

Connie shook her head. 'No, up at the main lodge where

28

the family and staff live. I've not been lucky enough to spend a night in one of the tents yet.'

'We got woken up last night by a hippo grazing outside, we think with her baby,' Oscar said. 'We couldn't see a bloody thing though could we, it's so dark here at night, just heard them.'

'I don't think I've ever been anywhere so romantic, and Oscar did propose in Paris.'

'Wow, nice. Wait until you get to Mchanga, I think it might top here for romance.'

Alice placed her knife and fork on her empty plate and looked at Connie. 'Have you been married?'

'Alice, hun, that's a bit personal.'

Connie sipped her wine and placed it carefully on the table. She wafted away an insect with the back of her hand. 'I was; we're divorcing and my aunt suggested I came out here to escape the UK and all the crap there. A bit of time out is exactly what I need.'

'I'm sorry.' Alice placed her hand on top of Connie's.

'No need to be, I'm well shot of a toxic relationship.' Connie took a deep breath. 'But this is really not what we should be talking about seeing as though you two have just got married!'

Alice laughed. 'I'm always too nosy. It comes from growing up as one of four sisters.'

'Wow, your poor parents. That sounds like quite a handful.'

'It was. I'm the youngest and so life has always been hectic. It's an even bigger family now. Me and Oscar are the last to get married – all my sisters are married and have at least one child, my eldest sister has four, so it's pretty crazy, isn't it?' She turned to Oscar.

'You could say that. Coming from a family with just one older brother it was a bit of a shock to begin with. But I love it.' He took Alice's hands in his. 'And we hope to add to the grandkids next year, don't we?'

Even in the candlelight Connie could see Alice's cheeks flush. The way she gazed back at Oscar, her eyes filled with love, made Connie's heart thud faster. She tried to still the palpitations with her breathing, her own life flashing past, of her and Felix on their honeymoon, their own hopes for married life as she remembered feeling as excited about the future as Alice and Oscar.

Aware of the silence she forced herself to bury her feelings and picked up her glass of wine. 'To your future.'

'Cheers,' Alice and Oscar said, knocking their glasses against hers.

'And to your future too.' Alice looked at Connie. 'I hope your time in Tanzania is exactly what you need.'

With Alice and Oscar heading back to their tent for an early night, Connie realised however lovely they were, making friends with a loved-up newly married couple was the last thing she needed. But Mtazamo was filled with married couples, much the same as Mchanga. Despite being thousands of miles away from home, she wasn't going to escape having what she'd lost rubbed in her face, even if people like Alice and Oscar didn't mean to and had no clue about what Connie had been through.

She left the table and pulled up a stool at the bar. She leant her elbows on the smooth wooden surface and gazed across the lit pool to the remaining couples finishing off their dinner. The air was still and warm, only a touch cooler than during the day. Along with the chatter from guests, the clink of cutlery on china and the whirr of ceiling fans, the air was alive with the rustle of insects and the grunts of frogs.

'Evening, Connie,' one of the barmen said as he finished cleaning a glass and placed it on the shelf behind him. 'What can I get you?'

'A ginger and whisky, please.'

'Make that two.' Jamil slid on to the stool next to her.

'Where have you been all evening?' Connie asked, as the barman poured two shots of whisky and topped them up with a generous splash of ginger ale.

'I had work to do back at the lodge.' He took hold of the two drinks the barman had poured and slid one along to

Connie. 'What have you been up to?'

'I've spent the evening chatting to loved-up newly-weds on their honeymoon.'

'Poor you, this place does get a bit sickening with seriously in love couples fawning all over each other.'

'It was actually a lot nicer than it sounds – they were friendly and wanted me to gatecrash their romantic dinner.'

'Rather you than me.'

Connie turned to Jamil, taking in his profile, his dark skin, handsome face and strong neck leading to broad muscular shoulders – the perfect mix of Geoff's ruggedness and his mother's Tanzanian beauty.

'Where's your mum?' Connie swallowed a mouthful of fiery ginger and whisky. 'I haven't seen her yet.'

'She doesn't work here any longer.'

'Oh?'

'Her and Baba aren't together any more. You know how he is – not one for sticking with one woman for any length of time.'

'Well, I'm sorry to hear that.'

'Are you?' Jamil turned, his leg brushing against hers.

'Hey, that's unfair. Just because your dad treated Bella the way he did, has never made me want your mum to suffer the same fate.'

Jamil put his hands up. 'I'm sorry, that was uncalled for. Bella still maintains a civil enough relationship with Baba despite all he's put her through, so I guess there's no reason why you would hate my mum.'

'Is your dad with anyone else?'

Jamil shrugged. 'There have been other women.' He glanced sideways at Connie. 'There have always been other women, but honestly I have no idea if he's with anyone now or if he even wants to have a serious relationship again. You know what he's like – too self-absorbed to really share his life with anyone in a romantic way.'

Connie had no idea what to say. Jamil understandably sounded down about the situation – his mum cast aside by a father he adored but one who could perhaps never be happy.

Jamil nodded towards the lounge area. 'Let's go somewhere more comfortable.'

They took their glasses and sat down on a sofa. Only one couple remained with their back to them on the far side of the lounge, curled up together looking out over the bush and down to the fast-moving river, shimmering in the moonlight.

'Don't you go stir-crazy here?' Connie leant back and gazed up at the thatched roof. The air was warm and heavy in the lamplight with barely a breath of air filtering through. 'I mean I know it's an incredible place to live and work, but what about a life – a social life?'

'Are you thinking back to the last time you were here and if poor twelve-year-old Jamil ever got laid?'

'God no.' Connie spluttered as she placed her glass next to a bowl of pistachios on the wooden chest in front of her. 'I didn't mean it like that, I just meant being surrounded by couples, it's not an ideal place for a boy to grow up.'

'Don't feel sorry for me, Connie Stone, I get plenty of action.'

'I so didn't mean it like that.'

Jamil laughed. 'I know you didn't.' He took a sip of his drink and leant forward, his bare arms resting on his thighs. 'Is your name Connie Stone or do you still have your married name?'

'My married name was Vaughn, and technically it's still my name – that's what it says in my passport – the divorce isn't quite finalised, but Connie Stone is how I want to be known from now on.'

'Do you know Bella never took Baba's name? She's always been Bella Stone. Suits her. Stone suits you too.' He pulled open the shell of a pistachio and popped the nut into his mouth. 'Did you ever consider keeping your maiden name?'

Connie shook her head. 'No. I was in love and was desperate to be Mrs Connie Vaughn. I had no idea how things would turn out.' She scooped up a handful of pistachios. 'Now using his name feels wrong.'

'Baba should never have married Bella. He's not the marrying type. But even so, he's always had a soft spot for

32

her.'

'It's a shame he had to screw her over the way he did. I know you were the result and obviously if he hadn't had an affair you wouldn't be here, but…'

'Everyone knows what he's like. Nothing changes. But it makes me think I'm not suited to marriage either. Staying single might be way more fun – gives me the freedom to travel; Baba wants me to be the 'face' of Mtazamo. I meet with travel agents, go to travel conventions, work closely with other luxury camps in East Africa. I'm not lonely, if that's what you're worried about.'

'I'm not worried, Jamil, your love life is really no concern of mine.'

'You're a lot easier to tease than you were sixteen years ago.' Jamil knocked his glass against hers. He had the darkest brown eyes that bore into her – she knew his type. She'd married a man like that, undressing her with his eyes, imagining the what if… but wasn't that exactly what she was doing? He was everything she needed to avoid.

'There are local girls who work here, plenty of girls to meet if I'm in Dar or Zanzibar. I went to Sydney for a couple of weeks last year and trust me, Australian girls are hot.'

Connie picked up one of the bird spotting magazines from the chest and whacked his arm with it.

He took the magazine from her, his fingers briefly touching hers. 'And occasionally,' he said, placing the magazine back down. 'A hot and single woman escaping her life in the UK will stay here for a few days and that's always a treat.'

His hand found its way to her thigh and crept upwards, creasing the material of her thin linen skirt and sending a shiver through her. She glanced behind at the other couple but they were oblivious, arms curled around each other, talking quietly. Before she could react, Jamil's lips were on hers, his kiss firm and purposeful, his hands at the top of her thighs. He tasted of whisky and ginger. His skin was smooth against hers, salty and spicy, overloading her senses. She kissed him back, her tongue flicking against his, her heart thudding, desire coursing through her that she hadn't expected. His hands crept higher until they rested around her waist, his thumbs caressing the sides of her stomach.

Connie froze and pulled away.

Jamil frowned. 'What's the matter?'

'I can't do this.' It was too soon, her emotions too raw and uncontrolled, memories flooding back of Felix and all the hurt he'd caused.

'You didn't enjoy it?' Jamil leant back against the sofa, his arms folded across his chest, his biceps and shoulder muscles shown off to great effect in the subtle lamplight.

'It's not that, it's just, we shouldn't…' Connie stood up, her head swimming.

'Why not?'

For so many reasons, she thought, not least of all because she wasn't ready for someone to touch her in that way, to make her feel that she could give in to those kinds of feelings ever again, not after what she'd been through. 'You're much younger than me.'

'That's a lame excuse,' Jamil said, standing up and sidling over to her until his face was only inches from hers. 'And you know it.'

'I've always thought of you more like a brother.'

'Well, trust me, I've never thought of you like a sister.'

Connie felt a rush of heat flood through her, well aware of the longing a young Jamil had for her.

'I'm heading back. Night, Jamil.'

He grabbed her arm. 'Not on your own you can't.'

With the realisation that he was right, Connie waited while he retrieved his rifle from the locked cupboard behind the bar. The barman who'd served them earlier winked at her.

'Come on,' Jamil said, pausing on the steps that led to the dusty path. 'I promise I won't try and seduce you on the way back.'

Chapter Five

The air was still as Connie left the staff lodge at six in the morning and walked with one of the safari guides through the camp. After a pleasant sleep with the night-time temperature dropping and the ceiling fan providing a constant and welcome breeze on her skin, the early morning sunshine was already warm on Connie's arms. She'd dressed as simply as she could in a khaki coloured capped-sleeved T-shirt, loose linen dark grey shorts and comfortable trainers. The stillness of the air in the camp made it seem hotter than it really was and Connie felt relieved that she'd never visited in January or February when the temperatures crept higher and the mugginess could be unbearable. The guide left her when they reached the guest lodge, heading towards a jeep parked beneath the shade of trees, while Connie took the steps two at a time up to the raised bar.

'Morning,' Connie said, joining Hilary, David, Alice and Oscar in the lounge area.

'Morning,' the four of them replied. They were sat on sofas around a large battered leather chest with maps and books about Selous sprawled across it.

Hilary beamed at her. 'I'm so pleased you're joining us this morning.'

'I wouldn't miss a walking safari for the world.'

'To be honest, I'm surprised you're up so early,' Hilary said. 'What time did you get to bed last night?'

'I look that bad, do I?' Connie said and laughed.

'Far from bad, love, just a little tired.'

'That was my fault, keeping her up.' Jamil stepped up on to the deck with a rifle slung over his shoulder.

Connie's cheeks flushed. She sat down on the empty sofa next to the one Hilary and David were on and caught Alice's eye and slightly raised eyebrow.

'We had lots of catching up to do,' Jamil explained, perching on the arm of the sofa next to Oscar and smiling at everyone. The guide who'd walked with Connie sat next to her.

Jamil gestured towards him. 'This is Mboto who's going to be the other guide this morning along with me.'

Mboto smiled and nodded at everyone.

'So,' Jamil continued, 'our walking safari – there are a couple of rules. When we leave camp we're going to walk in single file with myself leading and Mboto bringing up the rear. At no point leave the group and wander off on your own. Even from camp you can see the amount of animals there are out there.' He stood up, smoothing down the material of his khaki shorts. 'We need to be as quiet as we can, so please keep talking to a minimum. These are the hand signals I'll be using.'

As Jamil showed them the signals for stop, get down and follow, it took Connie right back to sixteen years before with her first experience of a walking safari led by Geoff.

'I know you've done this before, but are you paying attention, Connie?' Jamil said with a wink.

'I certainly am.' She met his deep brown eyes as laughter filtered around the group.

'And do you remember what the most important rule on a walking safari is?'

'Yeah,' she said, looking from Jamil to Hilary and David, then Alice and Oscar. 'Don't run.'

'Perfect. That's it then, stay close and don't run.'

Jamil strode ahead, his fitted beige T-shirt showing off his dark skin and muscles to perfection. Connie remembered the lanky kid who'd joined her on her first walking safari – he hadn't been the one leading with a rifle, simply an enthusiastic twelve-year-old eager to learn about the animals and the bush. Fast forward sixteen years and he was very much the one in charge – he looked the part, knew his stuff and had an ease and a way with the guests.

With Jamil leading, followed closely by Hilary, David, Oscar, Alice, Connie and then Mboto, they took the track that led directly from Mtazamo, away from the river and into the surrounding bush. Connie's wide-brimmed hat shaded her face from the sun and there were patches of shade as they walked beneath trees. Although there wasn't the stifling humidity of the rainy season, the still air and walking pace made them work up a sweat. Jamil occasionally raised his hand to stop to show them plants or point out a bird's-nest high up in a tree. At one point he brought them to a halt by a thin but well worn track that he explained was a hippo highway, the route the local hippos took to reach the river, although the only thing on the track was a line of marching ants.

They walked for an hour and a half, with Jamil pointing out giraffes in the distance, a waterhog by a muddy pool and spotting a wild dog chasing an impala into the undergrowth. They stopped for a rest in a clearing and sat on a fallen log to drink water from their pouches. There was companionable silence, Connie as happy as anyone to sit and quietly take in their surroundings, squinting through the heat haze and trees thinking she could spot an animal. David asked Jamil lots of questions, particularly about the birds and Connie listened to Jamil's assured replies, impressed by his depth of knowledge. She realised just how much he'd learnt since he'd been an eager teenager.

Refreshed, they set off again, walking in the same order as before, padding across dried earth and grassy areas, each of them keeping a look out for anything to spot through the trees. A growl like a dog's sounded ahead. Jamil signalled for them to stop and then turned to them, putting his finger to his lips before motioning to follow. Silently, they crept forward entering a small tree-lined clearing where they stopped again, Jamil pointing towards a tree on the far side. Mboto tapped Connie's shoulder and pointed in the same direction. A wild dog was sleeping in the shade.

'I think there are two of them,' Mboto whispered to Connie.

Up ahead, Jamil beckoned them forward. The ground beneath their feet was dry and covered with leaves and twigs and their footsteps made soft snapping sounds as they crept. Beneath the tree the wild dogs got to their feet, revealing four of them, their ears alert. They sloped off together, disappearing into the thick undergrowth.

They continued on, the sun creeping higher in the sky and the heat rising the further they walked. Connie's calves began to ache and she was longing to sit down and put her feet up when they rounded a corner and they were by a lake. Grass sloped down to the still edge of the water where a table for six had been set up a little way from the shore and two waiters, plus one of the cooks from the camp, were waiting for them.

'Wow,' Alice said, a grin spreading across her face.

'I remember this from last time,' Connie said, as they walked down to the table where the waiters handed them each a cold flannel.

'Breakfast out in the wilds.' Jamil pointed towards the peaceful lake.

'Are there crocodiles around here?' Hilary frowned, glancing along the sandy shore.

'There can be.' Jamil pulled out a chair for Hilary. 'Mboto's going to keep a look out, but we've never been bothered by a crocodile yet. Sometimes, if we're lucky we get to see an elephant wander down to the lake to drink or even swim across.'

With hands and faces cooled by the towels, Connie and Jamil took the end two seats furthest away from the lake. The two waiters served tea and freshly brewed coffee, while the chef cooked bacon, sausages and frittata on a camping stove a little further along the shore.

'I never want to leave,' Hilary sighed, dabbing the side of her mouth with a napkin and taking a sip of pineapple juice. 'I didn't think anything could top our love of Mchanga, but this...' She swept her hand towards the lake.

'Don't let Bella hear you say that,' Jamil said.

'Have you not done the walking safari before?' Connie asked, stabbing her fork into a slice of mango.

'No, never,' Hilary replied. 'And I've got no idea why not – we've done the boat and jeep safaris numerous times before.'

Jamil dropped a spoonful of sugar into his coffee and stirred it. 'To be fair, it was Bella's idea when she lived here to surprise guests with breakfast out in the open after the walk instead of going straight back to camp.'

Hilary clapped her hands. 'Well, it's a stunning idea.'

With the promise of having dinner together on their final evening before Connie headed back to Mchanga and Hilary and David continued on to Zanzibar before returning to the UK, Connie vowed to do nothing for the rest of the day. It was incredible how reading a book on the veranda of her room, having lunch, a swim in the pool and then a sleep could make the day go so quickly, but soon enough Jamil was knocking on the door of her room to see if she wanted to walk with him to the guest lodge.

'You're going to have to come and stay with us again before you go back to the UK, you know.'

'Well there's time; I'm not planning on going back for months,' she said as they reached the door of the staff lodge and stepped out into the dusk of early evening.

'I know. But I also know how easily time can slip by here. Before you know it you'll be on a plane back home.'

Connie bit her lip at the mention of home. She had no idea where home was any longer. Her old life in the UK felt distant and her new life in Tanzania – well, she was still trying to work it out. It had only been a few days after all.

'You've gone quiet. What have I said?'

'Nothing,' Connie said as they reached the guest lodge. 'I'm just in a reflective mood, that's all.'

She did love the relaxed and sociable evenings in Tanzania. It was the same at Mchanga as it was at Mtazamo – guests and staff mingling with drinks before sitting down to a freshly prepared three course meal.

Connie joined Hilary and David at their table and listened to them chat about their holiday and about their grandchildren back in the UK, in-between tucking into skewered prawns followed by tomato and caper chicken with roasted sweet potato and cauliflower.

Connie leant back, resting her hands on her full stomach, then immediately moving them back to the table. That was what she'd done when she'd been pregnant. Even in early pregnancy, despite her not having a bump, it had felt a natural thing to fold her arms protectively over her tummy, imagining cradling a growing baby. She took a gulp of wine and tried not to think about it.

'Do you know,' she said, glancing between Hilary and David. 'Today was the first time since I split with my husband that I hadn't thought about the pain he's caused me. I had other things to take my attention such as wild dogs, breakfast by the lake and good company.'

Hilary reached her hand across the table and took Connie's in hers, her tanned fingers stacked with gold rings. 'Oh Connie, I do hope your stay out here gives you the time to get over him and move on with your life.'

'I hope so too.'

'Well, if anywhere is going to help ease the pain of a divorce then it's Tanzania. I can't tell you over the years how often we'd arrive at Mchanga our shoulders heavy with the stresses and strains of life and two weeks later we'd leave feeling like new people, didn't we, David?'

'We certainly did.' He leant back in his seat as their waiter arrived at the table carrying three plates.

'I hope you have room for some more,' the waiter said, placing a plate in front of each of them containing a passionfruit tart.

'Oh, go on then.' Hilary flashed a smile back at him.

'Bella was telling us about her and Geoff's plans for a beach retreat on Zanzibar,' David said, leaning his grey-haired, tanned arms on the table. 'Wasn't she, Hilary?'

Hilary nodded and took a mouthful of the passionfruit tart. 'When it comes to fruition we'll be the first ones there, won't we, love?' She looked across the candlelit table at her husband.

'Absolutely. We do enjoy our usual resort on Zanzibar but it's not a patch on Bella's hospitality. A Zanzibar beach resort run by Bella would be just wonderful.'

'She's not talked much to me about it yet but I know her and Geoff have already leased out the land and are working on plans, so it will happen at some point.'

'Well, we'll be back next year, so tell her to get a move on.' Hilary raised her glass and waited for David and Connie to do the same. 'To you, Connie, and your amazing time in Tanzania!'

Chapter Six

'Connie, love,' Bella said, greeting her with a hug and a kiss as Connie climbed out of the jeep that had brought her back to Mchanga from the airstrip. 'It's good to have you back. Hungry?'

Connie nodded and hooked her arm in Bella's as they took the sandy path that led up the hill and away from the beach. They puffed their way up the shallow steps cut into the hillside and walked past the path that led to the staff cottages, then continued along the winding path to Bella's villa set alone at the highest point of Mchanga. 'I asked for some lunch to be brought up here so we can eat together in peace.'

They reached the villa and Bella kicked off her sandals and padded bare-foot across the outside deck with its plunge pool, and in through the open veranda doors. Connie did the same, leaving her flip-flops on the sandy path.

The coffee table in front of the sofa was filled with little dishes of seafood and salads.

They sat down and Bella clinked a glass of pineapple juice against Connie's. 'So, how was it?'

Connie leant back and sighed. 'Where do I start? It was so good to go back, although it felt like a lifetime ago since I was there. I was twenty-one then and now I'm thirty-seven. How the hell did I get so old?'

'You're hardly old, Connie.' Bella frowned. 'If you're old, then I'm ancient. You shouldn't have left it so long to come back.' She held up her hands. 'I know, I know, you didn't have much choice in the matter, but sixteen years is a long time before returning to a place you love. A lot changes, but mainly a place stays the same and the person changes. Like you from a single girl, just graduated from university with the world at your feet. The choices we make can affect our life for years.'

'Are you okay, Bella?'

'Just rather thoughtful. You being here has reminded me a lot of the past too.' She reached for a skewer of grilled prawns and handed one to Connie. 'And I'm a little out of sorts, that's all. I'm always sad when my regular guests leave – David and Hilary are good friends; people I'd genuinely see sociably if we lived near each other. They come back every year, but a year is a long time to wait.'

'You have friends here though, don't you?'

'Sure I do, but here is a place that people visit rather than live – unlike me of course, I chose to make my life here all those years ago because I fell in love with everything about Tanzania.' She laughed and waved her hand in front of her. 'You get reflective as you get older.'

'I can understand that – that's pretty much what I'm doing at the moment.' Connie pulled off one of the prawns and squeezed lemon over it. 'I totally agree with you that sixteen years is a long time to not revisit somewhere I love so much, but that's because I was in love with someone and he'd taken over my life – in a good way to begin with. Now I'm questioning all the time I lost and what I could have done instead.'

Bella took Connie's hands. 'You really can't go thinking about things like that. Life doesn't always work out the way you want it to, but that doesn't mean to say that time you spent with Felix was wasted. You loved him and you built a life together. We don't always know how things will play out and having a bastard husband who cheats on you and turns your life upside down is the shittiest thing in the world at the time, but sometimes it makes you stronger and sends your life in a different direction. Different can be good – it was for me.'

'Oh Bella, I can't even imagine how tough it was for you with Geoff.'

Bella shook her head. 'It's in the past, I've moved on and that's what you need to do, but I know full well that healing takes time. Talking of my bastard ex-husband, how was he?'

'You know, the same, hasn't changed a bit. Still a charmer, a little older, hasn't really mellowed. You still talk to him?'

Bella grunted. 'Of course, for business things. Our personal relationship might have died a death but professionally we still work well together. He often asks after you though – he's always had a soft spot for you.'

'You told him about my divorce.'

'Sorry, yes, I told him you were coming over and staying for a while and I explained why.'

'That's okay, Jamil knew and asked about it.'

'How did you get on with Jamil?' Bella took a forkful of coleslaw and popped it into her mouth.

'I know I shouldn't be surprised but I can't believe how much he's changed.'

Bella snorted. 'I should say – a twelve-year-old to a twenty-eight-year-old who is well aware of just how good looking he is.'

Connie remembered his dark eyes looking at her beneath long lashes and the way his hands had crept up her thighs. She blinked the image away. 'I barely recognised him to begin with; I was still thinking of him as a boy rather than a man. He seems to have quite a reputation according to Hilary.'

'Oh that I know,' Bella said. 'Don't go getting yourself into anything you're not ready to be a part of.'

'I'm not.' Connie shook her head. 'Jamil was just a kid when I knew him and I still think of him that way.'

'Indeed. Except he's inherited his father's charm and ability to seduce anything with a pulse.'

'Well, he didn't seduce me. We get on well; we did all those years ago too. It was nice to see a familiar face, that's all.'

Connie wondered if Bella's opinion of Jamil would always be tainted by her opinion of Geoff and the fact that he was the son of the woman who had stolen her husband away from her. If the woman Felix had an affair with had ended up having his baby rather than her husband's, Connie would probably have as much disdain for it as Bella did for Jamil.

Connie couldn't blame Jamil for his parents' affair, but she could understand why Bella would struggle to come to terms with him or accept him, particularly as she'd never had children of her own.

Would that be her, Connie thought, childless, an aunt or godmother to everyone else's kids, but never a mum? Maybe she should talk to Bella about how she coped living and being on her own. She met Bella's eyes, watching her intently.

'Why are you lying to me, Connie?'

'I'm not.'

'Okay, fine, I don't want to pry, but you know you can talk to me about anything, don't you?'

'I know, thank you.' Connie downed the rest of her pineapple juice, placed the empty glass back on the coffee table and bit her lip as she gazed out towards the ocean. 'We kissed, well he kissed me and I kissed him back. It was an impulsive moment. I'd had a bit to drink and he made a move. I responded but stopped him.'

'I'm not telling you off, Connie, heaven knows I'm in no position to do that and it's up to you who you sleep with…'

'I didn't sleep with him; it was a drunken kiss, that's all.'

'The last thing I want is for you to get hurt again.'

Connie turned back to Bella, nodding. 'I know. I know what Geoff is like and I know what a charmer Jamil is – that was obvious when he was twelve, let alone now. He made me feel good and I haven't felt like that for a very long time. In fact, I didn't expect to feel like that ever again.'

'Oh Connie, you need time to heal.' Bella shuffled closer, wrapping her arms around her. 'What made you stop?'

'With Jamil?'

Bella let Connie go and looked at her.

'It was too soon – I went from feeling desired to terrified. That's not right.'

'No, it's not, but it is understandable after what you've been through.'

'Also, he's far too young.'

Bella laughed. 'Age is just a number, Connie, never forget that. There's only what, nine years between you? That's nothing.'

'Except he's in his twenties and I'm heading towards forty.'

'You're not forty for another couple of years by which time he'll be in his thirties.'

'Why are you encouraging me, Bella?'

'I'm not. Really I'm not. His age shouldn't be what puts you off but his casual attitude to relationships. Anyway, enough about my ex-husband's philandering son. Take the rest of today to relax, get acclimatised to the place again and then you can start work tomorrow.'

Past the tops of the trees, the ocean looked endless, stretching to the horizon where sky and water merged in a hazy line of contrasting blues. The last time she'd been here, Connie remembered not being able to decide which view she preferred: the ocean with its crashing waves foaming on to pale sand, or the view of the bush leading down to the fast flowing Rufiji River with its crocodiles and elephants at Mtazamo. Either way, Bella was beyond lucky to wake up to this every day.

'Seriously, Bella,' Connie said, waving her hand in front of her. 'How do you manage to get any work done around here?'

'Trust me, it gets harder with each passing year.' She laughed. 'Maybe it's my age. I finally feel the need to slow down, which is why I employed Theo. Best decision I ever made.' She squeezed Connie's arm. 'And now of course I have you here too – although I'm more pleased about getting to spend time with you than having an extra pair of hands around the place.'

'I'm pleased to be here and see you too, Bella. I wish I hadn't left it so long, but there we are, I can't change the past.' She didn't need to say any more for Bella to understand, particularly as Bella's own marriage had ended because of a cheating husband.

'You know the ropes here pretty much,' Bella said. 'But perhaps for the first few days you can shadow Theo and me.

But organising day trips, and taking guests over to Zanzibar or Chumbe would be something extra we can offer – a tailored, more personal experience. That's what I've always wanted Mchanga to be all about and hopefully is. Go relax and we'll have dinner together tonight.'

Connie walked back down the winding, sandy path towards the restaurant. High up on the hillside away from the lodge and the staff cottages, were the suites, seven of them, even more luxurious than the beach villas – more spacious, beautifully appointed with decked verandas, private plunge pools and an ocean view. Connie was going to make the most of the time she had in her beach villa before it got booked up again. She stepped up on to her deck and slung her rucksack on the daybed – she'd unpack later.

It was quite easy, even with twelve beach rooms, seven hillside suites and dozens of staff, to go the whole day at Mchanga without seeing anyone until the evening. Connie left her villa and wandered down the sandy path that led to the beach, her feet sinking into warm sand as she passed the other villas half hidden by foliage and trees. A couple were lying on a pair of sunloungers close to the path that led to the restaurant and she smiled at another couple having lunch, catching sight of Theo talking to someone at the bar.

The pool was set away from the restaurant, overlooking the beach and the dense wood that stopped where the sand started. Connie took the path that led beneath the trees from the beach, the refreshing breeze immediately replaced by a sticky heat. The crash of waves on the sand was added to by the rustle of insects in the undergrowth and the call of birds high up in the trees. Connie walked along the path, the sound of her flip-flops muffled by the sandy earth and dried leaves coating the ground. She'd heard the stories about how elephants once roamed the area, and were often spotted right next to the beach. Now they'd moved away, leaving the undergrowth and trees free for colobus monkeys, their black and white coats easy to spot against the browns and greens of branches and leaves.

It was the first time, Connie realised, since she'd arrived in

47

Tanzania that she'd had time to be alone. Arriving in Stone Town and then Mchanga there was her aunt and other people she'd known from her previous time here. Then in Selous, when she wasn't with Geoff or Jamil there was David and Hilary, Alice and Oscar. Now, peace at last, what she'd been longing for.

Back in the UK she'd had friends who she'd leant on when her life fell apart. The last person she'd seen before flying out to Tanzania had been the one person she should have hated, but couldn't. Despite the fact Pippa had everything Connie had hoped and longed for – an intact and happy marriage and a newborn baby following a third successful cycle of IVF, she had wanted to see her and meet her baby.

Connie stalked on, sweat dribbling down the sides of her face and her back as she headed deeper into the trees and the heat intensified. Not only did Pippa have everything Connie had hoped for with her beautiful baby daughter, but she had a sister who had stolen Felix away from Connie. The chances of what had happened and the two women's connection were so slim, and yet the irony was, Connie's new-found friend and support throughout fertility treatment was related to the woman who'd been screwing her husband. Despite hers and Pippa's lives being so different, she wanted to stay in touch with her.

Connie spied two colobus monkeys in the treetops before she emerged back out on to the sand, her hot and sweaty body soothed by the breeze. She cooled off with a shower and had a siesta on the daybed before going for a swim in the pool. Walking back to her villa with a beach kaftan thrown over her wet bikini, her growing contentment began to give her an uneasy feeling, yet she had no idea why.

Chapter Seven

'Morning, Connie,' Maria, Bella's marketing and PR manager said from behind the desk as Connie entered the airy reception.

'Morning, Maria.' Connie smiled. Maria was in her twenties, Scandinavian with incredibly blonde hair and an almost permanent smile on her face.

'Bella said you're starting work today.'

'Yeah, I'm kinda eager to be doing something. Relaxing is all well and good but it's not in my nature to sit around and do nothing.'

'I know that mentality well.'

'Is Theo around?'

'Can't say I've seen him yet this morning.'

'I'm here!' Theo stuck his head around the side of the open entrance that led towards the beach. 'Trying to fix a leak on the tap out here. Maria, show Connie the upstairs office could you? I won't be long.'

'Don't you have a maintenance person to fix stuff like that?' Connie asked Maria after Theo disappeared behind the building again.

Maria closed her laptop and stood up. 'We do. He lives in the village and can fix just about anything but he only does a few hours each day and so if something goes wrong when he's not here, someone else does the job.' She stepped out from behind the wooden desk. 'Or should I say, attempts to fix whatever's gone wrong until he gets here.' She walked across the reception and Connie followed. 'The amount of times I've seen Bella first thing in the morning walking around the place with a spanner in her hand. It's about time she took it easy.' They began to climb the spiral staircase at the back of the building. 'It's been great since she took on Theo – he's helped her out so much.'

Upstairs was open-plan with four computer desks. Large windows ran along two sides, looking directly out into the trees with a glimpse of the beach and ocean beyond.

'Monkeys quite often come and sit on the window ledge, so don't leave any food lying around.' Maria walked over to the only desk that didn't have papers and pens scattered across it. 'This used to be Bella's, although she usually works up in her villa these days, so it can be yours now. Theo's is next to the window, our admin and the HR manager work across from you. I presume you've met them both already?'

'Great,' Connie said. 'And yes I have, briefly.'

She followed Maria back across the room. Maria pushed open a door.

'The kitchen so you can make yourself a drink. The fridge is always stocked with fruit juice and soft drinks for when you can't be bothered to go down to the bar. Theo should be up to explain everything else soon.'

'Thanks, Maria.'

Maria clattered back down the stairs and Connie went over to Bella's old desk and sat down. The wood was smooth against her fingertips. The view of sunshine filtering through the leaves was so different from the red-brick wall and pots of flowers she used to gaze out at from her shared work space in Cardiff. The only sounds were waves folding on to the shore and the creak of branches in the breeze.

Connie opened the desk drawers, finding pens and pencils, paper, empty notebooks, and other stationery.

Footsteps sounded on the metal stairs and Theo appeared, his beige shorts smeared with dirt, the sleeves of his T-shirt rolled right up to his shoulders. His tanned cheeks were flushed and his dark hair wind-swept.

'I'd better change before greeting any guests today.' He headed into the kitchen and returned clutching two bottles of water. 'Want one?'

'Thanks.'

He handed her one and sat down at his desk.

'Your job encompasses a lot more than your title suggests,' Connie said.

'Ha, yes, camp manager. It's the nature of working in a place like this. It's a luxury retreat but not quite the same as a luxury hotel in say Italy or Spain. It's what I love about working in East Africa, each day is different and unpredictable. I wouldn't have it any other way.'

'You sound just like Bella.'

'I think that's why she hired me.' He unscrewed his bottle of water and took a gulp. 'And seriously, you're going to be a massive help. There are things Bella has wanted to do for ages but we just haven't had the capacity to do anything with the staff we have.'

'So what exactly do you want me to do?'

'We want to encourage guests to stay here for longer. It's easier having one couple for a week, than two or three couples spending just a couple of nights. What lots of people do is use Mchanga as either a start or end point of their two week holiday because they want to go on safari or visit Zanzibar. So, our thinking is, by offering day trips or even overnight stays at The House of Stone while they're staying here, will hopefully encourage guests to book for longer. But we need someone to facilitate this, someone who will take guests to Zanzibar or Chumbe or wherever, so it's easy and luxurious. You'll likely be travelling about a fair bit – hope you're okay with that?'

'Absolutely.' Connie felt a tightening in her chest at the thought of a new job to get to grips with. 'I just hope I'm the right person.'

'You will be; Bella has every faith in you.'

'I know, but I'm in this position because I'm her niece – you have no idea whether I'd be right for the role, I've not been interviewed and I'm guessing employing someone in that kind of capacity would have been down to you?'

'It would have been down to both me and Bella and trust

me, I'm very happy to have you on board. And Connie, relax,' Theo said with a smile. 'You know this place and Stone Town.'

'I did, sixteen years ago.'

'Not a lot has changed really apart from this place is more luxurious and a little bigger than it was when you first came here and Stone Town is a little more decayed around the edges but just as vibrant. If Bella has faith in you, so do I. You know full well what's she's like – even if you are her niece there's no way she'd give you this job without believing you're up to it and can do it well. It's the reputation of her resort on the line.'

'No pressure then.'

Theo banged the palm of his hand against his forehead. 'Duh, just realised what I said. Trust me, you're going to be great. I didn't mean to freak you out.'

Connie laughed. 'It's fine, I'm up for a challenge.' She leant back in the chair. 'So, how do I get started?'

The next few days flew by for Connie, a blur of getting to grips with how Mchanga was run. Most of the time she shadowed Theo, starting at six in the morning and working through until the last guest had gone to bed. Connie's job was to get to know every guest and find out what they would love to do, and then attempt to make it happen. As jobs went, it was a pretty special one. Connie relished getting to know both the guests and staff better. Alice and Oscar arrived after their stay on Zanzibar and Connie enjoyed seeing their friendly faces around the place and ensuring they had the best possible time and end to their honeymoon. Mchanga was a small enough place for everyone who worked there to get to know each other, with most people living in the staff accommodation on the hillside, apart from the staff who travelled in each day from the village. The camaraderie was something Connie had missed working by herself as a freelance jewellery designer.

'How's it going?' Maria asked as Connie reached the bottom of the spiral stairs that led down from the managers' office.

'Apart from my brain being overloaded, I'm ready to do my first day on my own tomorrow.'

'Good for you.'

'Are you coming for drinks up at Bella's this evening?'

'Most definitely.'

'She hosts drinks for the staff every month?'

Maria nodded. 'She tries to, for whoever's not working or who can escape for an hour. A night at Bella's is always a highlight.'

A middle-aged couple who were at Mchanga to celebrate their silver wedding anniversary walked up the steps from the beach. The man knocked on the wooden side of the building.

'Afternoon,' Maria said, beaming at them as they walked across. 'How's your day been?'

'See you later,' Connie said to Maria, nodding at the couple as she went past.

So far, evenings at Mchanga had been a mix of socialising with guests, quiet time spent in her beach villa and a late night drink with Bella, Theo and any other staff members still around. It was often just her and Theo left by the end, chatting until late about work and travel and growing up in two different countries. He was easy to talk to and as the days went by they relaxed into each other's company and she'd look forward to seeing him each day.

Connie kept busy and that was exactly how she liked it – little time to dwell on the past and the what could have been. Her thoughts were focused on living in the moment, getting to know her new colleagues, spending time with her aunt, and walking a path she hadn't planned on taking but was one that was keeping her sane after an awful year. It was well into September and while the UK was heading into autumn, Connie got to spend each day in the sunshine, where it was normal to wear flip-flops to work and a bikini beneath shorts and a T-shirt. The days were getting hotter not cooler as the Tanzanian weather heated up, in anticipation of the short rains at the end of the year. If it wasn't for the circumstances that had brought her to Tanzania in the first place, she would have been having the time of her life.

She walked the now familiar route along the sandy path that cut through the heart of Mchanga with its bar, restaurant and pool and joined the path that led to the beach villas. Even with the shrieks from monkeys high up in the trees and the waves thundering on to the sand, her villa was an oasis of calm and a place she relished coming back to. Drinks at Bella's weren't until eleven, late enough for the guests to have finished their dinner and when many of Mchanga's staff could come along. Connie had a few hours to kill. She'd raided Bella's bookshelf not long after she arrived, so flicking through the handful of books she'd brought to her room, she chose a light-hearted novel about a woman inheriting a dilapidated cottage in Cornwall, grabbed her hat and sunscreen and headed to the beach to soak up the last rays of the day.

It got dark early close to the equator – the long light summer evenings back in the UK had been replaced by sultry dark evenings at Mchanga. From the deck of her room, Connie could see lanterns lining the edge of the beach where the sand met the forest. Further down she could make out the welcoming sight of fairy lights strung along the edge of the bar's thatched roof. Lamplight shone across her bed and she pulled down the mosquito net so it entirely covered her bed. She went into the bathroom and splashed her face with cool water, slicked on deodorant and a brush of lip gloss and mascara. Her face was already lightly tanned from just over two weeks in the sun and she looked much healthier than she had when she first arrived, when the toll of the previous few months had been evident in her pale face and grey-ringed eyes. She pulled on colourful palazzo trousers and a simple black vest top and headed along the path and up the hillside.

It was open house at Bella's. Her hillside villa was strung with lights, and the decked area surrounding the plunge pool lit by lanterns, flickering warm light on to the water. Connie smiled at the two ladies who ran the spa where they sat by the side of the pool, and looked beyond into the dimly lit lounge where a handful of other staff mingled.

'Connie!' Bella beckoned her over.

Connie weaved her way across the decking and sat on the sofa next to her aunt.

'I still keep pinching myself that you're really here,' Bella said.

'Can you tell she's missed you?' Maria said from the armchair next to the sofa.

Connie laughed. 'Just a bit.'

Bella waved at Theo who'd appeared on the deck. He walked around the edge of the plunge pool saying hello to the staff outside before sitting down next to Connie.

'You managed to get away, then.' Bella cracked open two bottles of beer on the edge of the wooden coffee table and handed one to Theo, the other to Connie.

'Cheers,' he said, knocking it against Bella's glass of wine and Maria and Connie's bottles.

'And now you can relax.' Bella smiled. 'It's ironic really, that a place renowned for being so relaxing and romantic has the hardest working staff.'

'That's why guests find the place so relaxing, Bella, because we work hard at making them have the best time.'

'And I appreciate the hard work more than you could ever know.'

'Bella,' Maria said, placing her hand on Bella's arm. 'You work harder than anyone I know.'

'It's not really hard work when it's your life.'

Theo held up his bottle and looked at Bella. 'To you and what you've worked hard for.' He took a sip and wiped away the droplets of beer on his beard with the back of his hand. 'I can't tell you how much I've been longing to sit down with a cold beer.'

Bella playfully slapped his leg. 'See, I'm not the only one who works too hard. I'll have none of this slow down bullshit.'

'As if anyone would dare say that to you.' Connie smiled at her aunt from over the top of her beer bottle.

'Oh, you'd be surprised.'

Connie glanced between Theo and Maria. 'Did you have evenings like this where you two used to work?'

'Sort of,' Maria said, nodding towards Bella. 'Not as nice as this and not in the owner's home, but there used to be occasional get-togethers in the staff lounge after guests had gone to bed.'

'Where was that?' Connie asked.

'When I worked at a resort on the Gold Coast.'

'You worked in Oz?' Theo leant forward and looked past Connie to Maria.

'For a few years before coming here. That's where you're from, right?'

Theo nodded. 'From Sydney originally but to be honest I've spent the whole of my adult life working abroad. I've kind of forgotten what it feels like to live there.'

'You said you worked at a safari camp before coming here?' Connie asked.

Bella waved to someone out on the deck, and stood up. 'I'll be back,' she said and headed outside.

Theo sipped his beer. 'Yeah, in Kenya, running the place. It was a pretty small and exclusive luxury camp and it was mostly couples who worked there along with local guides. A different vibe to here, even though this place is far from large.'

'What made you leave?' Maria asked. 'If you don't mind me asking.'

Clutching his beer in both hands, Theo stared out towards the staff sitting and relaxing on Bella's deck.

'No, I don't mind you asking,' he said slowly. He took another sip of beer. 'My relationship ended – we worked together as the camp managers and even though she was the one to leave, I just couldn't stay. Too many memories. I know Geoff.' He glanced at Connie and then Maria. 'Bella's ex, and he knew Bella was looking for a manager and recommended me.'

Connie leant back on the sofa, her hands clasped around her beer bottle. She listened to Theo and Maria talk about the countries they'd travelled to and worked in. It had only been a couple of weeks since she'd left her old life behind, and meeting new people, throwing herself into an unfamiliar yet interesting job and spending time with Bella had been a complete tonic.

'I'm going to get another drink.' Maria stood up. 'Either of you two want one?'

Theo shook his head. 'No thanks.'

'I'm fine too.'

Maria retreated to the kitchen area behind them and Theo turned to Connie. 'So, how are you enjoying the job? I know it's only been a few days of you getting to grips with how the place ticks.'

'Seriously, I'm loving it, more than I thought I would. I mean, I felt pretty nervous at the beginning of the week but you and Bella have been great and so patient with me asking a million questions.'

'What did you do back in the UK?'

'Nothing like this.' Connie took a handful of crisps from the bowl on the coffee table. 'I was a self-employed jewellery designer, so most of my working day was spent on my own designing, creating and working on commissions. This sense of camaraderie is something I missed working by myself. It's nice to finally have colleagues.'

'I get that.' Theo reached for a crisp too. 'You gave up your business to come here?' He frowned.

'Sort of. I've got a backlog of jewellery still available on my Etsy store that a designer friend is dealing with on my behalf and taking a small cut from each order.'

'And when that stock runs out?'

Connie shrugged. 'I'll see what I feel like when that happens. Either way I'm going to be here for six months until the end of February and Mchanga closes for the rainy season.'

Theo nodded and sipped his drink. She sensed he was desperate to ask her more and she wondered how much Bella had told him about why she'd come to Tanzania. It was the same for her as well – she was stopping herself questioning him further about the break-up of his relationship. She

57

wouldn't want to be put in that position and questioned about Felix, and she doubted he did either about his ex.

'I can easily start it up again. Think of it like I'm taking a sabbatical, it's just with my own business rather than being employed by someone. It's risky what I'm doing but necessary. Trust me, it's the best thing being here and seeing Bella again.'

'She didn't visit you in England?'

'Rarely. She came over when my brother got married and then when I did, but that was about it. There's no love lost between her and my father.'

'Oh really?'

'She's younger than him – not that their age difference should matter but perhaps it's a generational thing. Their personalities couldn't be more opposed. My father has always thought of Bella as reckless despite the fact she's a success and has created all of this.' Connie waved her arms in front of her. 'He's never seemed interested in what she's achieved or is doing. To be honest he's up his own arse most of the time.'

'Doesn't sound like there's much love lost between you and him either.'

'That's because I'm more like Bella than him, and he's never liked that. I've never really been that close to my parents or my brother.'

'I get that. I'm not close to my dad either – he left when I was eight and my mum raised me and my older sisters on her own. He got remarried and had two more kids, but he didn't stay in touch. I'm close to Mum but felt stifled growing up in a big city – my sisters were quite happy to get married and settle down young, so I felt okay about leaving home and travelling. I had seriously itchy feet – couldn't wait to leave.'

Connie placed her empty bottle on the table and relaxed back. Theo leant back next to her, their shoulders just touching.

'Do you go back and see your mum often?'

'When I get those two months off in the rainy season I go and see her most years. I Skype with her a lot. She's remarried, so she's not on her own and my sisters are popping out grandchildren like they're going out of fashion.'

Theo's shoulder was firm and warm against hers. Some of the staff were chatting on the deck. Bella put a hand on the head chef's arm and laughed. The tops of the trees that surrounded Bella's villa were dark shadows against the lighter sky with its nearly full moon and gleaming stars.

'She's so happy you're here.' Theo moved his arm until it rested on the edge of the sofa behind her, his skin brushing the back of her neck and sending a shiver through her. 'I know I've only been here a few months but there's been a noticeable difference in her since you arrived. You're good for her.'

Connie turned her gaze from Bella to Theo and met his blue eyes. 'She's good for me too.'

Chapter Eight

'There's a new guest in villa two,' Theo said, catching hold of Connie's arm as she swept past him clutching a pile of leaflets about The House of Stone to her chest.

'Just the one?' She put the leaflets on the side of the reception desk and turned to Theo.

'I know, a bit unusual, eh. A single guy, here for three nights. I wasn't available so Maria checked him in.'

'He's had time to settle in?'

Theo nodded.

'I'll head over there now.'

'Apparently he's already mentioned about going diving – he might want a trip to Zanzibar or Chumbe organised.'

'I'll see what I can arrange.'

Connie headed back out into the sunshine. Only ten in the morning and the heat smothered her and with no breeze for once, it was a day for doing as little as possible.

Connie liked the position of room number two; not quite at the furthest point from the main guest areas, it was tucked back into the trees a little more than the others, yet still had a glimpse of sand and ocean through the greenery. Connie took the path that wound behind the villas, before turning down the sandy path that led to the front of villa two. She waited at the bottom of the steps that led up to the deck and coughed.

'Hello?'

An empty rucksack lay on the floor next to one of the daybeds and a handful of shorts and T-shirts were piled on the bed. Connie stepped up on to the veranda and walked past the plunge pool, thinking how much she'd like to dive in.

'Hello? Anyone here? It's Connie, Mchanga's Guest Advisor.'

'That's a fancy title,' a man with a Welsh accent said, walking out from the bathroom at the back of the villa and into the bedroom.

It took only a second for Connie to clock the familiarity of the accent, the black curly hair, the buff body and muscly arms beneath a fitted white T-shirt. Yet time stood still, as the trauma of the last few months flooded back.

'Felix?'

Felix wiped his face with the flannel he had clutched in his hand, dropped it on the bed and walked towards her.

Already hot, Connie's face flushed hotter as rage raced through her. She staggered back, feeling as shocked and upset as she had when she'd confronted him seven months ago about his affair and when she'd found out she was miscarrying another baby. Their baby.

'What the hell are you doing here?' She held on to the post at the edge of the villa, partly for support, partly to stop herself from turning back and punching Felix's face.

'I needed to talk to you, Connie. I want to tell you how sorry I am for everything that's happened over the past couple of years.'

'What the hell's wrong with picking up a phone or emailing.'

'You know full well you'd ignore that. You *have* been ignoring my attempts to communicate with you.'

'You sound surprised.' Connie wiped beads of sweat from the sides of her face with the back of her hand. If she'd felt smothered before it was nothing compared to how she was feeling now. 'I was getting over you. I am over you.'

'You really mean that – you're over me?' Felix walked towards her and held his hands out. 'I love you, Connie, I always have done and always will.'

Connie shrank back, aware how much her heart was thudding in her chest, hating herself for letting her eyes linger a little too long on his defined jaw and those big hazel eyes that she'd fallen stupidly in love with years ago.

She made herself look away, out into the wildness of the trees and undergrowth that surrounded the villa.

'How can you even believe that after what you did?' She folded her arms, wanting a barrier between them. The last time they'd stood like this was in their apartment when she'd confronted him about his affair. 'If you truly loved me there's no way you'd have done what you did. No way.'

He took another step towards her. Connie held her ground.

'I was confused and angry,' he said. 'I felt a failure not being able to give you a baby, the thing you wanted most of all, being the one, you know, who couldn't get you pregnant.'

Connie clenched her fists. 'But you did get me pregnant.' She forced herself to remain calm and not kick him in the nuts or punch his handsome face. 'Not in the conventional way, but I was pregnant with your baby, twice. Don't give me a sob story about finding your infertility difficult to deal with. I was the one undergoing the actual fertility treatment. I had two miscarriages while you were off having fun screwing someone else's wife. If you really loved me there's no way you'd have behaved like that. You can get yourself on a plane back to the UK today. I'll book and pay for it myself if I have to.'

She turned to go.

'I have no intention of leaving,' he said. 'And you have no way of making me. I'm a paying guest and as you know, this place isn't cheap.'

She swung back to face him. 'You're a bastard, you know that.'

'Whether you talk to me or not, I'm staying here for the next three days.'

'Go to hell, Felix.' She stalked down the villa's steps and on to the sandy path that led to the beach.

Bella would have something to say about Felix being here, but then Connie remembered Bella had left early in the morning for Dar es Salaam and wouldn't be back until the afternoon before Felix left.

Tears mixed with sweat streamed down her hot face by the time she reached the start of the path from the beach to the main guest area. Not wanting to risk seeing anyone until she'd calmed down and composed herself, Connie continued to walk across the hot sand. Two guests were already set up for the day on sunloungers beneath one of the thatched umbrellas and Connie waved back when they waved at her, but kept walking until she reached the shipwreck. She stood by the edge of the ocean and let the surf wash over her toes. With her hands on her hips she took a deep breath and gazed across the wreck to where the ocean reached the sky, a myriad of blues and sea greens. The slightest of breezes dried her tears, leaving her skin feeling tight. She knelt down and scooped a handful of salty water and splashed it on her face, attempting to wash away any trace of upset. Felix was not going to beat her down; she wasn't going to allow him to taint the love she had for this place; or derail her healing. She wasn't going to let him win. How dare he follow her here when she'd left the UK to escape him, his betrayal and his lies. How dare he.

'Did you arrange anything with the guest in two?' Theo asked when Connie popped her head into the office on her way back to take some other guests up the coast for a picnic on the beach.

'He wasn't there,' Connie said calmly. 'I'll find him when I get back later.'

'Okay, no problem, we can catch up with him at dinner this evening and see what he fancies doing over the next couple of days.'

Connie nodded and left, unable to say anything else, afraid the hatred she had for Felix would be evident in her voice. She hated that she'd just lied to Theo but how could she even begin to explain her relationship to him without the past couple of years of her messed up life unravelling – nothing she was ready to share with anyone apart from Bella right now. This place had been her escape. How she was going to get through the next thirty-six hours with Felix here she had no idea.

Evenings at Mchanga were full of food, laughter, music and twinkling lights. The view from the open-air restaurant and bar disappeared at night, save for the moon reflecting on the ocean and waves tumbling on to the shore. In place of the view, the thatched bar area was lit by fairy lights and lamps, and the tables flickered with candlelight sheltered from the breeze in coloured glasses. Since arriving at Mchanga, Connie had loved socialising with the guests, ensuring they were having the best holiday possible, but that evening she had a feeling of dread at having to face Felix again, and be charming and sociable.

After changing into a flowing white skirt and wine-coloured vest top, her long wavy hair pinned up off her slender neck, Connie entered the bar from the pool side, relieved to see all the guests were still on the deck eating. Candlelight flickered further down the beach, a trail of lamps creating a makeshift path through the sand to where a couple were having a private dinner.

'Hey, Abasi. What's on the menu tonight?' Connie asked one of the barmen who was pouring an orange and red liquid into cocktail glasses. He pushed a menu towards her. She picked it up, leant against the bar and pretended to read it, while her attention was drawn to the tables. There was a mix of new guests and those who had been at Mchanga for a few days. Waiters were busy taking plates brimming with food to the tables and Theo was being his usual affable self, making sure everyone was enjoying themselves. Connie's heart skipped a beat when she clocked Felix on a table on his own, facing the dark ocean, his back to the bar area and her.

Once the guests had finished their dinner, most of them made their way to the bar. Connie took drinks orders and chatted to guests, talking about what they had done that day and making a mental note of what they fancied doing for the rest of their time there. This was Bella's life, ever the gracious host when she was there, enjoying a cocktail or a glass of chilled white wine with her guests. Connie was in mid-conversation with an American couple in their fifties when Theo appeared next to her with Felix by his side.

'Evening, Connie. Bob, Martha.' He nodded towards the American couple. 'This is Felix who arrived this morning. He was telling me about his job in marketing for an advertising company back in the UK, Bob, and I said that's the field you work in over in New York.'

Bob shook Felix's hand, his wife smiling sweetly as she sipped her Prosecco. 'Good to meet you, Felix. Who do you work for?'

Felix started chatting, avoiding eye contact with Connie. Once Theo moved on to talk to other guests, she quietly slipped away, intending to talk to anyone who wasn't her lying, cheating bastard of an ex. Somehow, without making it obvious, she managed to avoid having to talk to Felix for the rest of the evening; instead she flitted between guests, constantly on the move, eager to take bar orders and not stay still long enough to get trapped into talking to him. It was the first time since she'd been at Mchanga that she longed for the evening to be over, and by about ten, when guests started to head back to their beach villas or hilltop suites she breathed a sigh of relief.

On her way to the bar with an order, she brushed past Theo perched on the arm of one of the sofas chatting to Bob and Martha. He glanced at her and she smiled, aware that Felix was looking in their direction from where he sat on the far side of the bar. Theo was good looking in a less arrogant way than Felix – dark brown hair that was naturally windswept and sun-kissed skin. They were comfortable with each other and had naturally gravitated to each other once all the guests had gone to bed.

Connie looked at Bob and Martha. 'Can I get you anything from the bar?'

'No thanks, honey,' Martha replied, laughing. 'We have to walk back up the hill yet.'

Theo leant towards Connie, his hand finding the small of her back. 'I'm just going to have a quick chat with the remaining guests; fancy a drink before you head back to your room?'

'Would love one,' Connie said.

Theo, an effortless host, chatted with everyone who hadn't yet headed to bed, but Connie noticed he spent a lot of time with Felix – with good reason, being a guest on his own – but him chatting to and laughing with her soon-to-be ex-husband left a bitter taste in her mouth.

She was beginning to think that Theo had forgotten about his promise of a drink when he made his way towards her at the edge of the bar, where a gentle breeze floated in from off the ocean.

'Nice chap that Felix,' he said as he sat down next to her. 'I invited him over for a drink with us but he's calling it a night.'

Connie nodded and mumbled 'uh-huh' into her drink before taking a sip and hoping Theo hadn't noticed the way she avoided talking about him.

Felix stood up, downed the last dregs of his pint, and with the briefest of glances towards her and Theo, walked away with his hands planted firmly in his shorts pockets.

'He said he's in the middle of a divorce – wanted to get away from all the crap in his life back home.'

Connie clenched her teeth. 'Is that so.'

'Poor guy.'

Connie downed her drink, not trusting herself to say anything without laying into Felix and giving away who he was. She wasn't ready to tell Theo all the horrible things that had happened to her during the past year. Felix was all the crap in *her* life she'd been trying to escape from.

The bar was finally empty, the bar staff clearing away the remains of drinks and cleaning behind the bar. Theo slid his arm along the ledge behind Connie, his fingertips brushing her bare shoulder. She held her breath and then relaxed back until she could properly feel his fingers against her skin.

Theo stretched his legs out, resting them on the low table in front of them. 'Well, this is the place to come if you want to forget about stuff.'

'True.'

Everyone had gone. Felix was the last to leave, and the bar staff had disappeared round the back of the bar. Tucked away in a corner, the light dim, they were alone. Connie took a deep breath and leant closer to Theo, alcohol making her lose her inhibitions. She kissed his lips and held back for a second, her heart pounding, waiting for him to pull away and go 'what the hell?'. He didn't. Clasping the side of her face in his hands he kissed her back, more passionately than she'd done.

He stopped and looked at her, his hands still cupping her face. 'We can't do this, not here,' he said, glancing towards the bar.

Theo took her hand and led her down the steps from the bar. They stumbled and giggled together up the hill, past a wood-clad building housing shared en suite bedrooms, a communal kitchen and living area for staff, next to the four management cottages. Theo led Connie to the largest cottage at the end.

'Make yourself at home.' He turned on the lamp on the sideboard and poured them each a large glass of cognac.

Connie sat down on the sofa that faced the open doors leading to a small veranda. A breeze filtered through, wrapping itself around her. She'd drunk too much, which after her experience with Jamil and being teetotal during the past couple of years while she and Felix tried for a baby, was not the wisest of ideas. Taking the glass Theo handed her as he sat down, she shoved the thought to the back of her mind.

'You took me by surprise down there.' Theo knocked his glass against hers.

She took a sip of the sweet cognac and then downed the rest. She didn't want to think straight, she wanted to be impulsive, uninhibited, hurt Felix as much as he'd hurt her. She took the glass from Theo's hand. 'I surprised myself too.'

She kissed him, emptying her mind of everything, ignoring the sensible side of her that was screaming stop. She'd endured an evening of Felix invading her life again when she had been getting over him. She was hurting too badly and the last thing she wanted to do was be sensible. Even if that was exactly what she should be doing.

Theo kissed her back, pushing her gently down until she rested against the sofa. She closed her eyes as Theo's hands explored. Her hands discovered his body too, dipping beneath his linen shirt, the strangeness of touching an unfamiliar chest. The sensation of him kissing her in places only one man had for the past twelve years both thrilled and terrified her. He pulled her to her feet and led her through to his bedroom. He slipped her skirt off, leaving it pooled on the wooden floor by the bed and wriggled her vest top up and over her head. Her fingers worked deftly, undoing the buttons of his shirt. His skin glowed in the moonlight. And then, without even realising it, they were both naked, their bodies pressed together as they kissed.

She lay down on the bed, the ceiling fan sending the gentlest of breezes over her hot skin. Theo knelt on the bed, held her hands in his and pushed them until they were above her head, touching the headboard. She closed her eyes as his lips found her throat and the heat of his body pressed against hers. She emptied her mind of everything, all the pain she'd felt over the past couple of years with Felix, and gave into the longing she had for Theo, a feeling that had been building ever since she'd met him.

Connie had no idea how late it was by the time Theo wrapped his arms around her, hugging her naked body against his. Lying on top of the sheets she stared out through the open bedroom window at the night sky, a deep midnight blue flecked with silver stars. She listened as Theo's breathing slowed and became more rhythmic as he fell asleep, his arm increasingly heavy where it rested on her hip. Connie's heart pounded. She willed herself to relax into a dreamless sleep, but thoughts swirled around her head. Her not yet divorced husband was lying in bed less than a two minute walk from where she was lying with a man she'd only known for a couple of weeks, a man she'd just had sex with out of anger, frustration, hurt – a decent man she'd used purely to get back at the son-of-a-bitch she'd once loved. Fighting back the sobs that threatened to wrack her body she let tears slip silently down her cheeks and on to Theo's pillow.

Chapter Nine

Connie woke with a start, memories from the night before invading her head like a bad hangover. She turned on to her side but the bed was empty, the sheet crumpled. She was naked, apart from a sheet covering her, and she shivered despite the warmth of the morning. She could hear clattering in the next room and the smell of coffee brewing.

She sat up and groaned as pain thudded across her forehead. With the sheet pulled up to her neck, she swung her legs out of Theo's bed and reached for her underwear that she'd discarded on the wooden floor. She dressed and ran her fingers through her long, tangled hair. She paused by the closed bedroom door. In the cold sober light of day it felt strange being in Bella's old room. It was furnished the same – a wooden double bed facing doors out on to the small deck, wooden chest of drawers, even the pictures on the wall were identical – photos of animals a regular guest and professional photographer had taken while Bella had been living in Selous. Gone was Bella's jewellery and framed photos displayed on top of the chest of drawers. There was nothing evident in the room that was personal to Theo.

Connie took a deep breath, the realisation of what she'd done the night before flooding through her like a chill. She liked Theo, she really did, and she undoubtedly found him attractive but, there was no question that she'd used him. If Felix hadn't showed up, would last night have happened?

She pushed open the door. Theo had his back to her, pouring coffee into two mugs. He turned at the sound of the door shutting behind her.

'Morning,' he said and smiled.

'Morning,' Connie replied, taking hold of a steaming mug of coffee that he passed to her. He brought his own mug across to the coffee table, along with milk and a bowl of sugar cubes.

'I was going to let you sleep for as long as possible,' he said, sitting on the sofa.

Connie sat down next to him, without a clue of what to say. The easy way they'd been able to chat together up until this point destroyed by a reckless decision on her part.

Theo poured milk into his mug. 'I always start my day with a coffee and look at this view.'

'That's what Bella used to do.' Connie poured a generous amount of milk into her strong coffee and stirred it.

Theo sipped his coffee and Connie did the same with hers, giving herself time to think through what to say. He was dressed for work in his khaki green shorts and Mchanga T-shirt.

'About last night,' she said, unable to look him in the eye, conscious that she'd seen him naked and had done things that were far from professional to do with her boss. 'I don't normally behave that way. I'm sorry if…'

Theo placed his hand on her thigh. 'Connie, I'm not sorry. I like you and I assume by what happened last night you like me too. Nothing to be sorry about.'

Connie bit her lip and nodded. She really did like him but guilt flooded through her knowing that seducing him had happened out of anger at Felix, and an overwhelming desire to hurt him a fraction of how he'd hurt her.

'Maybe keep last night between ourselves though.' Theo stroked his thumb across her thigh. 'Probably best if the staff don't have us to gossip about. Or your aunt finds out.'

'Of course,' she replied. 'Goes without saying.' She gulped a mouthful of the hot coffee. Theo's hand was still caressing her leg, yet her desire was mixed with panic. If only she could rewind time to before she'd first kissed him. She downed the rest of her coffee, ignoring how it scalded her mouth and throat, and stood up. Theo's hand dropped from her leg.

'I should head back to my room and get changed.' She met his eyes, conscious she was wearing the very clothes he'd taken off her only hours earlier.

She turned to go and he caught her hand in his. 'Last night was great.' He pulled her closer and gently kissed her. 'We should do it again sometime.'

'I'll see you down at the office.' She was at a loss of how else to respond.

She left his villa, oblivious to her surroundings as she concentrated on putting one foot in front of each other on the steep path. She made it down the hillside and back to her beach villa without falling over, bumping into anyone and definitely without seeing Felix.

Connie showered, relishing the cool water pummelling her body as she washed off the lingering scent of Theo from her skin – his aftershave and sunscreen and sweat. Not that she felt dirty, not in that sense. It was an overwhelming feeling of guilt that consumed her for using him in the way she had. She wrapped a towel around herself and dried her hair before stepping out of the bathroom, which was screened off at the rear of the villa, and into the bedroom.

It was nearly seven in the morning already, so she dressed quickly, pulling on clean underwear, a floaty, pale-grey skirt and a black vest top with the Mchanga logo on it and headed towards the managers' office. This early in the morning, most guests were still in bed or relaxing on the decks of their rooms, watching the foaming surf or listening to monkeys chattering together on the roof of their room. There was one couple eating breakfast but Connie walked quickly past.

'Hey,' Theo said, as Connie appeared in the office doorway.

'Hey.'

His hair was still messed up and she fought back the image of how she'd run her hands through it and across his toned chest now hidden beneath a T-shirt.

'You've got a busy day,' he said, flicking through a pile of papers on his desk.

She liked how he was being normal with her. If he was distracted by the thought of them together the night before, he was dealing with it way better than she was.

'Yeah, I know.' She smiled and tried to rid her head of inappropriate thoughts. 'Snorkelling around the wreck and a picnic on the beach. How many couples are going?'

'Two couples plus Felix – when I was talking to him last night he was at a loss of what to do today, so I suggested he joined you. I get the feeling he doesn't want to be on his own.'

'Great,' Connie said, gritting her teeth in an attempt to contain the re-emergence of anger building at the mere mention of Felix. She took the guest list and itinerary from Theo, their fingers brushing against each other's as she did. 'I'll see you later.' She turned and left the office.

The day would have been perfect if only Felix wasn't there. It was in Connie's nature to please people. For years she'd worked as a designer, making bespoke jewellery often commissioned by a boyfriend about to propose; a mother celebrating her children with a necklace featuring their birth stones; a grieving son or daughter wanting the stone from their mother's wedding ring incorporated into a piece of jewellery to commemorate their loved one's life; or a celebratory bracelet for a graduation or a special birthday. But taking loved-up couples, as well as her nearly ex-husband for a walk along the beach the morning after she'd slept with her boss out of anger at her ex, was so very wrong.

Leading the way across the sand towards the shipwreck she focused on putting one foot in front of the other as the mid-morning sun caressed her bare shoulders. She tried not to think about anything, least of all Felix sauntering behind her or the image of Theo that kept filtering into her head and the way he'd kissed her and the feel of him against her as they'd curled up together and slept. She shook the thought away and pulled her sun hat further down so it fully shaded her neck.

The advantage of being with other people was that she and Felix couldn't talk – at least not about themselves, their past or anything else Felix seemed intent on discussing with her.

Connie kept herself busy, ensuring the two couples and Felix were relaxed and happy with a steady flow of drinks to enjoy on the sunloungers in-between snorkelling around the shipwreck and body boarding on the waves. At lunchtime, two of Mchanga's staff brought a large cool box and a bag to the beach and Connie helped them lay out picnic blankets on the sand. She set up bowls of salads and seafood for them to tuck into, with a couple of bottles of fizz.

'Cheers,' Connie said, as the six of them knocked their glasses of champagne together.

'You're both on your honeymoon?' Felix took a sip of his drink and glanced between the two couples.

'We are,' the husband of the younger couple said.

The wife of the other couple took her partner's hand. 'We're celebrating our third wedding anniversary and thought we'd take the opportunity to have a final 'big' holiday before hopefully starting a family.'

She just couldn't get away from it – happily married couples ready to start families – it was like they were drawn to her. She knew it was the nature of the place – as she'd said to Oscar and Alice at Mtazamo, Mchanga was probably one of the most romantic places in Tanzania, if not the whole of East Africa. Most of Bella's business came from honeymooners or couples celebrating wedding anniversaries. Ironic really, considering Bella's own marriage and love life had been far from happy.

'You're here alone?' the older husband asked, turning to Felix.

'Divorcing, not my choice. I needed to get away.'

'I'm sorry,' the guy replied.

Connie took a deep breath.

'Don't be.' Felix sat forward, resting his arms on his tanned legs, his hands clasping the stem of his glass. 'I hope we can work things out.'

The bastard had the nerve to make strangers feel sorry for him right in front of her, rubbing salt into her wounds.

'How come you chose to come here?' the wife of the

older couple asked.

'It was my wife's favourite place.'

There was an actual 'aah' from the couples – the men as well as the women. He was a salesman – he'd always been a smooth talker with the ability to charm. It had been what initially attracted Connie to him. Now his smoothness left her nauseous. He'd used his charm to seduce another woman while married to her, and he was weaving a charming lie to these people right in front of her.

'I hope you work things out,' the honeymooning wife said.

'Where did you have your wedding?' Connie asked her, desperate to change the subject.

The woman smiled. 'In a castle in Wales, seriously the most incredible place, wasn't it, Dom?'

'It didn't even rain,' he replied. 'Which is pretty much a miracle for Wales, isn't it?'

Everyone laughed. Connie smiled, well aware of the difference not just in the weather between where she used to live in Cardiff with Felix, but where they were now – the heat, the beach, the endless view of ocean and sky.

'Where in Wales are you from, Felix?' Dom asked.

And the conversation was back to him, his Welsh accent as much of a draw as the reason he was at Mchanga on his own. Connie took a strawberry from one of the bowls and zoned out. She heard Cardiff mentioned, something about Felix growing up in Wales…

'How about you, Connie? How did you end up working here?' the wife of the older couple asked.

Connie looked up from where she'd been staring at the strawberries. Felix's eyes were on her. She'd only poured herself a tiny glass of champagne, enough for a couple of sips and she wished she had a whole glass she could down.

'My aunt Bella, who you may have met, runs Mchanga.' She breathed deeply, debating whether to play the same game Felix was or not. Everyone's eyes were on her, including her ex-husband's. 'Much like Felix, I came out here to get over a divorce. Unlike Felix, I'm well shot of the son-of-a… well, you get the idea.'

They all chuckled, although Felix's distinct laugh was absent.

'So, you're not with anyone now?' the older wife asked.

Connie shook her head. 'Nope. Very much single and enjoying myself.' She allowed a glance at Felix. Was that a frown briefly creasing his forehead? She hoped so. Let him wonder. How much would she love to turn round and tell him that last night she'd slept with the manager of Mchanga. Completely unprofessional and she'd never really say anything, but she'd love to see the look on his face.

Chapter Ten

She managed to get through the rest of lunch, the conversation moving on from her and Felix to the couples' plans for the rest of their holiday, the excitement of a safari still to go and time on Zanzibar. Gone midday and the morning heat had intensified. With stomachs full of food and fizz, Connie called an end to the picnic.

'Stroll back to Mchanga, sleep, relax on the beach or have a drink in the bar. Whatever takes your fancy,' Connie said to the two couples, waving them off as she packed up the empty dishes, plates and picnic blankets.

'I'll help you carry them back.'

Bent over, zipping up the bag, Connie didn't look up at Felix. She'd managed to avoid being alone with him all day and now he had the nerve to hang back.

'No need.' She stood up and turned to him. 'The guys will come back and collect these.' She started walking, following the trail of footprints from the two couples strolling ahead.

Felix jogged to catch up with her and matched her pace. With her feet sinking into the sand she couldn't walk any faster.

'You can't ignore me forever, you know,' he said.

Despite wanting to stop and slap him, Connie kept walking. 'Actually, I can. I have nothing left to say to you.'

This was the man she once loved. The man she wanted to have children with. But now... Now, her skin crawled at the thought of him. She couldn't even look at him without anger searing through her and a whole multitude of feelings that she never wanted to feel again. To think that only the other day she'd been missing him. The hurt and pain she was feeling had to stop, even if that meant removing Felix from her life forever.

Trying to keep a fast pace along the beach sent sweat sliding down the sides of her cheeks. The afternoon sun was unforgiving and even with the slight breeze, it was time to do nothing and retreat to a cool room with a fan. Her mind flicked back to the night before and gazing up at the ceiling fan whizzing above Theo's bed – Connie's hands stroking his bare back; Theo's hands all over her. The thought of Felix ever touching her in that way again made her feel sick. She wanted nothing more to do with him. She stalked on, the sun pounding down, smothering her.

Mchanga was in sight, the thatched umbrellas providing a little shade for the guests. One of the beach attendants carried a tray of drinks down the steps from the bar and across the sand to a couple relaxing further along the beach. The breeze was a little stronger closer to Mchanga and wrapped Connie's long floaty skirt around her legs as she walked. The waves folded on to the shore, foam lapping at the feet of the honeymooning couple who'd been on the picnic as they walked along the edge of the ocean. She and Felix were once like them: in love, together, a team, happy. Now she couldn't even look at the man she once adored without wanting to hurt him.

The steps up to the restaurant and bar were only a few paces away. Connie slowed and half turned to Felix. 'Please, just leave me alone.' She took the steps two at a time, leaving Felix standing down on the beach.

'I love barbeque night.' Maria joined Connie by the bar as couples started arriving from their villas and suites to be seated on the terrace. 'Always so much fun and the highlight of the week.'

'You've finished for the day?'

'Yes, it's been quiet. Oh and by the way, a couple were supposed to arrive this afternoon but their plane was delayed and so won't get here until later this evening. I think Theo was going to talk to you about you welcoming them later if you're able to?'

'Of course I can. I've not seen Theo since this morning.' Connie willed her cheeks not to flush. No one at Mchanga knew what had happened between her and Theo and there was no reason for anyone to find out. There was no way anyone *should* find out.

She'd managed to avoid seeing Felix for the rest of the day and even though she knew he was around – sunbathing on the beach or relaxing in his room – the sight of him walking up the steps to the restaurant made her heart pound, but not in the way it used to. She watched as one of the waiters greeted him and seated him at a table overlooking the beach. It was a relaxed evening with guests getting up and choosing what they wanted from the selection of barbequed meat, chicken and seafood along with a range of salads on the table next to the barbeque. Most guests sat back down to eat at their tables but a few, including Felix, stood about with their plates brimming with food, a fork in their hands, chatting to Mchanga staff, many of whom were also tucking into the barbeque. Theo, ever the gracious host did the rounds, stopping by every table, chatting and joking with everyone, but she noticed he made a beeline for Felix, particularly if Felix was left on his own for any length of time.

Smoke spiralled up into the sky from the lit barbeque drums set out on one side of the deck. The smell of smoky charcoal and grilling meats as they sizzled and hissed above the glowing coals made Connie's mouth water. She realised she'd barely eaten anything all day – only a handful of strawberries at the picnic, and breakfast seemed a very long time ago. She was glad of a plate of food to stop her stomach rumbling and to focus on something else apart from Felix.

Maria introduced Connie to guests who had visited a couple of years before and Connie was relieved to have an excuse to avoid both Felix and Theo. It was late by the time she got a message over the radio from Mohammed that the guests whose plane had been delayed had finally arrived. With the party still in full swing, she made her excuses to the couple she'd been talking to, smiled at Maria who was relaxing with a bottle of beer up at the bar, and caught a glimpse of Theo sitting with Felix on one of the seats at the far side of the bar, deep in conversation.

Connie headed down the steps from the restaurant, leaving behind the chatter and laughter and smoked-meat smells. The path was lit by lanterns and she headed to the welcome building, quiet now with just Juma on security overnight.

'Evening, Connie,' he said with his usual grin.

'Evening,' she replied. 'Hope you've managed to have some of the barbeque?'

'Maria brought me a plate over earlier.' He reached behind the desk and handed Connie the welcome pack. 'You after this?'

'Yes, thank you. The new guests are in suite four, aren't they?'

Juma nodded. 'Took them up there myself.'

'Great, I'll head up there now.'

She tucked the basket under her arm and headed back out into the sultry night. The barbeque-smell filled her nostrils as she skirted the restaurant and made her way up the steep, sandy path that led to the hillside suites. She was halfway up when she heard footsteps behind her. She was about to turn to see who it was when an all too familiar voice said, 'So, you're shagging the manager then.'

Connie stopped and swung around to face Felix. 'What? What the hell, Felix?'

Her heart thumped despite the fact that this was what she'd wanted – for Felix to find out about her and Theo.

'Don't play innocent, Connie.'

'I'm not.' She clutched the basket to her chest and searched his face for what, she wasn't sure – hurt? Anger? Regret? 'I just don't understand what business it is of yours.'

Felix folded his arms and held her gaze. 'You're okay with *him* discussing having sex with you to one of the guests. Not exactly professional, is it?'

'Oh please, Felix, he banters with the guests. You're here on your own, you were both drinking and doing some male bonding and no doubt you gave him leading questions. I'm not stupid, I know what men talk about, so don't get all high and mighty about him being professional or not. Do I need to remind you that you were the one who was screwing another woman while we were married and I was pregnant?' Connie stepped towards him, hands clenched around the basket, a tightness spreading across her chest. 'The last time I checked I was single, so have done nothing wrong. You not liking how I spend my free time is none of your goddam business.'

'Technically we're still married.'

She turned and stalked away, panting up the hill, sweat coursing down the sides of her face in the night-time heat. She needed Felix out of her life. She needed him gone from Mchanga and back in the UK well away from her. She needed time to heal and to forget him. It was unforgivable that he'd had the nerve to fly out here and invade the place that she'd sought refuge. Why the hell did she feel guilty when they were divorcing?

Solar lights lit the path all the way up to the suites, small globes of warm light spilling across the sandy soil. Connie reached the top and stopped to catch her breath. Silence surrounded her and she sighed with relief that Felix hadn't followed. She waited until her breathing had slowed, patted her hot face dry with a tissue and made her way along the path that ran behind the seven hillside suites. The new guests were in one of the middle suites, not that it mattered as they were all set so far apart from each other on the hill, it felt like there was no one else around for miles.

Connie made her way down the narrow path that led directly to the private veranda at the front of the suite.

'Hello?' she called out, before stepping up on to the deck by the plunge pool.

'Hi there,' a female voice called back.

Connie looked across the plunge pool to where a couple were curled up together on the swing seat with a cocktail in their hands.

'Sorry to bother you so late in the evening. I'm Connie.' She walked across the wooden deck and shook their hands. 'It must have been a long day with your flight delayed.'

'We're here now, that's all that matters,' the woman said with a wave of her hand. 'And we were handed cocktails immediately on arrival, which made my day.'

Her husband smiled at her.

'I have a few goodies for you.' Connie placed the basket on the low table in front of them. 'And I just wanted to check if you have everything you need for tonight?'

'I think so,' the husband said.

His wife nodded. 'That's so lovely, thank you.' She tucked a stray hair behind her ear. 'The manager here, is it Theo? He's been so helpful all day making sure we got here okay.'

Connie was glad of the subtle lighting in the suite as her cheeks flushed. 'Good, I'm glad, you'll meet him tomorrow. Well, if you're fine for tonight I'll see you in the morning. Breakfast is between 7 and 10am down in the restaurant or up here if you prefer, and you'll find beach towels in the chest at the bottom of your bed if you want to relax on the beach or have a swim in the pool.'

'Thank you so much.'

'I'll leave you in peace. Enjoy your first night at Mchanga.'

Connie's head was filled with thoughts of Felix and Theo as she walked back down the hill. She hoped Felix had gone back to his room for the night, and she had no idea if Theo was expecting her to go back to the bar and have a drink with him or more, but that was the last thing she felt like doing, complicating her feelings any further. Instead of turning left towards the restaurant and bar at the bottom of the hill, she headed right and made her way to her room, to erase the thoughts swirling around her head with sleep. Bella would be back tomorrow – if Felix thought Connie had been angry, it would be nothing compared to the rage Bella would unleash on him as soon as she found out he was here.

Chapter Eleven

Connie woke earlier than usual after a fitful night's sleep. She pulled on a long white skirt and blue vest top and padded along the path at the back of the beach rooms, avoiding the restaurant where Theo usually grabbed a bite to eat before any guests arrived, and headed straight for the office.

'Morning,' Connie said. Maria was sitting at a laptop with a mug of coffee next to her.

'Hey, morning.'

Connie sat on the chair opposite her and leant on the table. 'Could you do me a big favour and ask Bella as soon as she gets back to come and see me before she does anything else, please?'

Maria nodded. 'Of course.' She placed a slender hand on Connie's arm. 'Everything okay?'

'Yes, a little complicated, but it will be – okay, I mean. I just need to speak to Bella.'

'Okay, sure, no problem, I'll let her know as soon as she arrives, although she's not due back until sometime this evening.'

'I know, thanks.'

Maria reached across the table and gave Connie's hand a squeeze. 'I know you have Bella, but if you do ever want someone else to talk to, I'd be happy to.' Her cheeks flushed a little as she met Connie's eyes. 'I've lived and worked overseas long enough to know how lonely it can be, spending so much time away from friends and family.'

'Thank you, I appreciate that.'

Maria released her hand from Connie's.

'I'd better get on.'

Connie left the office and headed down the path that led towards the beach villas. She turned the corner where the path split one way to the villas, the other way to the restaurant and ran straight into Theo.

'Hey,' he said.

There was no way she could keep on walking without ignoring him completely, so she stopped and smiled. 'Hey.'

'I feel like you've been avoiding me.'

'Not really, it's first thing in the morning.'

'How about at the end of last night?'

'I had those new guests to greet up at their suite.'

He moved closer and took her hand in his. 'You could have found me after.'

Conflicting emotions flooded through her as she met his eyes. His thumb rubbed against hers and half of her wanted to kiss him; the other half couldn't help but think about him discussing having sex with her to Felix.

'I know, I'm sorry, it was late, I was tired and I wasn't sure if you wanted to, you know...' She looked away from him, glancing along the path that led towards the restaurant, making sure no one was heading their way.

'Are you kidding, Connie.' His hands travelled up her arms, pulling her closer until his breath tickled her forehead. 'I loved the other night. But if it's, you know, too soon for you. I know you split from your husband not that long ago.'

Connie's head snapped up and she stepped away from him. 'We really shouldn't be talking about this here.'

He nodded. 'I agree. I'm just worried that what happened the other night was too soon. Trust me, I understand how hard it is to move on from a long-term relationship.'

She nodded and fought back the rising fear that Felix now knowing about her and Theo outweighed the brief satisfaction she'd felt at him finding out that she'd moved on from him. Except she realised, she hadn't. She wasn't over him or the hurt he'd caused. She'd simply confused things further by having sex with a man she actually liked and had slept with for all the wrong reasons.

'After we finish tonight,' Theo said. 'Come up and see me. To talk, nothing else if you don't want to.'

She nodded. 'Of course.'

Connie went through the day on autopilot. Everything she did felt like she was removed from the situation – there but not there at the same time. Felix and Theo constantly filled her thoughts leaving her in emotional turmoil. She met the couple she'd greeted late the evening before and helped them plan their five days at Mchanga. Then it was back to the office and a meeting with Theo and one of the admin staff. Theo was completely professional and at ease with her as they discussed guests, plans and excursions for the coming week. With new guests due to arrive that afternoon, Connie was glad to be kept busy. Theo needed to do paperwork so he tasked her with greeting and looking after the new arrivals. A late lunch – a bite to eat back at her beach room followed by a stroll around Mchanga checking the guests were okay, she somehow managed to not see Felix.

By late afternoon the radio clipped on to the elastic of her skirt crackled to life and Maria's voice said, 'Are you there, Connie?'

She unclipped the radio and pressed the button on the side. 'Go ahead, Maria.'

'The jeep's just pulled up with the new guests. I'll go and meet them.'

'I'm on my way over.'

The last thing she felt like doing was being sociable, greeting yet another happy couple and pretending she was fine. She fiddled with the bracelets on her wrist as she walked. The day was sultry and still and was doing nothing to put her in a better mood. She was desperate to take the bracelets off but didn't want the looks or questions that would come with the sight of the fading scar on her wrist. No one here, apart from Bella and Felix knew about them and she wanted to keep it that way, however uncomfortable or impractical they were in the heat.

Connie paused outside, took a deep breath and then stepped up into the welcome building, a smile on her face.

'Beverley, Simon,' she said with her hand outstretched. 'Welcome to Mchanga.'

Beverley was patting her face with the cool towel she'd been handed on arrival, but Simon shook her hand.

'Very glad to be here after a bloody long journey,' he said with a gruffness and London accent that reminded Connie of Geoff.

'It is quite a trek, isn't it,' she replied. 'But hopefully worth it and you can relax now.'

Simon handed Maria his cold towel and Beverley did the same.

'Mohammed will take your bags to your beach villa. If you'd like to follow me we'll go and have a drink and chat by the pool – it's about the only place today that's catching any breeze.'

Connie led the way, back down the steps and on to the sandy path that wound through the trees. With Simon and Beverley following behind she took the longer route and came up on to the deck on the far side of the pool.

'Wow,' Beverley said, as the view past the pool towards the beach and ocean revealed itself. 'That is incredible.'

'Pretty special, isn't it?' Connie said, watching Simon pull his sunglasses down to the end of his nose and gaze past her.

'You could say that,' he replied.

'Let's take a seat over here.' Connie led them to a daybed that faced the ocean, and she sat down on one opposite them. 'What would you like to drink?'

'What would you recommend?' Beverley asked, sitting down. She took a paper fan out of her handbag and wafted her face.

'The Mchanga house cocktail is amazing and the colour of the sunrise here.'

'Perfect,' Beverley said with a laugh. 'Let's start as we mean to go on.'

Connie radioed through the drinks order to the bar, adding a pineapple juice for herself. She didn't need to sell the place to Simon and Beverley, she simply explained the day to day running of Mchanga – when food was served, the options they had during the day and what she could organise for them. Once again she realised she enjoyed making people's dreams come true – exactly what Bella had been doing all her adult life, sharing the vision she had created with people wanting a slice of luxury and to escape from their normal lives for a week or two.

Connie had nearly gone through everything when Maria jogged up on to the decked area surrounding the pool. She slowed when Connie looked up and clocked that she was still talking to the new arrivals.

Maria skirted the edge of the pool and stopped in front of them. 'I'm so sorry to interrupt,' she said to Simon and Beverley. She turned to Connie. 'Bella's back already. She arrived early while I was on my break.'

'Oh really?' Connie glanced between Maria and the couple. 'Would you be able to find her and ask her to come here and see me?'

Maria clasped her hands in front of her. 'You might want to go and see her now,' she said, raising her eyebrows.

With her heart thudding, Connie turned back to the couple and smiled. 'Would you excuse me for just a minute?'

'You go ahead,' Simon said. 'We have cocktails and this view, you take your time.'

'Thank you. We're nearly done anyway, I'll get someone to come and show you to your room in a little bit.' Connie stood up and followed Maria off the decking and down on to the path that led towards the bar and restaurant. 'What's going on?'

'There's a bit of a commotion – Bella and one of the guests. She seems to know him and after what you said this morning, I got the feeling it might involve you.'

Connie was certain it involved her, and her heart sank as she paced after Maria. They clattered up the steps on to the raised area of the bar and relief flooded through Connie that there was only one couple sat on the far side sipping drinks. There were no other guests around but then there was no sign of Bella either.

'Where is she?' Connie glanced around.

'Down on the beach.'

Connie followed Maria over to the edge of the dining area, the sound of voices becoming clearer as she reached the wooden railings.

'You have the nerve to fly out here, believe you're welcome to stay at the place I call home. The place that is Connie's home for as long as she wants it to be.' Bella's voice drifted up from the beach below, simmering with anger.

Felix was half sitting, resting his elbows on the sunlounger, the toned and tanned skin of his chest gleaming with sweat in the sunshine. Felix's looks had been what had attracted Connie to him to begin with – had she really been so blinkered by his six-pack and lust that she'd overlooked his personality and ended up marrying a philandering, egotistical bastard?

'Lounging on my beach, upsetting my niece, after what you did to her,' Bella continued, stepping towards him. Her shadow fell across his chest. 'She's divorcing you. How you can believe it's okay to come out here and think you have a chance in hell of winning her back, I have no idea.'

A couple on sunloungers a little further down the beach, looked over but Connie wasn't sure they'd be able to hear what was being said, even though Bella's face and tone screamed disgust and hatred.

'You're leaving right now, on the next plane, even if I have to pay for it myself.'

'Don't worry, my flight's in the morning anyway.'

'Then I'll get someone to drive you to Dar – you can find a hotel there for tonight or sleep at the airport for all I care.'

Felix glanced up to the deck and met Connie's eyes. Her face flushed at being caught watching him. She gripped the wooden rail until her knuckles turned white and made her fingers sore.

Without taking his eyes off her, Felix calmly said, 'By the way, your precious niece is fucking your manager.'

Connie drew a sharp intake of breath, pushed herself away

from the railing and out of Felix's sight. Maria was still next to her staring intently at her feet.

'He's your ex-husband?'

Connie spun round. Theo stood a few paces away, his arms folded across his chest, his usual smile absent.

'I don't give a damn what Connie does in her own time,' Bella's voice drifted up from the beach. 'Or my manager for that matter…'

'Yes,' Connie said. 'He is. I'm so sorry I didn't tell you. I just couldn't, I was shocked and angry that he had the nerve to come out here.'

Theo rubbed his hand across his forehead and glanced at Maria. Without a word she slipped away, padding across the restaurant and out of sight. Bella was still talking, but had lowered her voice, and Connie was unable to make out what she was saying.

'The other night,' Theo said quietly. 'What was that really all about? Getting back at him?'

'No. No, of course not.'

'Stop kidding yourself, Connie. If you're still in love with him and hurting that badly, don't use me to punish him. I'm done with women messing with my life.'

He turned and walked away.

Connie had nothing left to say anyway. What could she say to make things better? She hadn't thought through what her actions would do to Theo. All she'd had on her mind was making Felix pay for what he'd done to her. The first person she'd slept with since Felix, a person she'd genuinely liked, and she'd disrespected him. She was better off alone, unable to mess up anyone else's life. She let tears stream down her face. The couple on the far side looked away when she glanced in their direction. Behind the bar Abasi was keeping himself busy, avoiding her gaze but she was pretty certain that he'd have figured out what was going on. There was only one thing for it. She took a deep breath, paced across the restaurant and down the steps that led to the beach.

Only Felix's towel remained on the sunlounger with a half-finished beer on the table next to it. Bella stood with her back to Connie, hands on her hips, her feet planted in the sand, staring out at the ocean. The couple on the sunloungers further down the beach had returned to reading their books.

Connie walked across the sand and stood next to her aunt. 'I'm so sorry, Bella.'

Bella turned to her. 'What on earth are you apologising for? You didn't invite him here. The nerve that man has. Does he not understand the damage he's caused?'

'I've messed up too; I feel awful about Theo…' Connie trailed off, her cheeks burning at the thought of Bella knowing about their night together and the way she'd used him.

'It's true then?' Bella asked. 'What Felix said?'

Connie nodded. 'Theo is mad and rightly so. He heard everything.'

'When did this happen?'

'Two nights ago. I was so angry at Felix and I wanted to hurt him so badly. I had no intention of hurting Theo… I've been stupid.'

Bella placed a hand on her arm. 'Oh Connie, love. Do you like him?'

'Yes.' Connie wiped away a tear. 'I only acted on impulse because I thought there was a mutual attraction.'

'You mean something would have eventually happened between you and Theo, you just instigated things earlier to get back at Felix.'

'That's awful, isn't it?'

Bella touched her arm. 'We all do things on impulse. Sometimes we make the right decision, other times we live to regret what we've done. That is life.'

Chapter Twelve

Bella remained true to her word. She refunded Felix for one night at Mchanga, contacted the manager she knew of a hotel in Dar es Salaam and booked a room for Felix that night. All that was left was for Mohammed to return with the jeep and drive Felix to Dar. With Bella back in charge and only two guests witnessing the scene on the beach, Bella sent Connie to her room. Connie wasn't sure if Bella was worried about what would happen if Connie and Felix came across each other, but she realised it was probably best to stay out of the way at least until Felix had gone.

She sat on the daybed on the open deck of her room and put her head in her hands. Mchanga had been an escape from all the crap of the past couple of years, from Felix and their divorce, from the physical and mental hurt she'd been through. It had meant to be her refuge, her place to heal, from both the physical scars on her wrist and the mental scars of not being a mummy to not one but two potential babies. Husbandless and childless at thirty-seven, and now her refuge had turned into another place she wanted to run from. Even once Felix had gone, she was still left with the situation with Theo.

The glimpse of sand and ocean through the trees wasn't any comfort. She rubbed her eyes and wished she could turn back time and react differently to Felix turning up. The noise of the surf was overpowered by the chatter of monkeys scrabbling around on the roof of her villa. The noise filled her head, suffocating her, despite usually being a soothing presence.

She couldn't sit and do nothing. She needed closure with Felix. She padded barefoot along the path that led behind the beach rooms, the feel of sand and dried leaves beneath her feet. Without thinking, she took the path that led down to room number two and stepped up on to the deck.

Felix was lying on the bed, his hands behind his head, staring up at the thatched roof above him. His feet were bare and his T-shirt had ridden up, revealing his toned stomach. Connie swallowed and fought back tears. He was achingly familiar, yet at the same time she felt so disconnected from him that it was hard to believe this was the man she'd been married to, the man she'd loved and had wanted to start a family with.

'Felix.'

'Why are you here, Connie? I'll be gone soon, isn't that what you want?'

He didn't move from where he was lying, or look at her.

She stepped further into the room to make sure he could hear her clearly. 'It's too late to be thinking about what I want,' she said. 'If you had, at any point in the last couple of years, stopped to think about me, rather than yourself, then maybe we wouldn't be in this situation. Maybe you wouldn't have had an affair; maybe you wouldn't have cheated on me while I was going through the worst time of my life; maybe you wouldn't have been screwing someone else while I was pregnant and then while I had two miscarriages. If you'd actually thought about me at any point, you wouldn't have come out here to try and "win me back".' Connie took a deep breath. Felix remained still, but she knew he was listening. 'What does that even mean? How can you seriously think I'm what you want, that being together again could possibly make either of us happy? It can't and it won't. I'm done with you. I made a mistake sleeping with Theo – not that I don't like him, because I do, very much, but because I slept with him out of rage at you. I seduced him for all the wrong reasons and I was an idiot. I have to live with that mistake just like you have to live with yours.'

She waited. He remained still, save for the rise and fall of his chest. Connie made to go but stopped. She was done hiding. She pulled off the thick bracelets that covered the scar on her wrist and dropped them with a clatter on the wooden deck.

She watched him leave. She hiked along a little-used path on the edge of Mchanga that led to the top of the hillside high above the staff accommodation, so there was no chance of bumping into anyone. She saw Mohammed drive through the gates to the welcome building, knew Felix would be there with his rucksack, Bella seeing him off her property. Connie heard the jeep door slam shut and then Mohammed drove out through the gates. She waited, until the sound of the engine had been swallowed by the rhythmic roar of the waves folding on to the shore.

Connie wanted to stay where she was forever, never having to face anyone again, Bella or Maria, any of the guests, or worst of all Theo. The view was incredible from this high up, just the tops of trees, the thatched buildings below blending into the surroundings, the white beach and shimmering ocean. Despite what had happened on the beach with Felix and Bella, and what Theo had heard, she couldn't hide away. With a sigh she headed back down the hill, joining the path that led directly past the staff villas.

It had been a long day but she knew that she was supposed to be mingling with guests in the bar, plus she wanted to make sure Simon and Beverley were okay after having abruptly left them by the pool.

The tables were all full with couples tucking into plates of seafood, candlelight casting soft light across their faces. She saw Simon and Beverley at one of the central tables and smiled. She noticed the table Felix had sat at the last two nights remained set for one. The barmen nodded and smiled as she passed – did they know about her and Theo? And then she saw him, his back to her, his broad shoulders hunched forward, arms folded, talking to Bella.

Bella caught sight of her and waved her over. Theo

turned, met her eyes and looked away. Connie reached them, her heart pounding, the chatter of happy couples surrounding her amplifying the awkwardness of the situation. In the lamplight the laughter lines to the sides of his eyes were accentuated, but there was little laughter in his eyes.

'We were just saying it's a particularly busy night,' Bella said, filling the silence. 'Everyone seems to have come to dinner at the same time.'

'I'm going to do the rounds.' Theo unfolded his arms.

'Is there anything in particular you want me to do this evening?' Connie asked.

'Ask Bella.' He strode over to the nearest table where a couple who'd been at Mchanga for nearly a week were tucking into their dessert.

'Evening,' he said, his voice filled with warmth, the opposite of how he'd spoken to her.

'Evening, Theo,' the wife said. 'Wonderful breeze tonight.'

Bella placed her arm on Connie's. 'He's pissed off, it's to be expected.'

Connie looked at her aunt and gave her a weak smile.

'You really don't have to be here tonight; in fact, it might be best if you're *not* here this evening.'

'You really don't want me here?'

'I don't mean it like that. Why don't you go to the office and write a Facebook post, put something up on Twitter?'

Connie bit her lip and glanced towards Theo, working his way around the restaurant, laughing with the guests.

Bella hooked her arm in Connie's. 'Walk with me.'

She led her off the restaurant deck and down the steps to the beach. Connie kicked off her flip-flops at the bottom of the steps and neither of them said anything as they passed the sunlounger Felix had been sat on earlier that day. The sand was cool beneath her feet as they walked away from Mchanga, her feet sinking into the soft grains.

Bella stopped when the music and chatter from the bar and restaurant had faded, overtaken by the waves pounding the beach. Connie could make out the villas through the trees behind them, the glow from the lamps on the decks welcoming in the darkness. With their arms linked and their backs to the dark ocean, the bar was a beacon of light in the inky blackness. Jutting out on the rock that overlooked the beach, warm light flooded from lamps and the candles flickering on each table. Twinkling fairy lights strung along the edge of the roof of the bar mirrored the stars glinting in the sky. The lights of Dar es Salaam were too far away to disturb the night sky and there was nothing else around for miles, apart from endless beach, forest and ocean.

Bella squeezed Connie's arm. 'Besides the view from my villa, this is my favourite spot, particularly at night.'

'It's stunning.'

'Whenever I'm feeling down or lonely or sad, this is where I come.'

Connie looked at Bella. The soft lines of her face were obscured by the darkness. 'I'm okay, Bella, really I am.'

'I know you are, love, because you've been through a lot worse. But I saw how sad you looked when Theo blanked you. I also know how much he's hurting and it's purely a gut reaction – he won't ignore you forever. It's one of those things that when you've been hurt emotionally, sometimes it's easier to not deal with it at all. That's exactly what he's doing.'

Connie swallowed, fighting back her emotions. 'How can we work together if he's not even speaking to me?'

'He just needs time and space, and so do you. That bastard ex of yours turning up was the worst possible thing to happen but we can't change that, so we're going to move on. We're all going to move on.'

'How?' Connie wiped her face with her free hand and looked at the restaurant through blurry eyes, thinking of Theo up there, being charming and chatting with the guests. If she hadn't been so reckless and thoughtless, that could have been her later this evening, curled up on a sofa having a drink with him.

'By taking some time out,' Bella said firmly. 'Theo has his two weeks' leave starting in a couple of days when our relief manager takes over. But I was intending to go to the new beach retreat on Zanzibar tomorrow to start planning how to inject some life into the place. Considering what's happened I'm going to stay here and you're going to go on my behalf.'

'You're trusting me with that responsibility?'

'Of course I'm trusting you,' Bella said, hugging Connie to her. 'You can of course get hold of me if you need to, and I know you have an eye for detail and wonderful vision. I want Baobab Beach to be the Mchanga of Zanzibar when we're finished with it. Geoff's going to be there too so you won't be making decisions on your own – although I'm not sure if that's a blessing or a curse.'

'I can't believe you're working with him again.'

'We've always worked well as business partners,' Bella said, continuing to gaze towards the restaurant. 'It was in our personal life that everything fell apart, mainly because he couldn't keep his dick zipped up – but you know that all too well with Felix. And you wonder why I hate him so much.'

'Oh Bella, I wouldn't ever want to get on the wrong side of you.' Connie leant her head against her aunt's. 'Geoff won't mind me being there instead of you?'

'I'm sure he'll be relieved. We might make great business partners but we're still fiery together. Just don't let him walk all over you.'

Chapter Thirteen

Connie left early in the morning, the sandy path behind the villas empty with only the monkeys playing in the trees and on the villa roofs.

'Hey,' Connie said as she entered reception and saw Maria behind the desk.

Maria looked up. 'Hey, Connie.'

'You're up early.'

'I like catching up on paperwork first thing before I get too busy and the day gets too hot.'

'Sounds sensible.' Connie hooked her rucksack higher on to her back. 'Is Mohammed around?'

'He's waiting with the jeep outside the gate. He didn't want to leave the engine running and risk disturbing the guests.'

'Okay great, I'll go find him.'

'Connie,' Maria said, before she had the chance to leave. 'Are you okay? I mean, I know it's none of my business, but I um, well you know I heard everything yesterday, and now you're leaving…'

Connie turned back to Maria. 'I'm so sorry you had to witness that…' Connie wasn't sure what else to say. The short time she'd been at Mchanga she'd started to think of Maria as a friend and yet had failed to confide in her.

'He's your ex-husband?' Maria asked, fiddling with a pile of leaflets, stacking them neatly next to her.

Connie nodded. 'Yes, my soon-to-be-ex.'

'Uh huh.'

'I know I didn't handle the situation well – I should have said something to someone about who he was, it's just he knocked me for six turning up here.'

The two women stared at each other. Maria picked up the leaflets again and tapped them on the desk.

'Well, I should get going if Mohammed's waiting.'

'Sure, yes,' Maria said, waving her hand. 'You know, I won't say anything to anyone about you and Theo…' Her tanned cheeks flushed.

Connie felt her own cheeks burn. What must Maria think of her? From her perspective, Connie, within three weeks of arriving had seduced Theo in the worst way possible to get back at her ex. Connie didn't know what to say – there was nothing she could say to make the situation any less damning.

'Theo's a good guy,' Maria said as if reading her thoughts.

'I know he is, I really do. That's why Bella wants me to give him some space. Me being here isn't going to help matters at the moment.'

Maria nodded. 'If you want to talk to me – when you get back – you can, you know.'

'Thank you.' With tears ready to spill, Connie turned and headed down the path away from Mchanga and Theo, to Mohammed and the jeep waiting to take her to the airport.

It was only going to be three days at most away from Mchanga, but to Connie it felt as if she'd been banished. If the situation with Felix and Theo hadn't happened, Bella would have gone to Zanzibar and Connie would have continued with her job at Mchanga, building on her relationship with Theo instead of destroying it through one stupid night.

Stone Town always took her by surprise – a melting pot of cultures and people, a steamy town filled with heat and smells. It was a place she loved visiting but was relieved to leave once she headed out of the compact town and further into the island where the air felt fresher.

She took a taxi from the airport, bypassing the heart of Stone Town, regretting not being able to spend one night at Bella's hotel and to gaze across the town from the hotel's rooftop bar, an oasis amongst the tightly packed crumbling buildings.

The roads were potholed and busy with people, cars and trucks carting goods across the island, but that didn't stop the taxi driver from tearing along the single lane roads. There was so much of Zanzibar she'd not explored yet. With Bella opening another beach retreat on the island, there was the potential to do so much more. She leant her head against the side of the car, relishing the rush of air through the open window. She must have nodded off because it seemed like no time at all until the car slowed and came to a halt on stony ground.

'There's nothing round here,' the driver said, looking out at the large gates they'd pulled up in front of, blue paint curling and peeling off from the wood of the broken sign above. 'The place closed a couple of years ago.'

'I know.' Connie handed him a wad of Tanzanian shillings and opened the car door. 'But it's going to be opening up again.'

The driver leant his head out of the car as Connie slid open the lock on the gate. 'Are you meeting someone here?'

Connie nodded. The gate swung open.

'I wait ten minutes,' he said. 'Just in case you need a lift back to Stone Town. If not, I go.'

'Thank you.' She waved and started walking down the drive. Palm trees lined the dirt road, the undergrowth from the surrounding forest crept on to the driveway. Up ahead, half hidden behind a domineering baobab tree, poked a two-storey once-white-now-dirty-grey building from amongst the surrounding greenery. It didn't take long to reach it and when she did, she realised a fresh coat of white paint and the flowers and bushes surrounding the building being tamed, would bring the place back to life.

Connie pushed open wooden double doors and stepped into a cool, dark entrance hall.

'Hello?' Connie called out. Her voice echoed back.

'Connie!' Geoff's voice boomed. 'We're out the back in the bar.'

She followed his voice, walking along a wide corridor until the place opened up and she stopped, her breath snatched away by the view. Wooden tables and chairs lay scattered across a decked bar area screened by trees but beyond was the whitest beach she'd ever seen. The ocean was turquoise, shallow and calm, a white- and blue-painted dhow half in half out of the water. It was a picture postcard perfect Zanzibar beach, the complete opposite of the wildness of the beach at Mchanga.

She pushed her sunglasses up into her hair. 'Wow.'

'That,' Geoff said, walking over and slapping a rough hand on to her shoulder, 'is exactly the reaction I wanted.'

'Walking through those entrance gates, I'd never have guessed the place would be this stunning.'

'All part of its charm.'

Connie turned at Jamil's voice. 'Hey, I didn't know you were going to be here.'

'Didn't know you would be either.'

Connie fought back the uncomfortable feeling of why she was here in Bella's place. 'Bit of a last minute decision.'

'Well,' Geoff said, squeezing her shoulder. 'I for one am glad you're here instead.'

'That's what Bella said you'd say.'

'I bet she did.' Geoff laughed, draping his arm around Connie's shoulder and leading her over to the bar. 'Come and have a drink.'

She sat on a stool next to Geoff, while Jamil went behind the bar and took a bottle of whisky from a shelf, poured a generous amount and pushed the glass towards Connie.

'The bottles were already here?' Connie asked.

'Yep, lots of stuff left.' Jamil leant his elbows on the wooden bar. With his deep brown 'come to bed with me' eyes, high cheekbones and dark and toned body he really was the last person – apart from Felix – she wanted to see right now. His biceps tensed as he lifted his drink. Inwardly Connie sighed, wishing she was alone. That was really what she needed and craved – total peace.

She sipped her drink, clenching her jaw as the liquid burnt

her throat on its way down. 'So, what's the plan for the next couple of days?'

Geoff drummed his fingers on the edge of the bar. 'To get a tonne of things done. Apart from making plans on just how we're going to turn this place into something even more special than it already is, we need to employ and organise the local villagers to clear this place up. Lots of them used to work here before it closed down, so we have plenty of eager new employees at our disposal.'

'Where is the village?' Connie asked, thinking back to the drive and that the place wasn't near anything.

'About ten minutes' walk that way.' Geoff pointed past the bar to the far side of the beach.

'We're staying here though, are we?'

'Yep, rooms seven and twelve have been cleaned and repaired enough for us to use while we're here. So, Connie, you take number seven, and me and Jamil will bunk together in twelve. Not sure why they didn't choose two rooms next to each other.'

'Baba, it was probably to keep you and Bella from being too close to each other.'

Jamil caught Connie's eye.

Geoff grunted, downed the rest of his drink and stood up. 'Right, I need to go make some phone calls and organise getting this place connected and up and running with electricity again. Jamil, show Connie around and start figuring out what the hell we're going to do to make this place appeal to the clientele we're used to at Mtazamo and Bella has at Mchanga. I'll be in the office.'

Connie watched him disappear into the dusky building. She turned to Jamil. 'Surely the appeal of the place is that.' She waved her arm behind her in the direction of the beach.

'It is,' Jamil said, looking past her. 'That's what's going to get people coming here in the first place, but it's what we need to do to keep guests coming back here year after year, because everywhere on Zanzibar is special. Barefoot luxury is what we're aiming for. The barefoot bit is easy; the beach, ocean and surroundings speak for themselves, but the rooms, well they're not what guests are used to if they've been to say, Mchanga.' He slipped out from behind the bar and brushed his hand against her arm as he passed. 'Come take a look.'

She left her drink and followed Jamil across the bar, weaving their way between the tables and chairs strewn over the wooden floor. They reached steps and a sandy path that led through the trees straight down to the beach. At the end of the path Jamil kicked off his canvas shoes. 'Barefoot remember.'

Connie slipped off her flip-flops and stepped on to the warm sand. It glowed a pearly white in the sunshine.

'I'm being completely serious when I say I think this is the best beach on Zanzibar,' Jamil said, 'and I've seen a lot of them.'

The beach was a perfect crescent, wide and long with plenty of space between the guest rooms each with a view towards the ocean. The beach wasn't empty though; palm trees dotted the sand providing shade with broken hammocks still strung between some of them.

Connie walked next to Jamil along the edge of the beach, the sun pounding down on her bare shoulders. Halfway along he stopped and turned to face the beach, his back to the ocean. He spread his hands out in front of him. 'This is it, really.' He pointed to the right, back the way they'd come to the bar area almost hidden by trees. 'The main building houses the restaurant, bar, offices and reception with staff accommodation on the first floor, plus there's the swimming pool on the other side of the bar by a narrower stretch of beach. Then there are eighteen beach rooms, bungalows, huts, whatever you want to call them and the beach. That's it.'

'The rooms could be more attractive, at least from the outside.' Connie shaded her eyes with her hand. The glare of the sun on the whitewashed rooms was too much even with sunglasses on.

'That's the problem. The insides aren't any better.'

Connie followed him up the beach, past a cluster of three palm trees casting long shadows across the sand.

Up close, the glaring white wall of room seven was a

shabby, slightly dirty white with paint flaking off. They went up wooden steps on to a small decked area that had enough space for a daybed, and then through the dark wooden door. Unlike the open-fronted beach villas at Mchanga, the inside of this beach room was dark, with only a tiny amount of sunlight filtering through a small dusty window.

'They wasted a huge opportunity when they built these rooms to not make the most of that view,' Connie said, walking across the small room. Many of the rusty-red coloured floor tiles were cracked and patches of mould stained the walls. The bed was small for a double, squeezed into a space with just enough room for a bedside table on either side.

Jamil stood in the middle of the room with his back to the window. 'The trouble was the owners who leased the land before us never spent any money on upkeep or improving what they originally built here. They were never going to get guests coming back year after year or be able to sell this as a luxury retreat despite having one of the most beautiful beaches on the island. By the way, this is one of the rooms that's had a clean.'

'Really?' Connie ran her fingers over the mattress. A clean-looking sheet covered it but everything about the room left her feeling like she needed a shower.

'Yeah, I know,' Jamil said, pushing open the door to the bathroom. 'Not great, is it?'

Connie brushed past him and into the small, dim bathroom lit only by a small window high up on the wall where leaves from outside curled through. Like the bedroom the floor was tiled but with blue tiles that went up the walls too. There was a sink, a loo and a shower head attached to the wall.

'This whole place needs knocking down and starting again from scratch,' she said.

Jamil left the bathroom. 'My thoughts exactly.'

Despite the stuffiness inside, Connie shivered. She turned and followed Jamil. Outside the brightness of sunshine, the turquoise shimmer of the ocean and the smell of salt air was a stark contrast to the dim musty room. 'My God, what a difference. In no way does that,' she pointed behind her, 'do justice to that.' She stared out at the gleaming white sand and the calm clear shallows of the Indian Ocean. Connie sat down on the top step. 'Is there enough money to do that much work?'

Jamil sat next to her, resting his arms on his legs, his thigh touching hers where they were squeezed together on the step. 'There's money, how much I don't yet know. It depends on what anyone feels needs to be done.'

'I could stay here forever. I didn't think anything could top the wild beauty of Mchanga but this…'

'Is what dreams are made of. Zanzibar at its best.'

'Pretty special, isn't it?' Geoff appeared silently next to room seven's deck. 'As with everything here, I can't get anything sorted over the phone so I'm going to Stone Town to get stuff done.' He wiped beads of sweat from his forehead with a handkerchief. 'Jamil, get that list written of everything that needs doing to get this place ready for guests.' He glanced at Connie. 'Start thinking how we can turn this into *the* place on Zanzibar for affordable luxury. No idea is too stupid or out there. Think out of the box. I'll be back later this evening. You kids take care of the place while I'm gone.' He winked and sauntered back along the beach.

'Baba is the type of person who likes to get things done. And quickly.'

'Well,' Connie said, 'there has to be a reason why he's so successful.'

'Yeah, that and pig-headed stubbornness.' Jamil glanced at her. 'He's not always the easiest person to work with, but his bark is worse than his bite, I promise.'

Stubbornness was a trait Bella had too. No wonder her marriage to Geoff had been a fiery one, even without Geoff's infidelities. 'As much as I'd love to stay here all day, I'll be burnt to a crisp in this heat.'

Jamil stood up and offered her his hand. She took it and he pulled her to her feet.

'Back to the bar then for a brainstorming session.'

~

They filled sheets of paper with lists and drawings, both of them getting carried away and ahead of themselves designing a new room that would make the most of the view and proximity to the beach and ocean. Connie loved the simple luxury of Mchanga and the idea of indoor/outdoor living and being one with the elements. There was nothing better than waking up to the sight and sounds of paradise.

They'd stuck to the pineapple juice that Jamil and Geoff had brought with them along with a few other supplies from Stone Town, but with the sun beginning to set, Jamil sidled behind the bar and cracked open a bottle of beer for each of them.

Connie put down her pencil and took a swig of her beer.

Jamil returned from behind the bar and sat on the stool next to her.

'When this place is up and running, who's actually going to manage it? Your dad's not going to leave Selous is he? And although it might be easier for Bella being on Zanzibar to keep an eye on here and The House of Stone, I can't see her really wanting to spend long periods of time away from Mchanga.'

'That's up for discussion,' Jamil said, resting an elbow on the bar and gazing out towards the ocean. 'I potentially could, except I travel too much to be the permanent manager here. We're probably going to need to employ a live-in manager or a couple – like Bella's done with the new guy at Mchanga.'

Connie felt a rush of shame. For a few hours, she'd managed to push what had happened to the back of her mind, lost in the task of imagining what this place could be like with some love, attention and a bit of creativity.

'Geoff?' A woman's voice called out.

Connie spun around on her stool. A smiling face appeared at the top of the steps from the beach. The woman had a colourful headscarf covering her hair and as she stepped on to the deck she revealed an even more vivid dress in a contrasting pattern.

Jamil slid off his stool and walked towards her, his right

hand outstretched. 'He's not here, but I'm Jamil, his son.'

'I brought some food from home.' Her voice had a melodic tone, her Tanzanian accent coating her words. 'I didn't want you all to go hungry, what with no way to cook anything here.'

She handed Jamil a metal caddy.

'It should still be hot, so eat soon.' Her skin was dark and so smooth. Only the lines around her eyes that creased when she smiled and her white hair showed her age.

'Are you from the village?' Jamil asked, shaking her hand.

The woman nodded. 'Cecile,' she said.

'I'm Connie.' She shook Cecile's outstretched hand.

'I'm so happy that this place is going to have life breathed back into it,' Cecile said. 'It was part of our village's livelihood.'

'Did many villagers work here?' Jamil asked.

'Lots,' she said, nodding. 'I ran a team of cleaners, although the rooms never seemed clean even after we scrubbed them from top to bottom.'

'Yeah, we noticed,' Connie said. 'Hopefully we can do something about that.'

She beamed. 'Well, I will leave you in peace. Enjoy the fish stew. My grandmother's recipe.'

'Thank you so much.'

They watched her weave her way back across the restaurant and down the steps to the beach.

'That sounds promising,' Jamil said, nodding in her direction. 'An eager workforce ready and waiting – that'll make life much easier.' He lifted the caddy. 'I'll see if I can find spoons and bowls. Why don't you head to the pool and we can eat on the deck there.'

Connie walked from the bar, catching sight of Cecile, bright against the sand in her headscarf and dress, as she made her way across the beach towards the headland at the end where the sand narrowed. Connie turned the other way, along the slatted wooden path beneath shady trees that led past the restaurant and opened out on to another raised deck and a kidney shaped pool that was empty apart from dirt and algae smearing the sides. Connie sat at the far end of the deck in the shade of a palm tree, her back to the pool, her legs dangling above the white beach that curved down to the perfectly clear azure water lapping the sand.

'Pretty special, isn't it?' Jamil sat down next to her, placing the caddy between them. 'I could only find spoons, no bowls.' He handed her one and popped open the lid. Steam escaped with the smell of spices.

Connie took a spoonful. 'That's seriously good.'

They ate in silence, the only sound the gentle foaming of the ocean on the shore and an occasional bird calling as it flew overhead.

'I'm glad you're here.' Jamil scraped the bottom of the caddy. He passed it to Connie. 'Have the last bit.'

'Thanks.'

'We seem to have lots of unfinished conversations from when you were in Selous.' He watched Connie take the last spoonful of the fish stew.

'We do?'

He nodded and rested back on his hands. Connie put the empty caddy down and turned her focus to the ocean shimmering in the fading light.

'Yeah, at Selous, whenever we got talking about you, you somehow managed to turn the conversation on to something else.'

'There were more interesting things to talk about than me. Do you think it'll cost a fortune to get this place up and running again?'

'There, my point exactly, you're avoiding the question.'

'Aren't we supposed to be figuring out what we're going to do with this place, not discussing my life history?'

'You came into my life sixteen years ago, blew my mind and then two weeks later disappeared out of it again. I'm intrigued by you, that's all.'

'You really want to know how my life panned out after my trip here all those years ago?'

'I feel like I know so little about you. Like, how did you get that scar on your wrist?'

Automatically, Connie turned her left hand over hiding the scar from view. She'd forgotten she'd taken off the bangles that had hidden it.

'That's a very direct question.'

'I know; sometimes it's the best way to get a straight answer.'

In many ways it was refreshing to have someone ask the question – someone who wasn't afraid, unlike her parents and her older brother who continuously tiptoed around the subject and avoided talking about anything to do with Felix, her divorce and how she was feeling.

She turned to Jamil and met his dark eyes. 'I tried to commit suicide, but I figure you'd already guessed that.'

He shook his head. 'Not really, no. I figured you wanted to hurt yourself but hadn't put you down for the type who'd actually try and take your life.'

'There's a type?'

He shrugged. 'Maybe, it's just *you* don't seem the type.'

'Maybe that's because you're remembering the carefree single twenty-one-year-old Connie with the whole of her life ahead of her. You don't actually know me. You didn't really know me back then either.'

'You obviously had more of an impact on me than I did on you.'

'That's only natural, isn't it? A twelve-year-old boy and a twenty-one-year-old woman.'

'True. You did make one hell of an impression on me. But trust me, Connie, you were happy back then and now…' He looked towards the ocean and the fast disappearing light, as he pushed his fingers through his black hair.

'And now what?'

'Now there's a sadness about you.'

Connie didn't say anything. What was there to say? She *was* sad, broken and lost. What she hadn't bargained for was someone she didn't know very well picking up on her sadness. She was thousands of miles away from home and the life and person who had caused her pain, and yet she was still unable to escape or convince people in a place that had once been filled with so much positivity that she was okay.

'So why did you try and kill yourself?' Jamil asked.

Connie shuddered. That word... it seemed so out of place, so alien to their surroundings. Her thoughts immediately went back to the moment, sitting on the kitchen floor of her and Felix's apartment – the feel of the cool-tiled floor beneath her, the thudding pain where she'd banged the back of her head hard against the cupboard door. And then peace, a feeling of release as she'd cut her wrist and watched blood, her blood, drip drip drip on to the pale grey tiles.

'If you really want to know, it's because in the hour or two before I hurt myself, my life literally fell apart – my husband confirmed he'd been having an affair and...' Connie stopped, unable to say out loud the other reason that had forced her to do what she'd done.

'And what?' Jamil asked, continuing to hold her gaze.

Connie looked away, back to the ocean. 'And it broke me.'

'You're talking to me like I'm your therapist,' Jamil said. 'Distancing yourself from your emotions.'

'I'd rather think of you as a friend.' Connie leant forward and brushed grains of sand from off the wooden deck. 'You did ask me, remember.'

Everything here was worn around the edges, faded, rustic – a certain charm but it needed tidying up, a sense of shabby chic added. Somehow they needed to retain its charm while restoring it and making it appeal to Bella and Geoff's clientele. She wanted to focus on the job of turning this run-down beach retreat into something fabulous and not be distracted by Jamil.

'I could make you feel a whole lot better, you know,' he said, pulling her back into the present.

Connie slapped his leg, immediately regretting it as her hand connected with his bare, muscly thigh and she realised it could be seen as a come on.

'You think I'm joking.'

Connie laughed, attempting to brush it off but she knew he wasn't. How had she managed to travel all this way to a place where she was supposed to be getting over a traumatic couple of years only to have her emotions messed about here too. Felix, then Theo and now Jamil. The last thing she'd wanted or had expected when leaving the UK for Tanzania was her lack of love life to change or get as complicated as it was beginning to feel.

'You were my teenage fantasy,' Jamil said. 'Seriously, for years after you left I used to think about you in that little red string bikini when I had a…'

'Woah, I get it.' Connie put her hand up. 'Maybe it's best if I stay that way.'

'A fantasy?'

Connie nodded.

'You're a hard woman to break, Connie Stone.'

'The trouble with fantasies is they rarely live up to your expectations.'

Jamil jumped down from the deck of the pool and landed in the sand. He turned to her. 'I'm pretty sure the sight of your nipples in a wet bikini – or without one even – would still live up to my expectations.'

The blood rushed to her cheeks. How had the conversation so quickly turned from her discussing her suicide attempt to Jamil undressing her with his mind?

'Never underestimate the effect getting out of a cool pool in a tiny bikini can have on a nearly thirteen-year-old boy, Connie.'

He'd done it again, knocked her for six with his ability to compliment her and make her squirm at the same time. She was flattered by the attention – he found her attractive and desirable. He was so intense, so charming, so attractive, reminding her of… She held back the thought, shaking it firmly from her head. Being good looking didn't make him a bad person or someone she should avoid.

Jamil moved closer and placed his hands on her thighs. She was relieved she was wearing linen trousers, yet even through the material she could feel the heat of his hands, daring her to push him away.

'I'm sorry I pried before, you know, about your scar,' he said, glancing down at her arm. 'But I don't get why you'd want to hurt yourself like that, even with all the crap going on in your life?'

Connie looked past him. The sky had darkened to a deep blue; soon it would be properly dark and there was barely any light to find their way back to the restaurant and hotel building.

Connie sighed. 'I guess unless you've been in a situation in your life where you've hit rock bottom it might be difficult to understand. But for me it was because I wanted physical pain to take away the emotional pain. Something tangible, something I could be treated for and recover from.'

'Fuck, Connie, that's messed up. You deserve someone so much better than your bastard ex.'

'And that person's you?'

'Hell no, I'm totally the wrong person, but a short term fix…'

'Having sex with you is not going to "fix" anything, Jamil.'

'Maybe not, but it would be a hell of a lot of fun.' He offered Connie his hand, pulling her off the deck, her feet landing in the soft sand next to his. 'You know what we need, a drink and a walk along the beach.'

Actually, that was the last thing Connie thought she needed, getting drunk with Jamil, but she followed him anyway. At least a walk along the beach would clear the fog of the past from her head.

Chapter Fourteen

Jamil retrieved a dusty bottle of white wine from behind the bar and they walked along the beach, finding their way by torchlight to the deck of room seven, the grains of sand cool beneath their feet. Unlike Mchanga where the waves were wild and fuelled by the breeze from the ocean, the air on this side of Zanzibar was still and remained hot and sticky once the sun had gone down.

They lit a candle in the lamp hanging outside the door and settled down on the daybed, each propped up on a lumpy pillow, gazing out at the moonlit beach. Jamil poured two glasses of wine and handed one to Connie.

'Cheers,' he said, knocking his glass against hers.

'It feels like we should be doing something productive towards getting this place up and running, not lounging around drinking wine.'

'If you hadn't noticed, it's pitch black and we have to do everything by candlelight or torch until we get the electrics back up and running.'

'How soon will that be?'

'Baba gets things done – he knows a lot of people in Stone Town. He's been in Tanzania for decades and understands how this place works. It's not likely to be tonight, but I wouldn't be surprised if something gets sorted tomorrow.'

Connie sipped her warm wine. She'd tasted better but it wasn't the worst and the location certainly took the edge off the vinegary aftertaste.

'Bella's like that, someone who gets things done.' Connie shuffled against the pillow until she was comfortable. 'I've always admired how she's managed to achieve so much and for having the guts to come out here on her own in the first place.'

'She likes to be in control of everything, which is why I was surprised when you showed up rather than her. She must really trust you.'

Connie sensed Jamil looking at her but she didn't turn to meet his gaze. Did Bella trust her or was this the only option she could see after the chaos Felix had caused back at Mchanga?

'Why are you really here, Connie, and not Bella?'

Connie sipped her wine and grimaced at the acidity. The moonlight caught on the gentle swell of the ocean and made it shimmer.

'You don't have to tell me if you don't want to,' Jamil said, stretching out on the bed. 'I love Bella, I really do, but I was very happy you showed up. Living out here you see the same people all the time.'

Connie took another gulp and shuddered as the warm liquid slipped down her throat. She turned to Jamil. 'I fucked the manager of Mchanga to get back at my ex-husband who turned up unexpectedly in a misguided attempt to win me back.'

'Okay,' Jamil said slowly. 'I was not expecting that.' He laughed.

'Jamil, seriously, it's not funny, I messed up big time. I acted like a teenager. I was stupid and rash.'

'I was only laughing because you surprise the hell out of me. I think I'm beginning to get to know you and then you tell me something like that.' Jamil leant over the side of the daybed and placed his glass on the deck. 'He hurt you that much, your ex?'

'Like you wouldn't believe.' Her hand immediately went to her scarred wrist.

'And Bella found out?'

'Yep, not that Bella finding out was an issue. It was Theo

113

finding out that I used him that was the problem.'

'Ouch, I bet he was pissed.'

'Jamil, you're not helping, I feel bad enough as it is without you making it worse.'

'Maybe this will help then.' He took her glass from her and placed it on the deck. He leant in and kissed her, softly at first, sliding closer until she finally responded.

She knew she should say no. Not because she didn't like Jamil, because she did, and not because he wasn't sexy, because that went without saying, but because he was too good to be true – the looks, personality everything about him, the perfect package. Yet he reminded her of when she'd first met Felix and that scared the hell out of her. The thought of Jamil playing out his teenage fantasy as his hands explored her body, travelling over the hollows of her shoulders and across her breasts sent shivers through her. Right this minute she felt beyond caring if having sex with Jamil was a good idea or not. His hands lingered on her breasts and she wondered if he was thinking back to her tiny red bikini… He moved downwards across her stomach and she willed herself to not flinch, her mind immediately flicking back to the memory of a tiny baby growing inside before it was snatched away from her… Her mind erased the thought as his hands moved lower undoing the button and zip of her linen trousers and easing her out of them.

Jamil slipped out of his shorts and dropped them on the deck before his hands slid along her bare legs, his fingers teasing her the higher he reached. She bit her lip and looked past the top of Jamil's head where he snuggled into her, kissing her neck. The lantern threw light across the whitewashed wall. Moths flitted against the glass, attracted by the flickering light. The wall reached up to the straggly thatched roof and the black sky beyond. Jamil was touching her in all the right places, just as Theo had done only a couple of nights before, and yet she felt disconnected, empty, not there in the moment like she'd been with Theo. A black shadow shot across the top of the wall, sending straw and grains of sand from the thatched roof tumbling down on to the bed.

'What the hell!' She sat upright, pushing Jamil off as she knelt, looking upwards.

'Shit, you scared me.' Jamil lay next to her on his back.

The movement on the roof sent more straw falling down. Something bigger fell and landed on the mattress between them, a rat-shaped thing dark against the white.

Both of them yelled and the rat froze then scampered across Jamil's legs, off the bed and disappeared into the darkness.

They both jumped off the daybed, their shouts turning to laughter as they hopped about on the deck. With her bare feet on the wooden boards, she was convinced she could feel sharp little rat claws sinking into her skin.

'What in hell's name is going on?' Geoff's voice boomed, and a torch light cut through the darkness further down the beach.

'A bloody giant rat is what's going on,' Jamil shouted back, still shaking his limbs as if the creature was attached to him.

'And what were you two doing to attract such unwarranted attention from your rat friend?' He glanced between Jamil and Connie.

'Nothing,' Jamil said. 'Talking and having a drink.'

Geoff grunted. 'Yeah okay. If you say so. Seems you both lost your trousers in all the excitement too.' He turned the torch beam from them and along the beach towards room twelve. 'I'm heading to bed. You kids keep it down.'

Connie clamped her hand over her mouth, stifling a laugh as she watched Geoff pad down the beach.

'That was not how I imagined tonight would turn out.' Jamil stepped towards Connie and tucked a stray hair behind her ear. 'We can always continue…'

'Jamil,' Connie said, not daring to meet his eyes, not wanting to allow him to seduce her again.

'Yeah, yeah, I know, the moment is lost.'

'You think?'

He laughed. 'You going to be okay sleeping in there alone

with that rat scampering around. You sure you don't need company?'

'I'm sure.' Connie put her hand on his arm. 'That rat is long gone, probably more scared of us than we were of it.'

'You know where I am if you change your mind.' He scooped his shorts from off the deck and stepped into them.

'Night, Jamil.'

'Night, Connie Stone.'

Connie considered sleeping on the daybed out in the open but kept imagining a rat falling and landing on her face. The mattress inside the room was hard but at least a mosquito net surrounded the bed. She listened to the near silence – only the slight sound of gentle surf on the beach disturbed the air. She lay on the bed in knickers and a vest top, her skin hot and sticky with no air filtering in from outside and the fan above the bed not working. How was she going to face Geoff in the morning? What the hell would he think of her? She felt like she was in her teens or early twenties again worrying about someone's parents, embarrassed by her actions. But why would Geoff even care? Jamil wouldn't be worried what his dad thought of him seducing her. By all accounts this was what Jamil did and he seemed to be taking after his father. The person she should be worried about was Bella and what she'd think of Connie almost having sex with a second man in the space of a couple of days. Connie was open-minded but her behaviour over the past week was out of character and not something to be proud of.

She slept fitfully. Beads of sweat covered her body and there were too many thoughts swirling around her head to give her peace. She woke early, put on a bikini, slipping shorts and a vest over the top and left the stuffy room. The beach was empty, no sign of Jamil and Geoff yet, and the sun was rising, reflecting on the distant still ocean. Connie padded barefoot down the beach and sat cross-legged in the sand, relishing the peace and beauty. Whatever they did, they needed open-fronted beach rooms, so guests could wake in the morning, sit up in bed and watch dawn breaking over the

Indian Ocean. The ocean was far out this morning revealing damp sand studded with rocks, fronds of seaweed and pools of water. The boat with peeling white and blue paint that had been bobbing up and down on the gentle swell when she'd arrived yesterday, was on its side on the sandy ocean floor. Further out, three women with patterned headscarves were reaching down, picking up clams and placing them in woven baskets that were hooked on their arms.

'You're up early.'

Connie's heart thudded against her chest as Geoff sat down next to her. 'God, you made me jump.'

'Sorry,' he said, resting his tanned, hairy arms on his legs. 'You couldn't sleep?'

'Not much.'

'Me neither. Too damn hot without a fan on. These enclosed rooms near enough boil you alive and it's not even properly hot yet.'

'I was just thinking how the rooms need to be rebuilt open-air like at Mchanga.'

'Couldn't agree with you more. I saw the plans you and Jamil drew up yesterday. Some great ideas.'

A tiny crab, almost invisible against the near-white sand scuttled in front of them. Even this early in the morning Connie felt the sun warming her skin, promising another blistering day. The silence between Connie and Geoff grew and all she could think about was Geoff stumbling across her and Jamil half naked, shouting and screaming over a rat.

She took a deep breath. 'About last night…'

Geoff waved his hand in front of him. 'What you and Jamil get up to is none of my business. Bad timing was all it was. Amusing though,' he chuckled.

Connie smiled and curled her arms around her legs. She wiggled her toes in the sand. Maybe it wasn't bad timing – not Geoff turning up, she could have done without him being witness to her and Jamil together, but the rat dropping down on to the daybed. How far would things have gone without the rat incident? How much would Geoff have witnessed if she and Jamil hadn't separated when they did? Perhaps the rat scaring the shit out of her was a blessing in disguise. At least Geoff was seeing the funny side – why wouldn't he? What would he care if Connie, free and single, slept with his son? After all he was the one who had countless affairs while married to Bella – with his reputation, he was the last person to judge.

The day was a long and hot but productive one. Sitting beneath the shade of the restaurant, Connie, Geoff and Jamil took the plans they'd started the day before and finalised them, after calling Bella to confirm she was happy for them to go ahead and put ideas into action.

'You guys certainly don't hang about, do you?' Connie put her pencil down and leant back in her chair.

'Time costs money,' Geoff said. He nodded towards the main building where a handful of men from the local village were painting the inside walls, revamping them from a murky grey to a fresher more vibrant yellow. 'And this place will eat money unless we get it up and running and filled with guests.'

Jamil had walked to the village to meet Cecile, the woman who'd brought over the fish stew, to recruit housekeepers to clean the rooms once they'd been rebuilt. Geoff had passed along Connie's drawing of what she thought the rooms should look like to an architect friend of his, along with some of his own and Bella's ideas. They even had electricity, although it seemed to be pretty temperamental, but at least it was a start.

'Are you staying here for longer or going back to Selous?' Connie asked.

'Back to Selous tomorrow. Jamil's going to oversee things here for a few more days. Bella wants you back?'

Connie nodded. 'I think she'd only planned on me being here for a couple of days anyway.'

'I'll book you a taxi for the morning.'

'Thanks.'

'You've been a huge help and a lot easier to work with than Bella.' Geoff took a sip of his beer, placed it on the table between them and wiped his mouth with the back of his hand. 'Don't bloody tell her I said that, will you?'

'Don't worry, I won't say a word.'

'You have a flair for design. Jamil said you're a jewellery designer back home; it shows.'

'Yeah, I've always been drawn towards doing something creative, so letting my imagination run wild on these rooms has been a joy.'

'Well,' Geoff said, standing up. 'I hope you stick around in Tanzania long enough to see your ideas come to fruition. Here he is.'

Connie looked along the beach to where Jamil was walking across the sand, his T-shirt slung over one shoulder, his dark muscular chest gleaming in the late afternoon sun. It took all of Connie's willpower to banish the idea of running her hands across his chest and kissing him again.

'Good news?' Geoff shouted. Jamil left the beach and took the winding path that led up to where they were sitting.

'Yeah, all sorted,' Jamil said once he reached them. 'Got a whole team of villagers wanting to work here. They've been struggling since this place closed. Housekeepers, waiters, musicians, washer-uppers, even a chef. You name it, they've got someone in the village who can do the job, and if they don't they sure as hell know someone who can.'

Geoff downed what was left of his beer and placed his hand on Jamil's bare shoulder. 'I'm going to do some work, make a few phone calls – for my sins I promised Bella an update, despite the fact you'll be seeing her tomorrow. I think she just wants to check that I tell her the same stuff as you'll be relaying to her when you get back.' He glanced between Connie and Jamil. 'You two kick back and relax. There's not a lot else we can do this evening. Take the hire car if you want and go for a meal. Or entertain yourselves another way if you know what I mean – you might just want to keep your antics behind closed doors this time…'

'We're really not going to be doing anything…'

Geoff waved. 'Aah, I'm teasing you, Connie. Go enjoy yourselves.' He threw Jamil the car keys and walked off across the restaurant, past the bar, and disappeared into the building.

'We good?' Jamil asked, looking across from the other

side of the table.

Connie frowned. 'Of course we are.'

'You fancy a meal somewhere?'

'Why not.'

They drove down the coast for an hour before cutting inland and skirting Jozani Forest with its red colobus monkeys before heading back towards the coast and the small fishing village and beach at Jambiani. Connie knew she was playing with fire again – was she leading Jamil on by going for a meal with him? They had to eat, they had nothing else to do, and perhaps getting away from Baobab Beach where they really had nothing to do was a good thing. If Jamil tried to make a move this evening, all she had to do was say no. The trouble was, he made her feel good about herself and she hadn't felt like this in a very long time, at least since her relationship with Felix had been happy and intact. Even with Theo she hadn't felt good about herself, mainly because she was conscious that she'd been using him for all the wrong reasons. Damn Felix for turning up the way he had and turning her life on its head yet again.

The beach was long and strung with hotels and restaurants that blended into the surroundings, spaced out from each other along the edge of the white sand. Jamil led them to a place right on the edge of the beach with an open-air upstairs that made the most of the view out over the ocean and the slightest of breezes that took the edge off the evening warmth.

They sat down at a table that overlooked the beach and once again Connie thought how far removed from her old life she was. There was no denying that the sun and exotic Zanzibar was a tonic after all that had happened over the previous few months. It was easy to forget how low she'd felt. Was she getting swept up in the romance of the place? The attention of a gorgeous and much younger man was undeniably attractive, but it had the potential for history to repeat itself.

Their drinks arrived and Connie reached for her white

wine, enjoying the cool dryness as it slid down her throat.

'They do incredible coconut fish baked in banana leaves here,' Jamil said, as the waiter returned.

'You choose for me, whatever's good.'

Jamil ordered and Connie gazed out at the ocean and the darkening horizon. It was a view she would never tire of, perfectly clear water lapping at white sand. With the intoxicating combination of salt spray and spiced food grilling over hot coals, she was in her element. Yet it felt like she was putting off the inevitable, dealing with her emotions, dealing with Jamil's desire, dealing with her misjudged liaison with Theo. Dealing with her past.

The waiter left and Jamil rested his arms on the table, leaning towards her. 'Just tell me – has Bella warned you off me – that I'm bad news, too much like my dad, got an eye for the ladies, et cetera, et cetera.'

Connie frowned. 'What makes you say that?'

'You saying no.'

'To us having sex?'

Jamil nodded, grinned and took a sip of his virgin pina colada.

'You seriously think Bella would tell me what to do? That she'd actually care if we had sex or not?'

'She cares about you enough.'

'Of course she does, I'm her niece and she doesn't want to see me get hurt, but she doesn't influence who I have sex with. She's pretty chilled out about that kind of thing.' Connie leant forward, aware of the other diners at the tables around them, and lowered her voice, 'For God's sake, Jamil, I'm nearly thirty-eight years old, I can make up my own fucking mind.'

Jamil held his hands up. 'Hey, I didn't mean it like that, I just meant don't let Bella's opinion of my dad and me get to you.'

'You're not used to being turned down, are you?' Connie folded her arms and sat back in the wicker chair. She didn't want to fight but there was a tension between them – whether sexual or other she wasn't sure.

'No, I'm not.' Jamil held her gaze with his big brown eyes. 'But I'm quite liking the chase.'

'It's a game to you, isn't it?'

'The women I usually go for want to be seduced – so no, I don't tend to get turned down because I avoid women who are likely to be difficult or complicated, or who want more than just a fling.'

Connie laughed. 'And here you are trying it on with me – a difficult and complicated woman.'

'You got that right.' He clinked his glass against hers. Still watching her he took a sip of his drink. 'I get it, Connie. You're not in the right place to be messing around with me. Just don't deny there's not an attraction between us even if you don't want to fully act on it.'

'What happened last night…'

'Yeah, yeah, that freaking rat.' He waved his hand. 'Let's move on from my ill-fated teenage crush on you, hey?'

The tension in Connie's chest began to dissolve. 'See, this is why I like you, your ability to not hold a grudge.'

'Apart from towards that damn rat.'

Connie smiled and knocked her glass against his. She relaxed back in her chair as dishes of lobster, seafood spaghetti and the baked fish with coconut were placed in front of them. She realised she would miss this – miss him. Jamil's company was easy and she couldn't deny there was a mutual attraction. She sighed and stabbed her fork in a prawn, firmly fixing the thought in her head that even when there was an attraction it wasn't always the wisest of ideas to act on it.

Chapter Fifteen

'What did you think of Baobab Beach?' Bella asked the moment Connie set foot in Mchanga.

'Nice to see you too, Bella.' Connie hugged her aunt and followed her to the bar.

'No seriously, did you like it?' She gripped Connie's hand as they headed along the sandy path. Bella led her to a seat facing the ocean and they sat down.

'Did I like it? I loved it. You couldn't have found a more beautiful place. I mean, this one is stunning.' Connie motioned in front of her. 'But Baobab, well it's a perfect Indian Ocean retreat. At least it will be when those hideous cottages are replaced.'

'Geoff emailed through a copy of the drawing you did of how you envisage the new beach villas to be.'

'And…?' Connie asked, holding her breath as she watched Bella.

Bella placed a warm hand on top of Connie's. 'And I love them.'

Connie smiled. 'It's been a really good couple of days.'

'I'm glad I sent you – I think you needed the time away.'

Connie flushed, remembering the reason why Bella had sent her.

'Back to work then.' Bella stood up. 'Lots to do particularly now we're able to get on with Baobab Beach.'

Connie got to her feet and smoothed down the front of her skirt. 'Is Theo around?'

'He's on his two weeks off. I think he was planning on

visiting friends in Kenya.'

Connie bit her lip.

'Throw yourself into work here and don't worry about anything else, particularly about Theo.'

'He's still pissed off at me though?'

'Oh Connie, love, he'll come around. A couple of weeks away will help him with that.'

Over the next few days Connie kept her head down and focused on the guests and making their stay at Mchanga the best it could possibly be. In the evenings, after the last guests had gone to bed, she'd occasionally have a drink with Maria or Bella, but she missed Theo's company and wondered where in Kenya he was, what he was doing and who he was with.

She did as Bella had suggested, throwing herself into work and taking advantage of being able to escape Mchanga on a daily basis by taking guests out to the local village school, or further along the coast to a good snorkelling spot. Four days after she'd returned from Baobab Beach, Bella met her in the welcome building, her cheeks hot and sweaty and a frown across her usual open and smiling face.

'What's up?' Connie asked.

Bella took her elbow and steered her into a room off the reception which contained a shelf of books and a computer for guests.

'What is it? You're worrying me.'

Bella closed the door behind them.

'My brother phoned while you were out.' Bella always referred to him as 'her brother', never as Connie's father, and always with disdain.

'I don't quite know how to tell you this besides just coming out with it, so I will. Your mother's ill and he suggested it'd be a good idea for you to go home and see her.'

'Ill in what way? Mum's always complaining about some cough or cold.'

'Seriously ill, Connie.' Bella put her arm around Connie's shoulders and pulled her close. 'Pancreatic cancer. Not diagnosed that long ago but diagnosed too late and aggressive by all accounts.'

'She's dying?'

'Oh Connie, I'm so sorry. It sounds that way. At the very least my brother thought it'd be a good idea for you to see her. I presume, just in case. He's a man of few words, certainly with me at least.' Still gripping Connie's shoulder, Bella pulled away. 'I'll get one of the girls to book you a flight.'

Connie's whole world felt like it had been turned on its head once again. So many times that year her life had come crashing down around her – everything she knew and understood taken away from her and her emotions tested. Walking back to her beach villa Connie thought how strange it was that she'd never been that close to her mum, and yet the thought of losing her was too much to bear; having lost so much already this year, she didn't know how she'd cope with yet another loss.

She reached her room, opened the wardrobe and started pulling out clothes and dumping them on her bed. To go back to England so soon after she'd sent Felix packing, felt as if she was chasing after him... She'd only recently returned from Zanzibar and with Theo away she hadn't been able to talk to him, to explain her actions, to find out if there was a chance he'd forgive her. To return to a place that had so many bad memories, when she was still battling to get past all that had happened between her and Felix with their fertility treatment and his infidelity, felt like a step backwards.

'Beyond selfish,' she muttered, rolling up her clothes and stuffing them into her rucksack. Her mum was seriously ill and here she was thinking and worrying about men. All three of them. Not only had she slept with Theo but she'd messed around with Jamil. It felt like she was rebelling, but against what? Her nearly ex-husband? Why did she need to prove anything to him? Proving that she was over him by having sex with other men wasn't smart. She was about to put the last pair of shorts into the rucksack when she realised that she was unlikely to need summer clothes back in the UK in late

September. But just in case she had to stay in the UK, she figured she should pack them. She faltered and then took her vest tops, shorts and cotton skirts back out and put them in the open wardrobe. She'd only take hand luggage with a change of clothes, and the jacket and cardigan she'd worn on the journey to Tanzania. She would be back.

Her mum would be fine; she was a hypochondriac and probably making out that things were a lot worse than they really were. She'd find out after a bumpy jeep ride to Dar es Salaam, a twelve hour-plus flight back to Heathrow and a two hour coach journey to Cheltenham. She swung her rucksack on her back, took a last look at the ocean view from the deck of her beach front villa and walked away.

Chapter Sixteen

Her parents' house looked the same as it had always done with its moss green Farrow and Ball painted front door and shiny silver knocker. Connie shivered in the chill morning air and made a mental note to buy warmer clothes and a coat. It had been too much trouble to think about retrieving her clothes out of storage in Cardiff. Depending on how long she needed to stay, she'd think about all that tomorrow. She had no idea how long she'd been up for – she'd slept on the flight as much as she could squashed in a middle seat between two people, and then there'd been an uncomfortable coach journey to Cheltenham followed by a taxi drive across the town. And here she was, standing on the doorstep of her parents' house, a house filled with bad memories.

The door swung open and Connie's brother, Alexander, stood in the dim light of the hallway. He always had been pale-skinned but he was ashen with dark shadows beneath his eyes.

'Oh my God, Alex,' Connie said, stepping into the house and hugging him.

'It's been quite a few days.' He stood back to let her past.

The large entrance hall was dark, with unopened post cluttering the usually tidy console table.

'How is she?' Connie left her rucksack on the floor and followed Alexander upstairs to their parents' bedroom at the front of the house.

'Not good,' Alexander said quietly, pushing the bedroom door open.

Despite it still being light outside, the thick dark curtains were drawn and there were only two lamps on, casting little light over the large, high-ceilinged room. It was the smell, though, that got to Connie – a staleness, as if the room hadn't been aired for weeks. Something her house-proud mum would be deeply ashamed of. It smelt of old food, medicine and, worst of all, death.

Her mum's shallow, rasping breath told Connie everything she needed to know before she even got close to the bed.

'Constance,' her dad said, barely looking at her. He clasped his wife's hand in his. His face was stonier than usual, the same grey tiredness as Alexander, but her mum looked a hundred times worse. Ashen-faced, sunken eye sockets, eyes closed. Despite the heat in the room a duvet was pulled up to her chin. Connie wanted to be back at Mchanga, in fact, anywhere but here.

She took a deep breath and forced herself to not run from the room, then leant over the bed and kissed her mum's cool cheek. The difference compared to the last time she'd seen her was startling. She had looked more drawn than usual and had seemed tired, but that could have been down to any number of things. Her mum always seemed to have something wrong with her and was constantly complaining about a niggling pain, headaches or tiredness, so much so that Connie tended to switch off. There was no denying that she really was ill this time.

Connie stood by the bed, unsure whether to sit on the edge of it or not. She remained standing and looked across at her father whose attention was solely focused on his wife.

'Is she sleeping?' Connie asked quietly.

'Yes,' her father replied bluntly. 'She wakes up occasionally but isn't making too much sense when she does. She needs to rest.'

Alexander placed a hand on Connie's elbow. 'Let's get a cup of tea. You must be tired after your journey.' He steered Connie back to the bedroom door and turned around. 'Do you want anything, Dad?'

'No, thank you.'

Connie followed Alexander back down the stairs and through the hallway, to the large kitchen at the back of the house with doors at the end leading out into the garden. The kitchen wasn't the same without her mum cooking or fussing over everyone. It was always spotless, always smelt of something delicious: freshly baked bread or coffee. Dirty plates and mugs were stacked next to the sink and Connie wondered if Alexander was cooking for their father who never cooked or washed up – in fact Connie had never even seen him clear the table.

Her brother flicked the kettle switch and turned back to Connie, who was leaning against the work surface opposite.

'She's not got long.' Alexander took two Earl Grey teabags from out of a tin and dropped them into their mum's favourite flowery National Trust cups. 'She went downhill really fast.'

Connie stared at the washing-up in the sink. Their Mum would hate the house being in such a state. Now she was here she would clear everything away, wash up, keep the house clean. The kettle boiling drowned out her thoughts and Alexander poured the water on the teabags. He put the cups on a tray and led the way through to the conservatory. He put the tray down on the coffee table and sat on the sofa with his back to the window. Connie shivered and sat on the armchair opposite.

'Why did it take you so long to let me know how ill she was?' Connie asked.

Alexander shuffled on the sofa. 'Mum didn't want you to worry. She's pretty much been in denial, plus she wanted you to have the time to yourself to get over Felix. You've had enough going on.'

'How on earth did you all think that keeping me in the dark was a good idea? I'm fed up of being lied to and being the last one to know about everything.'

'Connie, I wanted to tell you, I did...'

'But what?'

'Dad was reluctant to.'

'Really? Since when has he ever worried about upsetting

me? You know he was delighted to see Felix out of my life – he thinks I should suck it up, get on with life and not go running away to Tanzania.'

'I don't think it's being in Tanzania that's the problem.'

'Then what is? Oh, don't tell me – Bella.'

Alexander shrugged.

'He has no idea about half the stuff that went on between me and Felix. I needed to get away and Bella offered me an escape. I took it. I know none of you understand.'

'I do, Connie.' He looked at her. 'I know we've never been close but I get why you've gone to Tanzania. He broke your heart and your life fell apart. I understand why you needed to get away from here.'

Connie leant back and rested her elbow on the arm of the chair. 'How are you managing to be here? What about Rachel and the kids? Your job?'

'I took some emergency leave from work. Rachel is doing a fabulous job on her own with the children. Dad needed me here. He's a mess. I don't know how he's going to cope once, you know…'

Connie nodded and glanced out of the window at the grey light. The branches of the silver birch at the end of the garden were droopy with silvery leaves, the border was neat but colourless apart from varying shades of green, so different to the vibrancy she'd left behind at Mchanga with the deep blue ocean, the pale gold sand.

Connie turned back to her brother. He was playing with his watch, twisting it around on his wrist. She tugged down the sleeve of her cardigan, conscious once again of her scarred wrist. Alexander and her parents hadn't understood what had driven her to a suicide attempt. Her father had never warmed to Felix and believed Connie was well shot of him, certainly not worth committing suicide over. But then he didn't know the half of it. Not even Alexander knew about her pregnancies and subsequent miscarriages.

Connie cleared her throat. 'How long has she got?'

Alexander caught her eye and looked away. 'A few days, if that.'

Connie nodded. 'Are you staying here until, you know.'

'Yes. Rachel will be here later today with the children. I know they're too young to understand, and although I don't particularly want them to see their grandma like this, I think it's important that they say goodbye – that Mum gets to say goodbye to them at least.'

Alexander took Connie's rucksack up to the guest room that had once been her bedroom, and left her to unpack what little she'd brought with her. He retreated to his old room to phone Rachel. With her father not leaving his wife's side, Connie headed downstairs and cleared up the kitchen, filling the dishwasher and putting it on.

The kitchen clean, Connie made herself a coffee and went outside to sit on the paved steps that led from the patio down to the lawn. She pulled her thin jacket tighter and blew on her mug of coffee, her breath getting lost amongst the steam rising from the milky liquid. She gazed over the garden and remembered running around with Alexander when they were little and having a picnic on a rug in the middle of the grass with their mum. Faced with a future without her mother perhaps brought the good memories to the forefront rather than the arguments, the difficult times, the sense of not belonging.

Even in autumn, her mum's garden was a peaceful oasis, large and meticulously cared for with splashes of colour amongst the greens and browns. The large garden meant the tall and imposing white Georgian terraced house opposite was a long way off. The contrast to Mchanga was stark. It wasn't just the difference in temperature or even the view – she felt choked here, like her chest was constricting. Despite having had to deal with Felix in Tanzania, she at least felt like there was space to breathe, a future that hinted towards freedom and happiness, rather than a future threatening to suffocate her. But she'd always felt like that at her parents' house – a stranger in the place she once called home.

She sipped her coffee and plucked a leaf from the acer in the raised border next to the step, folded it between her fingers and flicked it down the steps. She no longer had a home in the UK. With the Cardiff waterfront apartment sold after she and Felix separated, she hadn't bothered to rent anywhere and she certainly wasn't in a position to buy a place. She had no idea what she wanted to do with her life, let alone decide on where she wanted to put down roots.

'Hey.'

Connie turned to see Alexander silhouetted in the kitchen doorway.

'Hey,' she said.

'You must be freezing.'

She shrugged. 'I wanted some fresh air. It seemed like a good idea.' She stood up and with her mug of coffee in one hand, brushed off dirt from her trousers with the other. She headed back into the kitchen and Alexander locked the back door. 'It seems a bit crazy going all the way to Cardiff to get some clothes out of storage – will you be okay if I pop into town and get myself a couple of things. A warm coat for a start.'

'Of course. Take your time – why don't you see a friend while you're out.' He placed a hand on her arm. 'You've still got friends in Cheltenham?'

Connie nodded. 'Are you going to be okay here?'

'Mum sleeps most of the time. Dad isn't saying or doing much. Rachel and the kids will be arriving late this afternoon – I'll be fine. Maybe we can all have dinner together later?'

Connie placed a hand on her brother's arm. 'I'll cook for us tonight.'

She hadn't gone clothes shopping in Cheltenham since she was a teenager, and even then she'd preferred taking the train to Bristol or Bath with a friend and going to River Island or Topshop. Now all she needed was a warm coat, a long-sleeved top and a pair of jeans – her usual quirky style meant she would normally visit independent shops to feed her love for wide-legged trousers, patterned tunics and floor-grazing maxi-skirts, but she wasn't really in the mood for browsing. She headed to FatFace and grabbed a padded military-style coat, a cream jumper, a pair of straight-legged jeans and pyjamas. She took the tag off the coat and swapped it for her summer jacket, shoving it into the bag on top of her new clothes. She set off for her friend Charlotte's house, a fifteen minute walk from the centre of Cheltenham.

Charlotte lived in a house much like the one she'd grown up in. Connie had enjoyed going round to Charlotte's for tea after school. Their house had been smaller than Connie's and it was evident that they weren't as well off and struggled to put Charlotte and her sister through private school, yet there was a warmth and homeliness about their house that Connie felt was missing from her own.

Connie stood outside Charlotte's front door – the small front garden was gravelled with a few shrubs planted behind the wall. The door was painted a pale grey. Connie rang the bell and stepped back.

Perhaps she shouldn't have just turned up like this. Although since having children, Charlotte was a stay at home mum, she was probably out doing something. The door swung open.

'Connie?' Charlotte looked at Connie, her frown turning into a smile as she pulled her into a hug. 'Oh my God. What are you doing here? Come on in.' She beckoned her into the hallway and closed the front door behind them.

'Sorry, I should have rung first. This is probably completely inconvenient. It was just spur of the moment.'

'No, honestly it's fine. I can't believe it's really you. I thought you were in Tanzania?'

Connie followed her through the hallway to a modern open plan kitchen-diner with sleek white units, polished concrete work surfaces and bifold doors leading to the garden. Charlotte's youngest son, Arthur, was on a stool at the kitchen island, paper and crayons strewn in front of him.

'I was,' Connie said, smiling at Arthur as he glanced up and straight back down to his drawing. 'Mum's ill, that's why I've come back.'

'Oh no, I'm so sorry.' She checked there was water in the kettle and flicked the switch. 'Is it serious?'

'Yeah.'

Charlotte looked across the kitchen at her. 'Really? Sorry, that sounds awful…'

Connie held her hands up. 'I know, I know, Mum's always complaining about feeling unwell, but this time she really is.'

Walking over to the island in the centre of the kitchen, Charlotte placed her hands on her son's shoulders. 'Arthur, love, can you take all of this into the living room and do your drawing there please so I can talk to Connie for a bit?'

Arthur slid off the stool. 'I don't want to do any more drawing.'

'That's okay, play with something in the living room instead then.'

'No, I don't want to.'

'Well, I want you to, please.'

'No.' He huffed.

The kettle began to boil and Charlotte glanced at Connie. 'As a special treat why don't you watch some Cbeebies?'

'Really?' He grinned and ran from the room. 'Thank you!'

'What can I get you? Tea? Coffee?' Charlotte asked, gathering together bits of paper and crayons.

'A coffee, milk, no sugar will be great, thanks.'

'Have a seat.' She motioned to the stool.

Connie perched up at the breakfast bar and watched as Charlotte set about getting mugs out and pouring hot water over the ground coffee in a cafetière. Charlotte brought everything over, set it down on the surface and sat down next to Connie.

'I should have been a better friend.'

'Don't be silly.'

'No, really, I let you down. I wasn't there for you when you needed me most. I was only talking to Tilda about this the other day – she feels the same.'

'You shouldn't feel like that,' Connie said, looking at her friend. 'I didn't actually want to talk to anyone. I felt so ashamed of how my life was falling apart around me and then I dealt with it by, you know…' She self-consciously ran her fingers across the bumpy scar on her wrist.

Charlotte nodded and put her arm around Connie's shoulders. What could she say to make things better? The truth was scrawled across Connie's wrist, a still-pink scar that Connie would live with for the rest of her life.

'Dealing with everything on my own perhaps wasn't the wisest choice,' Connie continued, 'but it was the only way I could deal with things at the time. There was so much of my life that most people knew so little about, I guess I didn't want to pile any more on top.'

Charlotte's forehead wrinkled. She tucked a loose hair behind her ear. 'What do you mean, other stuff going on? I obviously know about Felix and his affair...' She stopped, waiting for Connie to explain.

'You know the last time we met...'

'Mummy, Mummy, Mummy!' Arthur screeched, flying through the kitchen door and skidding across the tiled floor in his socks.

'What's the matter, love?'

'I don't want to watch *Bing*.' He stamped.

'I'm letting you watch Cbeebies and you're complaining?'

He folded his arms and stamped his foot again. 'I want *Chuggington*.'

'That is not how you ask, now is it?'

'I want *Chuggington*, *please*.'

Charlotte turned to Connie. 'Sorry, let me put something else on for him and then we might be able to talk in peace for twenty minutes.'

Connie watched Charlotte take Arthur's hand and lead him from the room. She knew what some people would say – that she was lucky to not be dealing with toddler tantrums or having to get up early every morning. She didn't have the endless routine of washing, cleaning, tidying up after a small child, negotiating meal times and bedtime, and yet all the things that came with having a family, however hard they may be, was exactly what she wanted. What she *had* wanted with Felix. She wiped away a tear and took a deep breath.

'Sorry about that,' Charlotte said, coming back into the kitchen and sitting down at the table. 'You were saying something about the last time we met?'

'Do you remember – me, you and Tilda met for lunch in Cheltenham.'

'Yeah, you seemed so happy, that's why I was shocked when I heard about you and Felix.'

'It was a weekend Felix said he was away with work.'

'But he wasn't, was he?'

'Nope, he'd gone to some secluded lodge somewhere to fuck the woman he was having an affair with.'

Charlotte glanced at the open kitchen door.

Connie blushed. 'Sorry, I didn't mean to swear, it's just…'

'It's okay, I understand.' Charlotte placed a warm hand on Connie's. 'Arthur wouldn't have been able to hear you. You really had no clue?'

Connie shook her head. 'Why would I?' She glanced away, out of the kitchen doors to a tree with a bird feeder hanging from one of its branches. 'What you don't know is that at the same time he was having an affair we were trying for a baby. Well, not exactly trying, we were having problems so were going through fertility treatment.'

'Oh Connie, I had no idea.'

'Very few people did, but that's how I wanted it… That's how *we* wanted it to be. Felix was adamant we didn't tell anyone about our struggles.'

'Yet he dealt with it by screwing around with another woman?' Charlotte said in a hushed tone.

'Go figure. His way of feeling like a man, apparently. The fertility problem was his. I've gone over and over in my head if there was anything else I could have done – supported him more, made him feel less like it was his fault I couldn't get pregnant naturally, but I know I didn't blame him, not in the slightest. In my mind we were in it together and would get through the challenges of infertility together, but he didn't think of it like that.'

'What an utter bastard.'

'There's more though…' Connie was unsure if saying more would help or not. She'd kept so much bottled up for so long that she worried if she opened the floodgates of her emotions she wouldn't be able to stop.

Charlotte took hold of her hand again and gently squeezed it. 'What is it, Connie?' She placed her other hand around Connie's so her hand was cupped. 'I should have been there for you. Sometimes it's difficult to know what to say when you see a friend's life fall apart. It didn't seem like you wanted to talk about it, so I stayed away. I'm so sorry. I realise now I could have been there for you without us having to actually talk about it.'

'It's not your fault, Charlotte, I really didn't make it easy for anyone to get close. It wasn't just Felix's affair or our marriage breaking up... The day we last met up I was actually pregnant. Almost six weeks pregnant thanks to fertility treatment. I wanted to tell you and Tilda, but I didn't want to jinx it before having the twelve-week scan. Crazy, huh?'

Connie could tell Charlotte was fighting back tears. The pressure on her hand increased. 'I had a miscarriage that weekend. I was alone at home, couldn't get hold of Felix because he was in the middle of nowhere screwing that woman. And despite me going through that, he still agreed for us to try another cycle of fertility treatment, all the while he was messing about behind my back. Confronting him about his affair when I was having a second miscarriage is what finished me off. I'd hit rock bottom. That's why I hurt myself.'

'Oh Connie, I wish you'd talked to me.'

'I did have someone to talk to. We went through fertility treatment together. She understood the pain of not being able to conceive and of losing a baby early on. I wasn't completely alone. I know you'd have been there for me if I'd asked. Tilda too.'

'The problem is, you shouldn't have had to ask.'

'Mummy!' Arthur yelled from the living room.

'Yes, Arthur?' Charlotte called back.

'I should go.' Connie stood up.

'Can I have a drink, please!'

'Don't feel you have to rush off, Arthur will be all right for a bit longer.'

'It's okay, Rachel and the kids are coming down from London today – Alexander's been here all week on his own. I said I'd cook a meal.'

'Well,' Charlotte said, as they left the kitchen and walked to the front door. 'I'm glad you came over.' She hugged Connie. 'Send my best wishes to your parents, won't you?'

'Mum's dying,' Connie said into her shoulder.

Charlotte squeezed her tighter. 'Oh God, Connie, I'm so sorry. About everything.'

Connie pulled away and wiped away the tears rolling down her cheeks with her sleeve. 'Can you tell Tilda, in case I don't get a chance to see her?'

'Of course.'

Connie set off down the path.

'Will you be going back to Tanzania?' Charlotte asked as she reached the gate.

Connie stopped, her hand on the metal gate. She turned to her friend. 'Yes, I'll be going back.' She stepped on to the pavement, shut the gate behind her and started walking back the way she'd come.

Why wouldn't she? There wasn't anything left for her here. She'd always been distant from her family. Even her close friends had moved on and had lives vastly different to her own. She had family in Tanzania too and over time would get to know people. Her thoughts returned to Theo and Jamil, Bella and Mchanga and Felix. There was so much that she hadn't told Charlotte. She longed to be back in Tanzania. She shivered in the chill air and picked up the pace as she walked back towards her childhood home.

Chapter Seventeen

Francesca and Tobin filled the house with laughter as only children could. At three years old Francesca was still too young to fully understand the seriousness of the situation with her grandmother, and eighteen-month-old Tobin was completely oblivious. With the arrival of Rachel and his grandchildren, Connie's father failed to raise even a little smile, but at least Alexander seemed happier. Connie noticed his spirits lifted the moment Rachel entered the house and he got to cuddle his children.

Connie kept busy in the kitchen making a lasagne for dinner. The feelings she'd been trying so hard to contain re-emerged the instant she caught sight of Alexander pulling Rachel and Francesca into a hug or Tobin toddled into the kitchen, Rachel hot on his heels. However selfish it made her feel, Connie longed to be back with Bella at Mchanga, the pain of being childless banished from her thoughts and away from a house where they were waiting for their mother to take her last breath. She shuddered and stirred the cheese sauce as it bubbled on the stove.

Alexander, Rachel and the children came and went, popping into the kitchen to grab a drink of water or a biscuit from the cupboard. Connie spooned meat sauce over the base of a large dish and neatly placed lasagne sheets on top before layering it with cheese sauce, more meat, more lasagne and a final topping of cheese sauce with extra cheese sprinkled on. This was proper comfort food for an autumn evening, with the sky already dark.

With the lasagne in the oven and a salad prepared, Connie set the kitchen table. Her mum always made sure they ate in the dining room when everyone was over, but Connie couldn't face the formality of sitting around the antique table. She'd always preferred the wooden kitchen table that looked out over the garden. She could hear little feet thudding along the landing upstairs and Rachel's stressed voice as she hissed at Francesca to keep quiet and get into bed.

Connie poked her head round the conservatory door that led directly off the dining room. Her father was sat in an armchair facing the garden. A book lay unopened on the table next to him and the cup of coffee Connie had made earlier was next to it, still full. Her father stared out at the darkness; there was nothing to see apart from the reflection of lamplight in the conservatory glass and the yellow glow of lights from the houses opposite.

'Dad,' Connie said, remaining in the doorway. 'Dinner's ready.'

Her father didn't turn. 'I'll eat later.'

Connie bit her lip. 'Are you sure? The kids are in bed – there's only us, Rachel and Alexander. I thought it would be good for us to talk.'

'Later, thank you.'

Without a word Connie left, unsure if she felt hurt at her father's refusal to join them or relieved that she wouldn't have to attempt to make small talk with him.

Alexander looked up as Connie entered the kitchen alone. 'He's not joining us?'

Connie shook her head. She placed the bowl of salad on the table next to Rachel and the baby monitor, grabbed the oven gloves, pulled the lasagne from out of the oven and sat down next to her brother.

'Well,' Rachel said, dishing them each a large helping of lasagne. 'This looks great. Thanks, Connie.'

Connie blew on a steaming forkful of lasagne, so different from the seafood and lightly spiced curries she'd been enjoying in Tanzania. Her thoughts flicked to Mchanga and what she'd be doing if she was back there, but immediately

Theo invaded her head, making her heart thud from shame or desire or both.

'Has Dad been eating?' Connie asked Alexander, ridding herself of Theo's image.

'A little.'

Rachel handed Alexander the bowl and Connie watched as he piled salad on to the side of his plate.

'You know what he's like, he doesn't deal with stress well and he's about as stressed as he can get right now.' Alexander shovelled a forkful of lasagne into his mouth. 'It was a complete shock for him. I think Mum knew something was seriously wrong but Dad didn't have a clue. Mum's always complaining about something. I've done it, switched off and not really heard or believed her when she's moaning about whatever ache or pain she has. We've all done it.'

'Except this time her complaints were for a reason.'

'Yes, but she didn't do anything about it until it was too late.'

They ate in silence, the scrape of forks on china plates loud in the stillness of the house.

'This is seriously good,' Alexander said, finishing off the last mouthful on his plate. 'My first proper meal since I was home.'

Rachel smiled at him. Connie took a sip of water. Despite their differing personalities and the fact that they'd never been that close, she was glad Alexander had his family and that stability in his life. He'd always been closer to their parents than she had and the toll it was taking on him was evident in the dark rings beneath his eyes and the creases across his forehead. Even though he was closer to their father than Connie had ever been, their father still wasn't an easy person to live with.

'She's missed you, you know.'

Alexander's words pulled her from her thoughts. She placed her fork down on her plate. Had she missed her? They'd never been close, but any chance of getting closer to her mum and making the most of their relationship was now gone.

'It's times like this that make you want to be close to the people you love the most,' Alexander said. 'You'll always be her little girl, even if you've grown apart as you've got older.'

Connie looked out at the dark, pinpricked by lights from the neighbouring houses. She fought back tears, aware that she'd never get the chance to repair their relationship now.

Rachel scraped back her chair and gathered the dirty plates together. 'I'll go and check on the kids.' She placed the plates next to the sink and left the kitchen.

Connie turned back to her brother. 'It was never Mum I was trying to escape from,' she said quietly. 'Or you. You know that, right?'

Alexander nodded. 'I know. I also know that Mum often wanted to back you up in arguments with Dad, but, well you know how he is – a formidable character and not easy to live with. I think Mum just wanted an easy life.'

'I feel like I let her down.'

'You didn't, and anyway, the choices were yours to make.' Alexander took a piece of cheese-topped lasagne from the dish on the table between them and put it into his mouth.

'I know, but I should have made more effort to see her – I always avoided spending time here, making excuses that I was busy working or Felix and I were away or doing other things. I guess the situation wasn't helped by Felix. He didn't really want to spend time with Mum and Dad and they never warmed to him.'

'She liked Felix, you know, secretly she did.'

Connie met her brother's eyes and frowned. 'Really?'

'I think she liked him because he was different to Dad.'

'I thought that was the reason she didn't approve of him.'

'To your face, yes, but from little things she said, I think deep down she was glad you married someone like him.'

'I bet she didn't feel that way as soon as my marriage fell apart.'

'Well, no, but then she was concerned about you. We all were.'

Connie glanced away from her brother, remembering the shame she'd felt when he'd visited her in hospital, the bandage on her wrist the evidence of how wrong her life had gone, the turmoil inside, the emotional scars and the loss of her baby at nine weeks, her pain to bear. Had she been right to not tell Alexander the whole story and to hide the truth from her mum? She would never know – it was too late to speak to her mum, and she wasn't about to put any more strain on Alexander.

'I need to talk to her.' Connie wiped her mouth with her napkin and left it on the table. 'I know she's in and out of consciousness and may not be able to hear or understand me, but there are things I need to say to her without Dad being in the room.'

'Sure,' Alexander said. 'She's usually more lucid in the evenings. I can stay with Dad down here if you want to have a bit of time?'

'Now?' Connie asked, panic rising in her chest. Despite wanting and needing to talk to her mum, she felt unprepared and out of her depth.

Alexander placed a hand on her arm. 'Connie, yes now, there won't be many more chances. Dad might want his dinner. I'll take him some. You go upstairs and say your goodbyes.'

There was such finality to saying goodbye, something she was unprepared for but had got used to over the past eighteen months. She'd lost two pregnancies, kissed goodbye to her marriage, her husband and a chance of having a family.

She paused in the dimly lit hallway. It had only been the Christmas before – less than a year ago – when Connie had stayed in the house with Felix. She'd carried on the pretence of being happy knowing full well her marriage was teetering on the edge after having found out about Felix's affair but not having confronted him. It had been Christmas Day morning when she'd learnt that she was pregnant for the second time. It had been news that had both scared and elated her and she had no one to share it with. If she'd been closer to her mum, wouldn't she naturally have been the person she could have – should have – been able to turn to? She'd known immediately the person she had wanted to confide in but she was thousands of miles away in Tanzania and the one person her father would have had a major issue with her contacting.

Connie's legs felt leaden as she made her way upstairs to her parents' bedroom. She paused outside the bedroom door, knocked lightly and entered. It took a moment for her eyes to adjust in the dim light. The nurse stood up and smiled at Connie.

'How is she?' Connie asked, immediately regretting the question, aware how meaningless it was considering the situation.

'She's been waking occasionally, asking after you and Alexander,' the nurse said.

'Would it be okay to sit and talk with her for a bit?'

'Of course. I was about to leave anyway and come back later.' She gathered up her bags from the end of the bed and turned back to Connie. 'Is Mr Stone downstairs?'

'Yes, in the conservatory.'

'I'll talk to him before I leave.'

She waited until the door closed behind the nurse. Despite the high ceiling and generous size of the master bedroom at the front of the house, with the curtains drawn and only one lamp on, the room felt as stuffy and oppressive as it had when she'd been there earlier.

She walked over to the bed and stood for a moment, stilling her breathing as she stared at the slight frame of her mum beneath the duvet. After a moment she sat in the armchair next to the bed.

'Mum,' Connie said, unsure how to continue. Her mum's ashen face was gaunt, her high cheekbones prominent, her eyes flickering beneath closed lids. Each laboured breath sounded loud in the stillness of the room.

'I'm here,' she said after a while. 'If you remember, I was in Tanzania, but I'm here now. I came back to see you.'

Connie paused again, unsure what else to say or if her mum could actually hear her. She couldn't remember the last time she'd sat down with her mum and talked properly – discussed what was going on in her life. Perhaps they never really had. They'd never talked about her mum's life either.

'I'm sorry I upped and left for Tanzania so abruptly – I needed to get away from Felix... from everything.' Her mum's eyes continued to flicker beneath closed lids. 'I know we never really talked and I'm sorry about that. I am okay though. I will be okay. I just need time to heal.' She glanced at the scar on her wrist, her permanent reminder of how desperate her life had got. She took a deep breath. 'I lost a lot of things in a short space of time, more than just Felix and my marriage... We'd been trying for a baby for a while, in fact we were going through fertility treatment. I should have talked to you about it, but Felix wanted to keep it to ourselves. I wanted you and Dad to be grandparents again, for Francesca and Tobin to have a cousin, but it wasn't meant to be.'

Connie remembered Christmas and sitting on her own in the living room. Her mum had bustled into the room, too preoccupied with making the house look perfect to bother with a 'happy Christmas'. If only Connie had made her sit down, had told her that she was pregnant, they could have shared such a special moment together, even if weeks later she'd have had to break the sad news that she'd lost the baby. Connie took another deep breath. 'I got pregnant twice but miscarried both times. I don't know why I'm telling you this now, maybe to make you understand why I hurt myself, why I wanted to take my own life. It was about more than just Felix...'

The fluttering of eyelids intensified and her mum moved her head to the side.

'Connie? Is that you?' Her mum's voice was little more than a whispered croak, her eyes barely open.

Connie shuffled closer and took her hand. There was no strength, and little flesh, only raised veins, bony fingers and cold skin.

'Yes, it's me. I've come back from Tanzania to see you.' She gently rubbed her thumb down her mum's hand, wanting to warm her up.

'Connie,' her mum whispered. Her eyelids fluttered open, revealing her watery blue eyes.

'Can I get you anything? A drink?'

'It's really you?'

Connie nodded, fighting back tears. 'It really is. I'm sorry I went off like I did, if I'd had any idea you were ill, I wouldn't have gone.'

'I hoped to see you again.' Her voice was so quiet, Connie needed to lean in to hear her properly. A tear travelled down her mum's cheek and Connie wiped it away with her thumb. Her mum's eyes closed and then opened again, focusing hard on Connie's face. 'I've always thought of you as my own. Always loved you like you were my own daughter.'

Connie pulled back, her forehead scrunching into a frown. 'What do you mean?'

'I want you to know…' her mum's voice faded, her eyes closing unable to keep them open any longer.

'Mum? Mum?' Connie said again, squeezing her mum's frail hand, but letting go immediately in fear that she'd break her fingers.

'Mum?' she said again. It was futile, her mum had slipped back into sleep, her moment of lucidity gone.

Connie paced across the room, her heart beating so hard and fast it felt and sounded like it was thumping against her ears, the same words playing over and over and over.

Always loved you like you were my own daughter.

Always loved you like you were my own daughter.

Always loved you like you were my own daughter.

Her mum was dying, her mind might be playing tricks with her, dosed up on so much pain medication. Perhaps she wasn't thinking clearly, was getting muddled. But perhaps at moments like this, the truth fought to the surface.

She needed to get out. Her whole body felt constricted, suffocated by the stale air and the dawning realisation of her mother's words. Within a space of a year, everything that Connie had been so certain of in her life had disintegrated around her: her marriage, her desire to start a family, and now she was questioning who her real parents were.

Chapter Eighteen

Connie closed the door to her parents' bedroom, leant against the landing wall and breathed deeply. Despite there being a three-year-old, a toddler and six adults in the house, it was eerily silent. The children were asleep in the spare bedroom at the top of the house next to Alexander's old room, and Rachel, Alexander, her father and the nurse were downstairs. Connie retreated to her old bedroom. She looked down over the garden where yellow light spilt across the patio and on to the grass from the conservatory and kitchen windows. She drew the curtains and sat down on the end of the bed, rubbing her forehead with her fingers.

She'd always felt different. For as long as she could remember, she'd felt an outsider within her own family. Was this the reason she felt she didn't belong?

Yet again, she was in emotional turmoil in this house. The last Christmas when she'd been here with Felix, she'd left him sleeping in the very bed she was sitting on, and she'd gone in the early hours of the morning to the bathroom to do a pregnancy test. Her uncertain reaction to the positive result was as confusing and emotionally destabilising as her mum's words, which she couldn't get out of her head.

Always loved you like you were my own daughter.

Connie lay on the bed and stared up at the ceiling, thinking through the possible reasons for her mother's words. She heard someone come up the stairs and her parents' bedroom door open and gently close. A little later cries from Tobin brought Rachel's light footsteps racing up the stairs to the top of the house to comfort him. Connie must have drifted off to sleep but woke shivering, the room dark, the house still silent, the bedside clock stating 01.17.

She stood up and took her clothes off, dropped them over the back of the armchair and put on the pyjamas she'd bought the day before. She was about to crawl into bed when a thought popped into her head. She shoved her jumper over her head, put her socks back on and crept from the room, attempting to avoid the creaky steps on the staircase but realising it was too long ago since she'd lived here to remember which steps were the noisy ones.

Her father's study was off the hallway on the ground floor, a snug room just before the kitchen. It was his domain but it was also where all the paperwork was kept, including her and her brother's school certificates and all the paperwork they hadn't taken with them when they'd moved out.

Connie clicked the door closed behind her, switched on the desk lamp and opened up the bureau next to the fireplace. Her father was methodical, some would say anal, and so an internal drawer was set aside for each family member. Connie opened the bottom one, pulled out a wad of papers, took them over to the desk and sat down in the armchair. She thumbed through them in the lamplight. Her mum had kept swimming certificates from school, Brownie badges, her GCSE and A-level certificates. She reached an A4-sized brown envelope and pulled out her birth certificate. She held her breath as she scanned it.

Date and place of birth: 11th November 1978, Cheltenham
Father's name: Edward Stone
Mother's name: Margaret Stone, née Turner
Father's occupation: Barrister
When registered: 7th December 1978

Connie looked at the birth certificate again and reread her parents' names and her correct date of birth. It made no sense. If her mum wasn't really her mother, then her dad wasn't her father either. Why then did her birth certificate have both their names on it? Could her mother be so confused and dosed up on pain relief that she wasn't thinking straight? With the certificate still clutched in her hand she leant back in the armchair and frowned.

If she'd been adopted, then surely her birth certificate would show the names of her birth parents – at least of her birth mother? She stood up and tucked the certificate back in the drawer of the bureau. Her parents were organised – methodical, liked things neat, particularly her father. No loose ends. Why then did it feel like something was hugely amiss, that the underlying feeling of not being accepted – at least by her father – while growing up had returned.

She crept from the study, quietly closing the door behind her, and walked straight into Alexander.

'Shit, you scared me,' Alexander said, clasping his chest. He was in stripy green, navy and white pyjamas much like the type their father would wear. 'What are you doing up?'

'Couldn't sleep. You?'

'The same. I was going to get a glass of water; you want to join me?'

Connie nodded and followed him down the hallway to the kitchen. He flicked on the under unit lights, took two glasses out of the cupboard next to the sink and turned on the tap.

Connie sat down at the kitchen table and watched her brother. They'd always been so different; apart from him being seven years older, which in itself had created a distance between them, he was like their father: serious and ambitious, although fortunately with their mother's more amenable temperament. Connie, on the other hand, was nothing like either of her parents: creative, wilful, far more like Aunt Bella… Her thoughts stalled as Alexander sat down opposite and pushed a glass of water across.

'Did you talk to Mum?' He looked at her. 'We didn't see you for the rest of the evening. I figured you needed some time to yourself.'

'Yes, sorry about that.' Connie sipped the water and placed it carefully back on the worn wood of the table. 'I talked to her but I'm not sure how much, if anything, she heard or was able to take in. She woke briefly.'

'She did?'

Connie nodded. 'Long enough to know it was me.'

'At least you got to speak to her before, you know…'

Connie looked away from her brother and stared out into the night. 'Do you remember when I was born?' She glanced back at him.

He frowned. 'What on earth made you think of that?'

'I don't know. Lots on my mind – I can't stop thinking about things.' Connie cupped her hands around her glass. 'So do you remember? You were seven; you must remember something.'

He nodded. 'I remember feeling very put out that I was finally going to be a big brother. I remember really wanting a brother or sister and constantly asking Mum but it never happened, so I think I was resigned to being an only child. Mum was poorly on and off when I was little – I vaguely remember her being in and out of hospital a lot.'

'Do you know why?'

Alexander downed the rest of his water and placed the glass back on the table. 'I don't think so. I don't think Mum or Dad wanted to talk about it – I guess I was too young to be told.'

'Have you ever thought to ask, I mean now you're older?'

'It's never seemed important.' Alexander stood and put his empty glass next to the sink. 'I remember Aunt Bella came to stay with us for a while – I think she'd come back from Tanzania because she was ill. I went to stay with Grandma and Grandad in Cirencester and when I came home again you were there.'

Connie stayed silent, digesting what her brother had said. 'I'm not sure I knew any of this?'

Alexander shrugged. 'I don't really remember much of the details. I just remember having a great time at Grandma and Grandad's and being totally spoilt and then feeling insanely jealous of you when I did come home.'

'Was Bella still there? When you came home?'

He frowned. 'I don't think so. She must have got better

and gone back to Tanzania. I'm sure I'd have remembered if she had been.'

'Were you born at home or in hospital?'

'At Cheltenham General, after a two day labour – Mum's always complained that I take my time with everything, like I kept her and Dad waiting.'

'But I was born at home?'

'I think so. Perhaps you arrived too quickly.'

Connie sat back in the wooden chair, the realisation dawning on her that she didn't actually know much about her birth. She was born at the end of the seventies – was it not normal like it was now to share birth stories? Even on birthdays she didn't remember her mum ever commenting about how Connie arrived into the world and yet Connie knew the ins and outs of all her friends' children's births.

'Do you think I look at all like Mum or Dad?'

Alexander stood with his arms folded, leaning against the draining board. 'What a bizarre question. Are you okay?'

Connie stood, scraping her chair across the tiled floor. 'It was just something Mum said to me – the last thing she said before going back to sleep.'

'And that was…' Alexander said, gesturing with his arms.

'She said that she always loved me like I was her own daughter.'

'Are you sure you didn't mishear? She's not exactly been compos mentis.'

'I'm positive.'

Alexander pushed himself away from the work surface and walked to the kitchen door. 'You look like Dad. You have the Stone nose and the exact same shaped lips as Dad and Aunt Bella do and Grandma Stone had.' He gave her a wave. 'I'm going to bed, Connie. You should too, it's stupidly late.'

Chapter Nineteen

The funeral took place ten days later. Their mother had died during the early hours of Thursday morning, not long after Connie and Alexander's heart to heart in the kitchen. Waking up to the news that she'd passed away threw the house into a flurry of emotion and planning for a funeral.

The church service went as well as it could. Connie, Rachel and Alexander, with Aunt Deidre, their mum's sister, had prepared a buffet and drinks back at the house after the service for friends and family. As she took a tray of drinks around, Connie spoke to most of the immediate family and her parents' friends – some she knew, some who introduced themselves as they took a glass of wine and offered their condolences. Bella had chosen to stay in Tanzania. It only seemed to be Connie who understood how difficult it was for Bella to up and leave at the last minute to travel back to the UK.

Connie had just filled another tray with drinks and had walked into the dining room when Rachel took hold of her arm and led her into the corner.

'I don't want you to freak out,' she said. 'But Felix has turned up.'

'He's what?' Connie's eyes searched the room.

'He's in the conservatory talking to Uncle Eric,' Alexander said, joining them.

'He has some nerve,' Connie said, fury building in her chest as she turned to Rachel. 'How the hell did he even find out about Mum?'

Rachel took the tray from Connie.

'I think that was my fault,' Alexander said. 'I put details on Facebook about the funeral.'

'Since when have you been friends on Facebook with Felix?'

'Since he sent me a friend request years ago. Facebook friends, Connie, pretty meaningless really.'

'Except he's managed to turn up at Mum's funeral.'

Alexander took hold of her arm. 'I know you're upset with him but this isn't the time or the place…'

'Oh for God's sake, give me some credit, Alex, I'm not going to make a scene.' Connie's face flushed – a combination of anger and the thought of the conversation that had played out between her, Felix and Bella on the beach at Mchanga.

Connie took a couple of paces into the dining room so she could see into the conservatory. Felix was dressed in a dark grey suit with a pale grey shirt and dark grey tie. He was the epitome of handsome and elegant, capturing people's attention, chatting to Connie's great-aunt and uncle in the conservatory doorway.

Rachel leant closer to Connie. 'Are you sure you're okay with him being here. We can ask him to leave.'

'No, it's fine, thank you.' She smiled weakly at Rachel, took the tray of drinks back off her and retreated to the living room. She made her way around the room making small talk with guests. Tomorrow this would all be over.

The tray empty, she went upstairs and locked herself in the bathroom. She stared at herself in the mirror; even in the dull October light that streamed through the bathroom window, her skin still looked lightly tanned from being in Tanzania and she looked a lot healthier than she had done just a few months ago. All she had to do was make it through the rest of the day and tomorrow she'd be heading back to Tanzania, once again escaping from her old life.

She washed her hands and dried them on the towel, gently patting dry the raised scar across her left wrist before she pulled the sleeve of her dress back down to cover it.

She unlocked the bathroom door and came face to face

with Felix, leaning against the landing wall, his hands in his trouser pockets.

'I was hoping I'd never see you again.' Connie sidestepped past him. The murmur of voices floated up from downstairs.

'Really? You didn't expect me to be here today?'

Connie stopped at the top of the stairs and folded her arms. 'No, why would I? We're not together any longer and you never liked my parents anyway.'

Felix took her arm and pulled her into her room. He shut the door behind them and turned to her. 'That's unfair; we may not have got on but she was still my mother-in-law for eight years and I wanted to pay my respects.'

Connie nodded. 'Fine, I accept that.'

They stood staring at each other, years of a shared history bubbling between them.

'How are you coping?'

She looked away from him, tears filling her eyes for the first time since her mum had passed away. 'How do you think I'm coping?'

'I know, I'm sorry, you've gone through so much this year, what with this and us and then the mis…'

'Don't you dare bring that up.'

He took a step towards her and held his hands up. 'I'm sorry, I really am. I know you hate me and I know you have every right to feel that way. If there was anything I could do to make it up to you, I would.'

'Then respect my wishes and leave me alone.'

'That's really what you want?'

Connie nodded, fighting back tears.

'I thought you might need a friendly face here today, even mine. I'm truly sorry about your mum. Although your parents and I had our differences, your mum was always kind to me and I appreciated that. I can only imagine how hard this past year has been for you. I'm so sorry for all the hurt I caused.'

Before she could react, his arms were around her, hugging her to his chest. Her body relaxed into him with the familiarity; the smell of his Hugo Boss aftershave, the feel of his hands on her back, the firmness of his chest pressing against her through her dress. She rested in the crook of his shoulder, a place where she'd laid her head countless times before, and the tears she'd been fighting slipped down her cheeks, staining his dark suit darker.

'Are you in love with him?'

'In love with who?' Connie pulled away from his warmth and familiarity. She shook her head. 'Theo? That really matters right now?' She pushed past him and opened the bedroom door, glad once again of the distance between them. 'How can you even ask that? How dare you even have the arrogance to assume me not wanting you must be because I'm in love with someone else and not purely because I'm no longer in love with you. For the last time, Felix, go to hell.'

She slammed the door and ran down the stairs, weaving her way through the people congregating in the hallway and kitchen until she was outside, the chilly air stinging her skin through the thin material of her dress. She was grateful that it was October and too cold and damp outside for guests to venture out. Apart from her father. He was sat on the bench at the end of the garden, his legs splayed, his elbows resting on them as he leant forward staring up at the house.

She faltered, uncertain if it was a good idea to go down and sit with him or not. She'd avoided him as much as possible since she'd been back in England, but she couldn't avoid him forever. She rubbed her hands up and down her arms as she made her way across the grass, still frosted in the places the sun hadn't reached. Her father didn't look at her as she sat down on the bench, the cold dampness of the wood seeping through her tights to her legs.

'It was a beautiful service,' Connie said, blowing into her hands in an attempt to warm them. 'Uncle Eric's reading was moving.'

Her father grunted.

'People will be leaving soon, if you want to say goodbye.' She thought of Felix in her bedroom and wondered if he was still up there watching. Today was a day for honesty. She did hate Felix for what he'd done to her and for the pain he'd caused. She would never forgive him and she would never take him back. Nearly thirty-eight and she felt well and truly confused, her life having fallen apart in the most spectacular way. Now, after losing her mum, she was even questioning who she was.

'Were you ever going to tell me?' Connie asked.

'Tell you what?' Her father sat upright and folded his arms across his broad chest, his legs still splayed and rooted to the spot.

Connie stared out over the garden, not making eye contact. She was leaving tomorrow, she had nothing to lose. 'This might not be the right time to say this, but then again I don't think there will ever be a better one.' Connie breathed deeply and blew out a plume of foggy breath. 'Were you ever planning on telling me that I'm not your daughter?'

Connie stole a glance at her father but he remained impassive, unwavering in his defiance, staring at the house, looking at anything but her.

'She told you then?' he eventually said and leant back against the bench.

Connie sucked in a sharp breath. He didn't even try to deny it. 'I'm nearly forty. How the hell have you managed to keep this a secret from me for all this time?' She swivelled to face him and folded her arms across her chest in a weak attempt to contain her emotions. 'If I'm adopted then why on earth does my birth certificate have yours and Mum's names on it?'

'You're not adopted.' He stood up, neatening the cuffs of the jacket beneath his overcoat as he did. 'But you're right about it not being the time to bring this up.'

'Mum told me, you know – she told me that she'd always loved me *as if I was her daughter*. That's the last thing she said to me. The trouble is, the more I think about it, *you've* never loved me *like* a daughter, have you?'

He looked at her for the first time and Connie could see through his clenched jaw and unsmiling eyes that he was trying to contain his emotions too, that tears were ready to spill. 'I have guests to say goodbye to.' He started to walk away but only got a few paces before stopping and turning around. He took off his overcoat, walked back to Connie and placed it around her shoulders. He lifted up her chin and met her eyes. 'If you have any questions, ask my sister.'

Chapter Twenty

After the freezing temperatures in England, the heat when Connie emerged from the airport in Dar es Salaam hit her, enveloping her in its warmth. The sun beat down, cars beeped, people shouted and for the first time in nearly two weeks she felt alive again. Waiting outside the airport she realised she felt wrung out – as if she'd been turned inside out and put back together again but all wrong. She didn't know what to think any longer, let alone how she should feel.

Mohammed pulled up in the jeep and she slid on to the back seat, wound the window down and enjoyed the breeze pummelling her face as they sped out of the city. After a wait for the ferry to take them across the water to Kigamboni, they were back on the coast road speeding towards Mchanga. Connie leant against the head rest and closed her eyes, allowing the multitude of thoughts tumbling around her head to play out. She had no idea how she was going to talk to Bella and what she was going to say to her. Since the conversation with her father in the garden, she'd had time to digest his words and, along with what Alexander had told her during their night-time chat, Connie had a pretty good idea of what had happened nearly thirty-eight years ago.

'Welcome back,' Mohammed said, crunching the jeep over the gravelled entrance to Mchanga.

Connie glanced at her watch. Lunchtime. She tried to work out where everyone would be.

'Do you know if Bella's around?'

Mohammed parked and turned off the engine. The jeep

shuddered into silence, the peacefulness of the place becoming immediately apparent.

Mohammed swivelled in his seat to face her. 'I believe she had plans to visit the local school with some guests today. She'll be back later.'

'Okay, great. Thanks, Mohammed.'

Connie stepped out of the jeep, pulling her rucksack off the back seat. She slammed the door shut, and retreated into the slightly cooler building with its ceiling fans whirring overhead. She needed to reacclimatise and have a cool shower to wash away the stickiness of almost twenty-four hours of travelling.

'Hey, Connie, you're back,' Maria said, a little too cheerfully from behind the desk.

Connie's smile covered the discomfort she felt at the memory of Maria being witness to the scene that had played out between Bella and Felix on the beach.

'Hi, Maria, it's been a while.'

'Are you okay?'

'Yes, fine thank you.' Connie wondered if she should try and ease the awkwardness she sensed between them, but figured she didn't have the strength or desire. 'I was away a bit longer than planned.'

'Talking of being away for longer.' Maria reached beneath the desk and pulled out a key. 'Whilst you were gone we had to clear out your beach room as it had been booked by guests from a week ago. Bella moved your things up to one of the staff cottages.'

'Oh, okay, that's not a problem. I figured I wouldn't be staying down by the beach for much longer.'

Maria handed her the key. 'Do you want me to get someone to show you up there?'

'No, that's okay, I can find it – which one is it?'

Maria's eyes shifted away from Connie's. 'The one second from the end, next to Theo's.'

With flushed cheeks and a pounding heart, Connie headed along the path that cut up the hillside to the staff accommodation. She reached her new home, pausing to glance along the path to Theo's cottage only a few steps away. She opened the wooden double-doors and went inside. Like Theo's cottage, the place was small but well designed. The living area and kitchenette made the most of the view, at the rear was a bathroom, and to the side of the living space was a bedroom. Connie dumped her bag on the coffee table and looked around. Her clothes had been brought up and hung in the wardrobe and neatly folded in drawers, and her wash things put away in the bathroom. She was tempted to stay up here for the rest of the day and restart her life at Mchanga the next morning... She ran her thumb along the bumpy scar on her wrist. She couldn't hide away up here. She made herself walk to the door and step out on to the sandy path.

She was about to make her way back down the hill, when she heard a clatter from Theo's cottage. She stopped, her heart thumping and turned back. Without thinking, she covered the short distance to the cottage.

'Hey,' Connie said quietly, hovering in the open doorway.

Theo had his back to her but she noticed his shoulders stiffen.

'You're back then,' he said without turning around. He dropped a teaspoon with a splash into a mug.

She bit her lip. Perhaps she should leave him be and keep her thoughts and turmoil to herself instead of involving him any more in her messed up life.

'Can I come in?'

'If you want, but I'm heading back down in a few minutes.'

'I need to talk to you.'

'Really?' He turned round to face her. 'I haven't got anything to say to you.'

'It's not about that...' Connie's heart thudded at how it must look to Theo – her literally screwing him the way she did and then disappearing first to Zanzibar at Bella's suggestion and then back to the UK out of necessity, leaving the situation between them unresolved. 'I know how this must seem to you but I really don't have anyone else I can talk to.'

'What, not even Bella?'

'It's about Bella, that's the problem.'

Theo exhaled a long breath and shrugged. 'Fine,' he said, gesturing towards the sofa that looked out over the trees to the ocean. He picked up his mug of coffee. 'Did you go back to England to see him?'

'No,' Connie replied, stepping into the room. 'Of course not. Did Bella not tell you why I went back?'

'Something about your mum being unwell but I figured there was more to the story than that and Bella was making up stuff.'

'And why would she do that?'

'Because you asked her to.'

They both remained standing, the sofa a barrier between them. She'd not seen Theo for nearly three weeks and looking at him now with his messy hair, neat beard, tanned skin and piercing blue eyes she wanted to fling her arms around him. Yet there was no smile, no warmth exuding from him like there had been during the blissful first couple of weeks she'd been at Mchanga.

'My mum died.' Connie placed her hands on her hips and blew air over her suddenly hot face. 'That's why I was in England for so long because I stayed for her funeral.'

'I had no idea, I'm sorry.' His voice softened and he motioned once again to the sofa. 'I only got back a few days ago and honestly Bella hasn't said much.'

Connie sat on the armchair and waited while Theo sat on the sofa and placed his mug on the coffee table.

'I think Bella's dealing with a lot right now – a lot of emotions she can't really talk to anyone about,' she said.

'Not even you?'

'Particularly not me.'

Theo frowned. 'I thought you two were really close. You seem close.'

'We are.'

Theo blew on his coffee and took a sip.

'I'm closer to her than I've ever been to my parents and that's why it all makes sense now.'

'What does?'

'That I'm her daughter.'

Coffee splashed as Theo put his mug down with a thud. 'What do you mean, you're her daughter?'

'It was the last thing my mum told me before...' She glanced away from Theo and wiped away a tear. She turned back to him. 'Before she passed away. I talked to my father and although he didn't admit to it, him *not* denying it told me as much. Along with a conversation I had with my brother, everything clicked into place.'

'Does Bella know that you know?'

Connie shook her head.

'Are you going to talk to her?'

'What if it changes our relationship?'

'I'm sure it will.'

'But what if it's not in a good way?'

Theo leant forward and placed his elbows on his knees, clasping his hands together. 'I guess the question you need to ask yourself is do you want to know the truth whatever the outcome?' He pointed to his chest. 'I've always found honesty to be the best policy. That way you have less chance to screw around with other peoples' lives.'

Connie looked away from him, the awkward tension that had briefly dispersed snapping right back. 'I've taken up enough of your time.' She stood up and headed to the door, but turned back. 'I can't even begin to tell you how sorry I am for the whole situation with Felix – if I could go back and change what happened, I would.' She faltered, unsure if she should say any more or not. 'The circumstances may have been wrong, but sleeping with you wasn't a mistake.' She didn't wait for a reply, but marched down the hillside, her thoughts and emotions in turmoil.

'Connie, love, you're back.' Bella strode across the restaurant and flung her arms around her. Connie hugged her. Bella pulled away and looked at her. 'Are you okay?'

Connie nodded, not knowing what to say.

'It must have been an incredibly difficult couple of weeks.'

'It was.' Connie knew there was no love lost between her

parents and Bella, and if she was upset at all about her sister-in-law passing away she was hiding it well. But why would she be upset, given what Connie had learnt over the past few days?

'Can I talk to you? Alone?'

'What, right now?' Bella frowned.

'Later, whenever you've got time, but tonight.'

'Of course, love.'

Once again, Connie was thrown into the role of hostess, being sociable and acting like she had no cares in the world despite feeling torn inside. Most of the guests were seated in the restaurant, tucking into their dinner when Bella hooked her arm in Connie's.

'Let's take a stroll,' she said.

They walked together down the steps and on to the beach, the sand sinking beneath Connie's feet as they headed away from the lights, music and chatter. They reached the last pair of sunloungers and endless sand and darkness took over. Bella unhooked her arm from Connie's and sat down. Connie sat opposite, her back to the thundering waves that were folding on to the beach, facing the twinkling silver lights from the bar and restaurant. She looked across at Bella's shadowed face. 'I can't begin to tell you how messed up my life feels right now.'

'Felix is gone, out of your life for good. You can begin to move on, Connie. Build a life here if you want to or choose to go wherever makes you happy.'

'It's not just because of Felix, the divorce and all the crap in my life leading up to this.' She rubbed her thumb over the scar on her wrist. 'It's not even about losing my mother, because I haven't really lost her, have I?'

Bella met Connie's eyes and frowned. 'What do you mean?'

'I've not lost the mother who gave birth to me.'

Bella's eyes shifted away from hers, her mouth opening slightly as if to say something. She reached her hand up to her face, covering her mouth, her eyes focused on the ocean.

'How? How do you even know?' Bella's voice was almost lost in the noise of the surf.

'A combination of things; piecing together what Mum said, from questions I asked Alexander, and then Dad's reaction. He told me to ask you.'

Bella's laugh was hollow. She wiped away tears with her fingers.

'It's true, isn't it?'

'Oh Connie.' She reached across the sand and took Connie's hands. 'I never intended you to find out like this.'

'Bella, I'm thirty-seven, I figure no one intended for me to ever find out.'

'I was twenty when I got pregnant. I'd planned to come out here for a few months but fell in love with the place and never wanted to leave. I fell in love with a man too. I was young and naive, got myself knocked up and he headed back home.'

'He knew you were pregnant?'

'Oh yes, but I don't blame him. I shouldn't have told him, but I did and of course he wanted no part of it. I only knew his first name and that he was from Stockholm but I'm not even sure that was true.'

'So I'm half Swedish.' Connie rubbed her temples, the enormity of the truth sending a band of pain tightening across her forehead.

'I guess you are.'

'No wonder I've always felt different; that I never fitted in at home.'

'Although I wanted to stay here,' Bella continued, either not wanting to or unable to focus on anything but telling her story. 'I realised I couldn't have a baby out here on my own – much to the disappointment of my family, my brother in particular.'

'Why on earth would he be bothered by that – I know having a baby when you weren't married was frowned upon then but surely Grandad would have been more pissed off about it than my father?'

'You'd think.' Bella stood up. 'I need a drink.'

She set off across the sand towards the trees and the beach villas. Connie followed, numerous questions unanswered. They trekked up the hillside to Bella's villa.

'I shouldn't have built this damn thing so high up,' she said breathlessly as she flung the doors into her living room wide open. She headed straight for the chest against the back wall, poured two glasses of whisky, handed one to Connie and then sank down on the sofa.

Clutching the drink, Connie sat next to her.

'Why was my father so angry that you were pregnant?'

'Because he felt it was unfair – that I, despite being unmarried and not intending to have a baby could get pregnant and have a healthy pregnancy, while him and your mother had been trying for another baby ever since Alexander turned one. Nearly six years of trying, and although your mother got pregnant three or four times that I'm aware of, she lost each pregnancy.'

Connie's grip on the glass tightened. 'She had four miscarriages?' Even saying the word choked her. She carefully placed her glass on the table and leant her elbow on the arm of the sofa, resting her forehead against it.

'At least four. She was desperate for another baby. I'm not sure my brother was, but he sure as hell wanted the torment your mother was going through to end. It seemed like the perfect solution…' Bella took a sip of her whisky.

'To give me up?'

'I never once thought of ending my pregnancy and yet I knew that I couldn't look after a baby – I was too young and hadn't figured out my own life, let alone be ready to be responsible for another person. I'd considered giving you up for adoption but the thought of never seeing you again was too much. I was certain of that even before you were born. I think my brother and your mother would have ended up legally adopting you, but as it turned out, you arrived two weeks early and quickly, took us all by surprise and I had you at their house. I was fine and you were healthy; there was no need to go to hospital. Circumstances were what made us agree to do what we did. Your mother was desperate for a baby and I was desperate for you to stay with them so I would always have a link to you. Crazy though it sounds, at the time our decision seemed like it was in everyone's best interest. Even yours.'

Connie clenched her fists and stood up, pacing the short distance to the deck. She breathed deeply. The lemongrass-scented candles flickering in lanterns on either side of the plunge pool sweetened the air along with a salty tang from the ocean. Everything here was so alive, so vivid. She had space and time to think, time to reflect on her life and what she'd chosen to escape from back home. Yet her past had once again chased her to Tanzania.

'What are you thinking? Please tell me, Connie.'

Connie turned away from the flickering candlelight and darkness beyond, back to her aunt. 'That you lied on my birth certificate. I couldn't make sense of it at the time. Mum and Dad's names are down as my mother and father, although that's blatantly not true. You passed me off as their biological daughter. You do realise that's fraud?'

Bella nodded. 'I know. We knew.'

'You took a huge risk. No wonder none of you ever told me.'

'Life is unfair, cruelly unfair as you know all too well. Was it the right thing to do, who knows? You were raised by two parents as part of a family with a brother – a life I didn't feel I could ever give you. But I also got to be a part of your life – I knew you were okay, well looked after, loved.'

'It didn't always feel that way – there were many times I felt distant from them, Dad in particular. So many times I wanted to come and live with you. Is that why he hates me? Because I was always drawn to you? It must have killed him to know that, when they were the ones who were raising me.'

'My brother doesn't hate you,' Bella said quietly. 'Far from it. He's never been one to show his emotions. I just don't think he knew how to handle a strong-willed teenage daughter who reminded him of me. I think he was probably worried that you would take the same path I did.'

'What? Get pregnant young? Or up and leave for Tanzania?'

'Both.'

Connie thought back to the conversation she'd had with him on the bench in her parents' garden. She'd always been frustrated by him being so reserved and always seeming to look down on her and never approve of anything she did, even if she was successful at it. Discovering the truth about her family had allowed her to understand where those feelings had come from. Yet, at the end of their conversation on the garden bench, she remembered how tenderly he'd draped his overcoat on her shoulders. A small gesture but one that spoke volumes.

Connie rubbed her eyes, stemming her tears. 'How? How is it even possible that you all got away with this? How could Mum have passed me off as her baby? I don't understand.'

Bella patted the empty space on the sofa next to her. Connie remained standing on the deck, the stillness of the night air hugging her.

Bella shrugged. 'Your mum was a stay-at-home mum and with all that she'd been through, with all the loss she'd suffered, she was pretty much a recluse. She'd stopped inviting friends over and they'd stopped dropping by. The neighbours kept themselves to themselves – if she didn't want to she didn't have to leave the house, and trust me, she didn't.'

'But she must have had to register me with a doctor? What the hell did they make of her suddenly going "ta da, here's a baby"?'

'Every time your mother had been to her doctor to say that she was pregnant or for them to confirm a pregnancy, she'd then gone on to lose that baby. She was naturally afraid of acknowledging a pregnancy. She passed off having a baby without anyone knowing because she'd been too afraid to jinx things. It sounds looney, I know, but women do get to that point.'

A memory flashed into Connie's mind and the feeling of utter despair that she'd felt sitting on the kitchen floor of her and Felix's apartment, her marriage and her future in tatters as she bled from miscarrying her baby and bled from the cut she'd made across her wrist.

'I can understand how the longing for a baby can drive

someone to do such a drastic thing. It doesn't make it right though.' She folded her arms and walked the short distance across the deck and into the living area. She sat down on the sofa next to Bella and tilted her head upwards, feeling the relief of air on her face from the ceiling fan whirring above. 'So, my father is actually my uncle, Alexander is my cousin, my niece and nephew second cousins, and Mum, well, I wasn't related to her at all. To be honest, it makes so much sense; now I understand why I've always felt like an outsider, why I was always drawn to you and why I'm like you. Nature over nurture, I guess. The thing that hurts the most is that Mum lived with this lie all her life and only felt able to tell me because she was dying.'

'And for that I will forever be sorry.' Bella plucked a tissue from the box on the coffee table in front of them. 'Giving you up and going back to Tanzania was the hardest thing I've ever done.'

Connie left Bella and walked down the hill towards the beach. The weight of secrecy she hoped would have been lifted by talking to Bella was still there, it was just now in the form of more questions and a different kind of unsettled feeling. Her place in the world had been turned upside down – everything she'd known and believed in for the past thirty-seven years had changed. She'd lost a mother and yet had gained one in the space of a few days.

At a brisk pace she stumbled down the hill and back out on to the beach, walking across the sand to the water's edge where it foamed on to the shore. She allowed her feet to be licked by the seawater, relishing the coolness while the rest of her felt hot, sticky and confused. She didn't have to glance behind her towards the restaurant and bar to know the evening was still in full swing – she could hear the music from here – jazzy and upbeat, a perfect accompaniment to late night cocktails by the ocean.

She didn't hear Theo until he was right next to her.

'Are you okay?' he asked, staring ahead. 'Did you talk to her?'

The moon reflected in the water, a distorted shape constantly moving with the ocean. The sky was clear and decorated with thousands of silver stars, an endless expanse stretching as far as the eye could see towards Zanzibar and beyond.

'I did.' Connie glanced at him. 'She confirmed what I thought.'

'That she's really your mother?'

'Yep.'

'Shit.'

They continued to gaze out at the ocean, the rush of the waves on to the sand filling their silence.

'Where is she?'

'I left her up at her villa.' Connie stepped backwards, the soft dry sand sticking to her wet feet. 'I think she needs some time to think things through. What are you doing out here?'

'I saw you on your own so I thought I'd see if you were okay.' He turned to face her. 'It's good you talked to her.' He held her gaze for a moment before heading back across the sand, his hands shoved into the pockets of his loose linen trousers. Connie watched him go, more confusion flooding through her at Theo's concern, yet acknowledging the disappointment that he was heading to the bar for a drink with everyone else and not her. What would it take for her to gain back his trust?

Chapter Twenty-One

Mchanga was packed with guests and so there was no time for Connie to brood over the events and revelations of the past couple of weeks. Theo was at least talking to her, even though their easy-going flirtatious relationship was a thing of the past. For three days after their heart to heart, Bella was unusually quiet, which was also noticed by other staff including Theo and Maria. She still engaged with guests and kept herself busy but she was a shadow of her usual happy and vivacious self. Although she was worried about her, Connie didn't attempt to take conversations with Bella any further than simply discussing the everyday running of Mchanga – she was done with ending up an emotional mess and she didn't want to push Bella any further, understanding that she had a lot to deal with too.

It was late afternoon and Connie had just returned from taking guests on a walk around the wood to see the colobus monkeys when Bella marched towards her.

'We need to talk.' Bella hooked her arm in Connie's. 'Not here, not right now. I need to get away – that's not something I ever feel like doing as Mchanga is the place I'm always drawn to, but I need a change of scene. You've got nothing planned with guests for tomorrow, am I right?'

Connie nodded. 'Nothing yet and I've finished for today apart from helping out this evening.'

'Good. We're going to have a night in Stone Town.'

'We are?'

'We are. Pack lightly – we're hitching a ride on a Cessna

taking a couple to Zanzibar. We leave in forty minutes.'

With no time to argue or question further, Connie panted up the hill to her cottage, chucked a change of clothes and a washbag in her small rucksack and headed back down to meet Bella.

'It's an honour to have you back, Miss Stone,' the head waiter of The House of Stone said, nodding to Bella and then Connie as they arrived at the open-air rooftop restaurant.

Bella sighed. 'Kwasi, how many times have I asked you to call me Bella?'

'Many times, Miss Stone.' He smiled and led them across the rooftop to a table by the whitewashed wall overlooking Stone Town. Bella nodded to guests and shook hands as she followed.

The waiter pulled out Connie's chair and one for Bella. A bottle of white wine sat in a cooler full of ice.

'What can I get you, Miss Stone?' Kwasi asked, pouring them each a glass of wine.

Bella waved him away. 'You're impossible. Go serve the guests and bring us a selection of dishes whenever you have a moment. No rush.'

He nodded and left them alone. Bella raised her glass.

'Cheers.'

'Cheers.' Connie took a sip of the cool wine and gazed across the dark rooftops. The shouts, laughter and music from down on the ground escaped into the night air.

'Sometimes I need the hustle and bustle of Stone Town to make me appreciate the peace and quiet of Mchanga,' Bella said.

Connie turned back from the view to find Bella watching her intently.

'It's a special place,' Bella continued, 'but when you work somewhere you love for as long as I have you get used to it, get complacent about just how beautiful the place is and how lucky you are to call it home.'

'Mchanga is where you've always wanted to live?' Connie asked. 'Not Selous or here?' She wafted her hand towards the rooftops.

'I love each place for different reasons, but yes, Mchanga will always have my heart. It's my success story – I built that place up on my own.' She unfolded her napkin and placed it on her lap. 'Mtazamo was always Geoff's, his baby for the want of a better word, and although I helped shape and turn it into the success it is today, for me it will always be shadowed by heartache. If that hadn't happened I imagine I'd never have left, but I did and I made my own way. Mchanga, The House of Stone and now hopefully The Baobab Beach Retreat are my passion.' She lifted her glass and tapped it against Connie's. 'But yes, escaping to a place that's filled with life and assaults the senses makes me feel fully alive. I need that right now.'

It wasn't just the sounds that filtered up from the depths of Stone Town, but the smells of street food cooking and lamplight casting weird and wonderful shadows over the decaying walls. In daytime the decay, the rubbish, the peeling paint on the houses was evident, yet after dark with dim lighting and star-studded clear skies there was a beauty to the place that Connie often felt was missing in the harsh glare of the sun. It was a place that intrigued Connie, left her wanting more, and yet made her feel relieved when she could escape to the quiet beauty of the coast.

'I've had a lot to think about over the past couple of days.' Bella folded her hands together on the white tablecloth. 'I feel guilty that I've selfishly taken the time to think things through when you're the one dealing with the shock of finding out the truth.'

Connie wondered if the other diners, mostly couples, along with a handful of families with older children, had any family secrets bubbling under the surface.

'I wasn't so much shocked about the fact that you're my birth mother – to me that actually makes sense and deep down perhaps I always knew. What I was shocked about was the fact that none of you – *none of you* – ever thought to tell me. What was I supposed to do with that kind of information while my mother was on her deathbed?' Connie stopped talking, aware that her voice was beginning to rise.

Kwasi returned and placed bowls of coconut crab soup and a plate of spiced lamb and rice in front of them, while Bella made appropriate ooh and aah noises. Connie stayed quiet and sipped her white wine.

'Thank you, Kwasi,' Bella said. He nodded, turned and left them.

Bella sat back in her chair for a moment, her eyebrows furrowed as if she was working out what to say. She sat forward and dipped her spoon into the bowl of soup.

'I was shocked that you knew.' She dabbed the side of her mouth with a napkin. 'I never for a moment thought that either my brother or your mother would tell you the truth. I know your mother always struggled with the fact that she was raising you, yet hadn't been pregnant or given birth to you like she had with Alexander. I thought she'd take that to her grave.'

'I'm not sure she intended to tell me.' Connie gazed once more across the rooftops, picking out the sounds of a bicycle bell tinkling from down on the ground amid the laughter and chatter from the diners. 'She really wasn't with it. She was in and out of consciousness, which is why I thought I might have been mistaken. A niggling feeling told me otherwise.'

'It was a confession,' Bella said quietly.

Connie's attention snapped back to Bella. The lines around her eyes and corners of her mouth were soft in the flickering candlelight.

'That's exactly what it sounded like,' Connie said, nodding. 'A confession.'

'You should try the lamb before it gets cold.'

Connie stabbed her fork into a piece of lamb losing half of it as it fell apart. She popped what was left on her fork into her mouth. 'Wow, that's delicious.'

'The hint of aniseed gives it a beautifully delicate but fragrant flavour, don't you think?'

'I don't remember the food being this good the last time I was here.'

'It probably wasn't. I've been able to employ better, more

renowned chefs as the years have gone by and the hotels have become more established and celebrated. I feel incredibly lucky that I haven't had to cook for myself in years.'

Connie smiled and dipped her spoon into the soup. It was quite a life Bella had chosen: owner of luxury hotels in exotic Tanzania and Zanzibar, compared to what could have been – a struggling single mother back in the UK. What would Connie have done? After the difficulties she'd been through over the past eighteen months to get pregnant, only to miscarry twice, she couldn't even begin to comprehend giving birth only to give up her baby. But then Connie was almost thirty-eight and a maternal urge had been strong for years, compared to twenty-year-old Bella in the late seventies pregnant with a baby she didn't want, when she was longing for a life of adventure in a country she'd fallen in love with. It didn't really compare.

Connie put her spoon down and reached across the table and took Bella's hands in hers. 'I don't blame you for what you did or for not telling me. I get that you were all trying to do the best for me. I am, however, glad that I've now found out the truth.'

Bella pulled one hand away and wiped a tear from her cheek. 'I'm glad you found out too.'

Connie released Bella's other hand and took another mouthful of the aniseed lamb. 'Does Geoff know you had a baby? That I'm your daughter?'

Bella shrugged. 'I never told him, and I have no idea if he had any inkling. I was young when I had you and my body bounced back into shape, but I still have the stretch marks to show that I carried you for nine months. That might have been a big enough clue for him but he never mentioned it either way. Him having a child with Inaya could not have hurt me more. I think he thought I'd forgive him and we'd rub along together like we'd always done, me turning a blind eye to his infidelities, but I couldn't, not when he became a father.'

'He had affairs with other women, other than Jamil's mother?'

'Are you kidding me? I lost count. A lot of single women worked at Mtazamo over the years – most were a lot younger than Geoff. He was a serial philanderer and for some reason it never bothered me. I guess I was so wrapped up in work, building our business that I couldn't care less what he was doing. He was still loving and affectionate to me, my companion and someone I could spark ideas off and enjoy late night talks with. But of course the arrival of Jamil changed that. I couldn't forgive him.'

'Did you not want to have children?' Connie asked. 'I mean, apart from me?'

'I've been pregnant three times.' Bella's eyes filled with tears. She turned away from Connie and gazed out over the rooftops. 'The first time with you and then twice during my marriage to Geoff, both times before Jamil was born. Geoff didn't know either time that I was pregnant and I had early miscarriages both times.'

'Oh Bella, I had no idea.'

'No one did.'

'How on earth did you keep it a secret from Geoff?'

Bella grunted. 'That was easy. Geoff has always been wrapped up in Geoff. His life revolves around himself. I don't think it would have crossed his mind that I was pregnant.' Bella wiped a tear from her cheek. 'We never really discussed starting a family – we just weren't careful. To be honest we were both too busy focusing on our businesses to be thinking about children, but I guess we didn't not want them either. Of course, Geoff's attention was taken up by more than just work. I knew how much of a wandering eye he had. It wasn't hard to hide what was going on in my life or my emotions. He was never very receptive to changes of mood unless I was actually screaming at him, which I naturally did after finding out Jamil's mother was pregnant with him.'

They talked late into the night, eventually leaving the tranquility of the hotel for the heat and humidity of the streets below. They wandered down to the waterfront with its dhows bobbing up and down on the black water. A festival was in full swing in the Old Fort and soulful beats floated on the air as they wandered, arms linked, a comfortable silence between them, each lost in their own thoughts. They headed back to the hotel, stepping out of the heady night-time warmth into the cool and peaceful lobby.

'Time to sleep. We'll leave early in the morning.' She kissed Connie's cheeks before heading up the stairs to her private quarters on the top floor.

Connie had one of the guest rooms for the night, and grabbing a local magazine from the sideboard in the empty lounge, she headed up the stairs to the first floor. 'Utulivu' the plaque on the door said, which meant 'tranquility'. She opened the bedroom door and locked it behind her. The wall lamps had been switched on and a warm glow emanated around the room. Above the bed a ceiling fan whirred and the shuttered windows were open, allowing the sounds and smells of Stone Town to float through. With white walls and a four poster bed draped with pale blue and turquoise chiffon fabric, the room lived up to its name. The bed faced the window and to the far side of the room on a raised platform stood a freestanding bath, the wall behind it covered in colourful pieces of glass that glinted in the subtle light.

She knew she wouldn't need to set an alarm for the morning. Bella or one of the reception staff would wake her, and she was confident morning prayers would pull her from her dreams. She stripped down to knickers and a vest and snuggled down in the bed, her head resting on the pillow that smelt of cinnamon and cloves. She pulled the thin bedspread up to her waist and closed her eyes, the thought of once again travelling back to Mchanga filling her head before sleep took over.

Chapter Twenty-Two

'I'll drive,' Theo said, slinging a small rucksack on to the front seat of the jeep.

Connie frowned. 'I thought Mohammed was driving?'

'He was, but he's not feeling well.'

'Won't you be needed here?'

Theo shrugged. 'Bella's insisting I go with you. She'll manage fine without me for a few hours.'

'I am capable of taking the guests out on my own, you know.' Her words came out harsher than she'd meant, but a week back at Mchanga after her and Bella's flying visit to Stone Town, and Theo was still distancing himself from her.

'I know.' Theo pulled himself up on to the jeep and into the driver's seat. 'But with Mohammed sick, Bella wants someone else with you – other than the guests. You got everything?'

Connie nodded. 'Just waiting for the couples.'

Truthfully, Connie was relieved she didn't have to do the driving as well as entertaining two honeymooning couples and making sure their full day stayed on track. Although a confident driver in the UK, it was a whole different matter driving a large and unfamiliar jeep along potholed Tanzanian roads and being responsible for four guests at the same time.

She glanced through the open passenger window to where Theo in khaki shorts and a cream T-shirt with 'born to be wild' scrawled across it, rested his head back on the seat, sunglasses shading his eyes.

'I appreciate the company.'

He glanced at her over his sunglasses. 'You're the one doing all the hard work. I'm just driving.'

It wasn't really hard work, Connie thought as they set off with two loved-up couples happily settled on to the back seats behind them, the windows wound down to make the most of the breeze. They took the road that led away from Mchanga and in the opposite direction to Dar es Salaam. This was new territory for Connie but with advice from Bella and the local staff, she'd tailored the trip to include snorkelling at a reef off a desolate stretch of beach followed by a picnic, a visit to a fishing village and Prosecco by the ocean before heading back to Mchanga in time for dinner.

They drove for an hour, the coast road winding inland, edged by looming trees, occasional corrugated iron shacks selling fruit, vegetables and bottles of fizzy drinks and water. Tracks led off from the main road, cutting through bushy undergrowth leading to villages. Then they skirted the coast again, the electric blue ocean shimmering in the sunlight, snatches of creamy sand stretching endlessly in both directions.

The couples mostly looked out at the view, hands entwined, occasionally chatting. Connie and Theo sat in silence too, Theo driving, his right arm resting on the open window as they sped along in the morning sunshine. At times Connie glanced back to let the couples know where they were and how much further they had to go and soon enough, directed by Connie, Theo pulled off the main road and down one of the bumpier tracks that led towards the ocean.

They parked in the shade of a cluster of palm trees at the edge of the beach. Connie pulled the snorkelling gear out of the back, while the couples clambered out of the jeep and stretched their legs.

'This is stunning,' Gertrude said to her husband, Hans, as they wandered on to the silky sand.

While the couples headed down to the ocean clutching snorkels and towels, Connie started unloading the rest of the stuff from the back of the jeep. Theo came round the back and slid the umbrellas out of the boot.

'Hey, I thought you weren't doing anything except driving?' she asked.

'I was joking, Connie; I'm here to help.'

Together they laid out a large picnic blanket between four sets of towels and cushions for the couples to relax on after their swim. Theo put up the umbrellas, shading the area they'd set up, and Connie unpacked plates, cutlery and glasses and got the cool boxes out of the boot ready for lunch.

The picnic was the perfect way to relax after a swim in the ocean – a delicious array of lightly spiced nibbles and seafood washed down with virgin mojitos the bar staff had made up in flasks before they'd left that morning. While Theo took photos of the couples splashing about in the shallows, Connie packed everything back into the jeep, and then they were off again, a short drive further along the coast to a fishing village where one of the fishermen who provided their daily catch to Mchanga lived and worked. While the honeymooning couples had a guided tour of the fishing boats and harbour, Connie and Theo sat on the bonnet of the jeep and watched the fisherman charm the guests.

'He's a natural storyteller,' Theo said, wrapping his tanned arms around his bare knees.

'Bella said he jumped at the chance of showing people around and talking about his livelihood. Quite a character.' Connie rested her arms back on the jeep, the hood surprisingly warm even in the shade. The view of the ocean was endless, stretching to the horizon.

Connie nudged Theo, her arm briefly connecting with his warm skin before pointing up the coast in the direction of Mchanga where dark clouds were encroaching on the blue sky.

Theo turned his head. 'That doesn't look good. Did you check the weather forecast this morning?'

'Rain was forecast but for overnight.'

'Maybe it's coming across early.' He frowned. 'Looks like a storm to me.' He pulled his mobile from his pocket, glanced at it and put it back. 'Bugger all reception around here.'

'Hopefully we'll make it back before the rain starts.'

The fisherman led the couples towards the edge of the ocean where traditional blue and white painted dhows filled with rolled up nets bobbed up and down with the swell of the water. Connie watched the clouds creeping closer and sensed Theo getting twitchy, eager to be on the road again. He slid off the bonnet and paced in front of the jeep glancing between the couples and the storm clouds.

'You're making me nervous.' Connie joined him by the side of a whitewashed building.

He glanced northwards to where the clouds consumed the blue sky. 'We're a long way from Mchanga.' He caught the fisherman's eye and beckoned him over.

The fisherman turned to the couples, said something and waved them ahead of him, up towards Connie and Theo.

'Storm coming in,' the fisherman said, flashing his white teeth as he smiled. 'Coming across fast too.'

'Think we'll have to save the Prosecco for when we're safely back at Mchanga.' Theo ushered the couples on to the jeep, everyone saying goodbye and thank you as they clambered on.

They set off, bumping down the narrow road from the village until they turned on to the main road that headed back up the coast. Moody grey clouds blanketed the sky, eating up the blueness, the brightness of the day diminishing the further they drove. The sun disappeared and the rain started, giant drops plopping on to the dusty road. The windscreen wipers couldn't keep up with the amount of water emptying on to them. Theo slowed right down.

'Shit.' Connie leant forward and squinted. 'Can you actually see anything?'

'Not really,' he replied, coming to a halt on the side of the road.

The rain lashed down, drumming on the jeep roof and splashing through the open windows at the front.

Isaac, the husband of the English couple, leant forward and put a hand on Connie's shoulder. 'What are we doing?'

'There's no way we can safely make it back if it continues like this,' Theo said, turning round to face the couples. He looked at Connie. 'We passed the sign to Coral Bay Resort a little way back. I reckon we head there and see if we can shelter in their bar until this passes. I've met the manager before so I'm sure it won't be a problem.'

Connie's heart thumped as fast as the rain slammed down. Theo did a three-point turn and they crawled back the way they'd come to a turning that headed towards the ocean. Water pooled into the pot holes and the dry, dusty ground was now a quagmire of muddy sand. The holes in the road sent them jolting from side to side. Connie gripped the edges of her seat and glanced at Theo leaning forward, his focus solely on the road ahead, his hands holding the steering wheel so tightly his knuckles were white.

They didn't even notice the hotel building until it was right in front of them – through the torrential rain, it blended in with the trees surrounding it. Theo skidded to a halt in front of the entrance and turned the engine off.

'Well done,' Gertrude said from the back seat.

Connie couldn't get her bearings and despite the hotel being a beach resort, she had no idea which direction the ocean was.

Theo turned to the couples. 'If you stay here we'll see what we can sort out – I'm going to try and reach Mchanga again; Connie, maybe you go and speak to reception?'

'Sure.'

The entrance to the building was only a few steps away but Connie was soaked by the time she dived under cover, her top sticking to her skin with muddy water splashed up her legs and on to her short skirt.

'*Jambo*,' the receptionist said, a Tanzanian with the biggest smile on his face and the perfect welcome for Connie escaping the storm. 'You're not with our new guests?'

'No,' Connie said as she reached the desk. Rain water dribbled down her face. 'We're from Mchanga up the coast on a day trip and have got stranded with this weather. Any chance of staying here until the storm passes?'

'Of course,' he said. 'I'm glad you made it to us safely.'

'If we can sit in your bar or restaurant, maybe have a bite

to eat that would be amazing, thank you.'

'I can do better than that as currently we do have two rooms free.'

'Thank you, but I'm hoping we won't need to be here that long.'

Theo entered the hotel reception with rain soaking through his clothes and hair, and water streaming down his face. 'I've checked the forecast with Maria and it's for torrential rain and storms for the next twelve hours at least. The sky's so grey out there it looks like it's night-time already.'

'Well, the good news is they have two rooms free here.' She turned back to the receptionist. 'I spoke too soon about not needing them.'

Theo leant a wet arm on the desk. 'Thank you,' he said. 'We have two honeymooning couples out there and I really didn't want to tell them they had to sleep in a jeep tonight.'

The receptionist smiled. 'It's our pleasure. With flights delayed the guests who were due to have those rooms won't be here until the morning anyway. I'll get my colleague to show you to the rooms so you can settle your guests.' He picked up the phone on the desk next to him, pressed a button and rattled something off in Swahili.

Connie glanced at Theo. 'We can sleep in the car.'

He shrugged. 'As long as the guests are comfortable I don't care where I sleep.'

The receptionist put the phone down and shook his head. 'Please, no need. There's an empty room in the staff quarters.'

'Are you sure?' Connie asked.

'Of course. It is no problem.' He unhooked two sets of keys from off a line of hooks behind him and handed them to Connie. 'If you get your guests from your car, my colleague will meet you in front of reception and will show you to the rooms. I think you might need to make a run for it.' He grinned.

Connie smiled back at him. 'Thank you so much.'

He reached into a drawer and handed another key to Theo. 'For your room. Follow the path from the restaurant away from the beach and you'll reach the staff accommodation off a path to the left. The bedding is clean and there are fresh towels in the cupboard by the door. I hope you don't mind sharing?'

'We'll be fine, thank you,' Theo replied smoothly. 'Appreciate your hospitality.'

One of the Coral Bay staff led the way along rain drenched paths and Theo went with Gertrude and Hans into the first beach villa they reached, while Connie continued a short distance further with Isaac and Claire to the second vacant villa. They were soaked through by the time they got inside.

'A bit more of an adventure than expected, but this place is lovely,' Claire said, looking around. 'I only wish we'd brought a toothbrush and a change of clothes.'

Connie pulled a packet of mints from out of her back pocket. 'I can help you with this,' she said, handing it to her, 'but not the clothes, unfortunately.'

'I'm sure we can manage going commando for a night,' Isaac said, sliding his arm around his wife's shoulders.

Connie smiled. 'Well, I'll leave you two to it – that's probably not the right choice of words,' she said as the couple laughed. 'There is of course everything else you should need in the bathroom back there, and you'll be pleased to know that the shower is indoors and in fact the whole place is a little less open to the elements than at Mchanga.'

'Thank you so much, Connie.'

Connie nodded and headed for the door. 'I'll see you in the morning.' She opened the door and was nearly blown off her feet. She struggled to shut it behind her and sheltered beneath the overhang of the villa, watching the rain lash down, pummelling the sandy path which was now swimming with water. There was nothing she could do apart from make a run for it. She splashed back along the path, water and sand soaking her legs and the rain plastering her clothes to her body. The glow of lamplight in the beach rooms as she passed was inviting and she was desperate to be inside in the dry.

She shot past the empty restaurant and took the path that led through the trees away from the beach, keeping her head down and watching her footing. She could barely see through the torrential rain, with the fat droplets hitting her and the path. Lights on the wall of the wood-clad building ahead were a welcome sight and she didn't stop until she reached the door. She pulled it open and entered, dripping water on to the tiled floor of the entrance hall. A trail of water led along a corridor and Connie followed it down to room seven and knocked.

The door swung open. Theo's chest was bare and damp, his shorts still dripping water on to the floor. He rubbed a towel through his hair and stepped back to let her in.

'Were Isaac and Claire okay with their room?'

'Yeah, they were fine. Think they're liking the adventure.'

'Gertrude and Hans too.' Theo closed the door behind her. 'Staff accommodation's not bad either.'

He went over to the sink and patted his chest and face dry with the towel.

A high up window looked out into darkness and rain, but the room itself was homely with a desk below the window and a lamp casting a warm glow around the room. A small double bed was next to the desk, with the sink on the left wall and a wardrobe against the opposite one.

'You're going to have to get out of those clothes if you want any chance of them drying out before the morning.'

'What are we supposed to wear instead?'

Theo threw her a white bath towel.

'You're kidding me?'

'Seriously, Connie, don't be shy, it's not like we haven't already seen each other naked.' He pulled off his soaking wet shorts and Connie turned away just as she caught sight of his bum as he tugged down his pants and wrapped a towel around his middle. He went to the sink and started squeezing the rainwater from his clothes.

Connie bit her lip. It was true, they had seen each other naked but that was different, that was a night fuelled by alcohol, passion and anger. Now, sober, in a strange room, in the middle of a storm, it felt very different. He was at the sink with his back to her. Connie sighed, realising she couldn't spend the night soaked through to the skin even if it was still unbelievably hot. She'd never dry out in the humidity. She peeled off her T-shirt and skirt. With a quick glance behind she unhooked her bra, stepped out of her knickers and wound the towel around her.

Theo finished at the sink and walked past her to hang his clothes up in the empty wardrobe. In the lamplight and against the white towel his skin was tanned, his arms and legs slightly darker than his chest. Connie caught sight of herself in the mirror above the sink, her dark hair plastered to the sides of her tanned and freckled face. Theo sat on the chair by the desk and looked at his phone. Connie rinsed her clothes and squeezed out as much water as she could and then did the same as Theo, hanging them up in the wardrobe. She took a spare towel out of a drawer, squeezed the water from her hair into the sink, sat down on the edge of the bed and started rubbing it dry.

Theo looked up from his phone. 'If I'd known how much time we'd have on our hands I'd have brought my laptop.'

Connie scrunched the ends of her hair to get rid of the excess water and turned to him. 'There's not a lot we can do apart from sit the storm out and hope it passes soon.'

Theo glanced back to his phone and thumbed through screens. 'By the way, there's a communal bathroom down the hall and a kitchen where we can make drinks if we want.'

Connie went back over to the mirror, rubbing her hair. What they needed was a TV; watching a film would be preferable than talking to each other or looking at their phones in silence.

'What time is it?' Connie asked. She dropped the wet towel over the side of the sink and began to untangle her hair with her fingers.

'Almost eight.'

She tugged out the remaining knots and let her damp hair cascade over her bare shoulders. She'd let it dry overnight and see just how curly and unmanageable it would be in the morning.

Theo placed his mobile on the desk. 'I think I might sleep.

I rarely get an early night at Mchanga.'

'I can sleep in the jeep if you feel uncomfortable us both being in here?'

'Why would I be uncomfortable? There's plenty of room.' He slid across the bed and lay down on the right-hand side, resting his hands behind his head.

Connie's eyes travelled the length of his body, relieved the room was dim in the lamplight as her cheeks flushed at the thought of only a towel separating her from his nakedness.

'I'll turn off the light,' she said.

'If you want.'

She padded across the tiled floor and switched off the lamp on the desk. Even without it on, there was enough light from the security lamp on the wall outside to make her way back. She swung her legs on to the bed and lay down, resting her head on the pillow. It was narrow for a double, with only a short distance between them. She normally slept on her side but if she did there was a good chance her towel would come undone.

Connie listened to the continuous rain drum against the roof. She could hear Theo's breathing, slow and steady, but sensed he was still awake. Her whole body felt tense and she had no idea how she was supposed to sleep with the noise, heat and tension between them.

A blinding white light flickered across the room followed almost immediately by a clap of thunder that sounded like the roof was falling in. Both of them sat bolt upright. Connie clutched hold of her towel before she lost it.

'Fuck, that was loud,' Theo said.

Another shaft of lightning flooded the room.

'It's right over us,' he said.

'No one's going to be getting much sleep tonight.'

'I'm sure our honeymooning couples will find another way to occupy themselves.'

Connie avoided his gaze, feeling her cheeks burn at the thought. She stared out of the window, watching the rain lashing down, visible in the light from the outside wall lamp. Another crash of thunder boomed, so loud overhead it seemed like the whole room shook.

'Well,' Theo said, leaning back on the bed and resting on his hands. 'This wasn't quite how I imagined today would turn out.'

Lightning lit up the room, accentuating Theo's toned chest and stomach, drawing Connie's eyes downwards to the towel covering his groin.

How many times over the past few weeks had Connie wished that she'd had the opportunity to be alone with Theo, to talk to him, to try and put right all the wrong she'd done him. He hadn't purposely avoided her – he did talk to her back at Mchanga, but out of necessity. Gone were those first blissful couple of weeks when they'd have a late night drink, chat and flirt. It wasn't ideal to be holed up in a strange room together in nothing but towels, but they had time now.

'Do you ever stay at Mchanga when you have your two weeks off or do you always travel somewhere?'

'Sometimes. Or I go over to Zanzibar for a few days. I've got friends in Kenya, which is where I went on my last two weeks off. I always go away in April and May when it's the rainy season.'

'Will you…' She was cut off by another boom overhead. She waited until it dissipated. It was followed by another silver flash. 'Will you go back and visit family in Australia then?'

'Probably, for a bit at least. My parents are divorced and both remarried and have new families. I have lots of half brothers and sisters. I guess that's why I don't feel so bad living abroad most of the time, my parents aren't alone. They've got plenty of kids and grandkids.'

They fell silent, their eyes shifting from each other, the rumble and flashes continuing overhead.

'We're being polite,' Theo said, sitting up and folding his arms across his chest. 'Avoiding mentioning the one subject I know we're both thinking about.'

'Maybe it's time we stopped being polite then.' She held on to her towel as she changed position, tucking her legs beneath her and leaning her weight on her hand. Theo's eyes briefly dropped from her face downwards and she realised how exposed she felt with just the thin towel covering her. She held on to the thought that this conversation needed to happen. They needed to clear the air, put the past to rest and move on. She took a deep breath. 'I meant what I said when I got back from England that what happened that night wasn't a mistake.'

That night... Just the thought of it filled her with conflicting emotions – both a desire to repeat it and to bury it away, never to have to think about how much she'd hurt him.

'Maybe not a mistake for you...' Theo hugged his arms around his knees, making his biceps flex.

'So, having sex with me was a mistake?' Despite being cold stone sober she felt brave, wanting to thrash this out, much like the storm was doing outside.

'You fucking me to get back at your ex was the mistake, Connie. You made the first move remember.'

Connie met his gaze. 'You didn't have to act on it.'

'Yeah right, a gorgeous and sexy woman like you makes a move – what the hell did you think I'd do?'

His nostrils flared as he glared at her. Another clap of thunder, a little further away; another shaft of lightning flooded the room with light.

Connie held her hands up. 'Okay, you're right. I wanted you to sleep with me and I wanted Felix to find out about it, but,' she pointed a finger between them, 'we'd been flirting with each other from almost the moment we'd met – that you can't deny. I only made a move that night because there was something going on between us.'

'Being fuelled by alcohol and anger is not a sensible reason to sleep with someone.'

'I know what I did was wrong, but I wasn't thinking straight and that had nothing to do with being drunk. I can't begin to tell you how much anger I had for Felix that night. And honestly, I don't love him any longer. In fact, I hate him, I really do and I've never felt that way about anyone ever. It scared me to death how much I wanted to hurt him and at the same time I really liked you. Like *really* liked you. I truly didn't mean to hurt you the way I did. If I'd been in a place

188

emotionally to think about my actions before actually acting on them I wouldn't have done it.'

'You wouldn't have slept with me?'

'Not that night, no, and not instigated by my desire to hurt my ex, no.'

'That still doesn't change what you did.'

'And I suppose you've never done anything you've regretted?' Connie folded her arms across her chest, immediately wishing she hadn't as the motion pushed her cleavage up above the top of her towel. Not that Theo would care being well and truly over her.

'Of course I've done things I regret. Plenty of things, but what you did was calculated. You wanted to make him jealous because you still have feelings for him.'

'Are you not listening to me? It wasn't jealousy I wanted him to feel but pain and anger – just a taste of how he'd made me feel with his actions. You're right about feelings though – but the feelings I had that night were for you, not him.'

Another crash of thunder made her pause.

'My life over the past couple of years has been complicated to say the least. Felix was my husband and I loved him. After what he did to me, while I was going through the worst time of my life, I'll never forgive him, let alone be able to trust or love him again. Him turning up at Mchanga, a place I'd sought refuge, incensed me.'

Theo looked away from Connie and nodded. 'I've been hurt before, that's why I couldn't stand the thought of allowing you to play games with me.'

'It was never a game to me… thoughtless yes, but I had no intention of hurting you. How can I make you believe me?' She automatically rubbed the scar on her wrist. She stopped, turning her wrist upwards and held it out towards him. 'Felix made me do this. I'd got to the point in my life where nothing made sense any longer, and honestly I had nothing to live for. I cut my wrist and overdosed on paracetamol.' She drew in a shuddery breath and fought back tears. 'You know that Felix had an affair, but what you don't know is that he was having an affair while we were trying for a baby, while I was undergoing fertility treatment. I had two miscarriages in the space of nine months while he was off screwing another woman. The second miscarriage was at the start of this year and that was the day I not only confronted him about his affair, but the day I tried to take my life. I don't expect you to forgive me for how I behaved and treated you, but I hope you can understand where my desire to hurt Felix comes from.'

Theo took hold of her hand and lightly rubbed his thumb across the scar on her wrist. 'I'm so sorry, Connie, I really had no idea. I thought it was just blokey banter when he chatted to me the night after…' He gazed across the room as if trying to remember something. 'We'd both had a bit to drink, he was easy as hell to talk to… I remember now he was the one who steered the conversation on to women. He didn't specifically ask about you, but yeah, he asked the right questions to get me talking about who I was with… fuck, I can't believe what I told him about us… the bastard… if I'd known…'

'You didn't know.' Connie placed her free hand on top of Theo's. 'And I'm so sorry I put you in that position to begin with.'

He stopped rubbing her scar and held her hand instead. 'It's easy enough to place blame when you don't know the full story. I got hurt by my partner – by my ex-partner. Life was sweet, too damn perfect in fact, we'd talked about trying for a baby, both got all excited about our future and then she dropped the bombshell that she only wanted to have a baby if we went back to the UK so she could be close to her family. I understand that it wouldn't be easy being pregnant and raising a child in a country like Kenya but ever since we'd got together she'd known about my desire to continue living and working in Africa. It's not like it came as a shock when I said I wanted to stay.'

'What happened?'

'She gave me an ultimatum. I guess I wanted to stay here more than I wanted to have a family with her, and she wanted a baby more than she wanted to be with me. She went back to the UK and I stayed, although I couldn't stay at the camp we'd been running together in Kenya.'

'Do you still love her?'

Theo's hand tensed. 'I'm not in love with her any more. It's been just over a year since she left and she's now living in London and pregnant with her new boyfriend's baby. The fact that she could move on so easily and have a baby with someone so quickly after throwing away a seven-year relationship spoke volumes. She was a huge part of my life for a long time, and like you felt about Felix, I thought she *was* my life. I imagined a life for us here, raising a family in Kenya. I know full well that would have its challenges, but she chose to live out here and she knew my heart belongs here.'

They fell silent, their hands entwined.

'The thunder's stopped,' Connie said.

Theo pointed to the ceiling. 'The rain's eased too.'

The drumming on the roof had slowed, more of a patter with larger drips splashing down from the roof and trees on to the ground.

'We might be able to sleep now,' Connie said.

Theo's hands slipped from hers and it seemed like he was about to turn round and lie back down when he paused.

'Don't you think after all that, sleeping would be a shame, not to mention a travesty to let all that heated passion go to waste?'

She looked into his eyes, the distance between them impossibly far when all she wanted was to feel his hands on her again and his arms around her. She smiled. 'What do you have in mind?'

Theo leant forward, resting his hand next to her on the bed so his arm brushed her towel-clad side. When he moved closer and put his lips on hers, her heart began to thud.

He kissed her again with more passion and this time she responded, kissing him back and sliding her hand across the hot skin of his back just above his towel. His free hand slipped beneath her towel and followed it up, his fingertips brushing her stomach and between her breasts to where the top of it was tucked into the rest of the towel. He released it allowing the towel to fall open and pool around her on the bed. He pushed her gently down until she rested her head back on the pillow. Sliding one of his legs between hers, the movement released the knot in his towel, so when the heat of his body connected with hers there was nothing between them except skin on hot skin.

Chapter Twenty-Three

Connie opened her eyes. It took a moment for her to remember where she was and when she did, she smiled. Theo lay on his front next to her, his breathing quiet and steady, his arm lying across her bare stomach. She turned her head to look at him, the memory of the night before flooding back. After snatched sleep, curled in each other's arms, their skin stuck together with the heat and humidity, and despite longing for a cool shower and clean clothes, Connie didn't want this moment to end.

Theo's eyes opened. 'Morning,' he said and stretched, his arm moving upwards from her stomach, his fingers brushing her breast.

'Morning.'

He shuffled closer until his forehead rested against hers. Cupping her face, he kissed her lips. She kissed him back, closing her eyes as his beard tickled her face, his body pressing into hers as he pulled her close.

'If it didn't resemble a furnace in this room I'd want to stay here all day with you,' he said.

'What time is it?'

He reached across her and picked his mobile up. 'Just gone six.'

'We have a little more time before the sun comes up and cooks us alive.'

Theo dropped his mobile back down on the bedside table. 'What do you suggest we do?'

'I can think of something,' Connie whispered as she crept

her hand down the length of his taut back and across his hip.

Pools of sandy water dotted the path and fat drops of water dripped continuously from the trees. They walked along the path in companionable silence. Everything had been said the night before, their actions saying more than they ever could put into words. Before getting up they'd phoned through to reception and arranged for breakfast to be taken to the honeymooning couples' beach rooms, and one of the restaurant staff had dropped off a breakfast of fruit, yogurt and pastries at their room too. They'd eaten it together on the bed, dropping flakes of pastry on to the sheet.

Although the rain had stopped and the storm clouds had passed revealing blue sky and sunshine, everywhere was drenched – trees hung heavy with water from the pummelling they'd taken overnight. The Indian Ocean paradise was a washout in the daylight. Despite feeling hot, sticky and in need of another cool shower and a change of clothes, Connie felt like a weight had been lifted from her shoulders and replaced with a contentment that she hadn't felt in a very long time.

Before they reached the hotel reception, Theo took her hand and pulled her into the shadow of a drooping palm tree around the side of one of the beach rooms. He slid his hands around her waist and his lips found hers, kissing her deeply.

He pulled away and smiled. 'I won't get the chance to do that again for a while.'

Connie held his face in her hands. 'Last night was amazing.'

'It was.' He grinned. 'Come on, let's go before anyone wonders where we are.'

They walked side by side along the path, their hands occasionally brushing against each other's as they made their way to reception. Theo went in to thank the manager and Connie unlocked the jeep and opened all the windows.

'Good morning,' Gertrude and Hans said as they reached the jeep and Connie took their rucksack from them.

'That was one big storm,' Hans said.

'Made for an interesting unscheduled stop,' his wife replied.

Connie smiled with the thought of just how interesting their overnight stop had been – a passionate night in the most unromantic of rooms.

Theo came out of the hotel reception as Isaac and Claire appeared along the path from the beach rooms.

'Did you get any sleep?' Theo asked as they clambered on to the jeep.

'Not much,' Isaac said. 'You?'

'A little,' Theo replied, catching Connie's eye.

She hoped no one noticed her face flush as she pulled herself up on to the passenger seat and looked ahead, unable to hide her smile as Theo sat next to her in the driver's seat.

The drive back to Mchanga was uneventful yet slow going due to the amount of rain that had been emptied on to the road overnight. Rivers of rainwater ran down the sides of the road and the potholes were mini pools that Theo did his best to avoid. As the sun rose higher in the sky and the day got hotter, Connie could see the water steaming up off the ground as it began to evaporate.

The gate into Mchanga was a welcome sight. Theo bumped the jeep down the track and pulled up in the shade of the trees.

'Home at last.' His hand left the gear stick and brushed Connie's fingers.

'Hey, thanks you two for getting us back safely,' Isaac said, followed by an echo of thanks from the others.

'Not a problem and all down to Theo.' Connie shifted in her seat to look behind her. 'It wasn't quite the end to a relaxing day that I had hoped for, but an adventurous twenty-four hours at least. We never did have that Prosecco on the beach, did we? How does meeting on the beach by the shipwreck before dinner sound?'

'We'd love to,' Gertrude and Hans said in unison, followed by nods and agreement from Isaac and Claire.

'First a shower, then a relaxing day doing absolutely nothing,' Claire said and they all laughed.

'You're back.' Bella jogged down the steps from the welcome building and shook hands with the couples before they headed off along the path that led up to the hillside suites.

Bella threw her arms around Connie and hugged her. She took Theo's hand and kissed him on the cheek. 'We were worried about you.'

'It turned out just fine.' Theo slammed the jeep door shut and they followed Bella inside.

'Hey there,' Maria called from behind the desk. 'Good to have you back safely.'

'Was everything okay here?' Theo looked around.

'Apart from it being a thunder storm from hell, we got off pretty lightly,' Bella said. 'Some of the thatched umbrellas on the beach got damaged and no one left their room all evening because it was just torrential. There's not a lot going on today, apart from clearing up. Guests seem to be quite happy to relax in their rooms or sit by the pool. You two go freshen up and get changed before starting work. Our new guests don't arrive until this afternoon and you can unload the jeep later – no one's going anywhere today.'

Bella ushered them away and Connie followed Theo, puffing up the hill and along the path to the staff accommodation.

'I was expecting chaos here but it feels quite calm and relaxed,' she said, unhooking her bag from her hot shoulder and dropping it on to the wooden step in front of her cottage.

'I think it probably felt worse for us being in a jeep stranded miles from here.'

'Well, we'd better get changed and see what we can do to help.' She turned to go but paused with her foot on the step. 'Maybe have a drink later?'

'Why not have a drink now – there's no rush.'

'Tempting, but I'm desperate for a shower and clean, fresh smelling clothes.'

'Is that what the smell is?' he said, laughing.

Connie whacked him playfully on the arm.

'I do have a shower in my place.' He caught her hand in

his, sliding his fingers between hers. 'And it's plenty big enough for two.'

Connie may have been in her late thirties and almost divorced but it didn't stop her heading back down the hill feeling as if she had 'I just had sex in a shower', blazoned across her forehead. She felt like a teenager again, heady with lust from a secret liaison, but as her feet hit the rocky path she calmed down, realising the feeling was because she was used to having a husband – not that the passion had ever gone out of their relationship, it's just they'd become so familiar with each other. With her and Theo everything was new: getting to know each other, his personality, his touch, his taste…

Bella appeared, walking along the path from the restaurant.

'Feeling better after a shower?' she asked, hooking her arm in Connie's and walking with her.

'Yep,' Connie replied, unable to say more as an image of Theo's naked body pressed up against hers in his shower, cool water splashing down on them, enveloped her thoughts.

'So,' she said, changing the subject. 'I'll unload the jeep, then I'll be free for when the new guests arrive. I'm going to organise Prosecco on the beach before dinner with the honeymooning couples we took out yesterday, but I could see if any of the other guests would like to join us?'

'That sounds lovely – we should make an evening of it.'

Connie settled back into the day to day running of Mchanga with ease, although her thoughts were firmly on Theo. She welcomed a Norwegian couple celebrating their twentieth wedding anniversary, and while she was walking with them to their beach villa, she caught sight of Theo dashing across the restaurant deck. Her heart skipped. After leaving the couple to settle in, she spent the afternoon inviting other guests down to the beach for sundowners and arranging for the bar staff to organise drinks.

Despite the sun setting behind them over mainland Tanzania rather than the ocean, when Connie headed down to the beach later that day, the darkening sky was streaked pink and amber. The sand was soft and cool underfoot, and down by the wreck the only sounds were the waves folding on to the shore and an occasional squawk of a bird flying overhead. Connie was the first one there and had placed lanterns at intervals along the beach.

With the arrival of the first guests, waiters with trays of drinks appeared along the candlelit pathway. Soon the stretch of sand by the shipwreck was filled with people chatting and laughing, sipping the head barman's secret recipe sundowner cocktail.

Gertrude and Hans, and Isaac and Claire came over and tapped their drinks against Connie's.

'Well,' Claire said. 'This certainly makes up for missing out on our sundowner yesterday.'

'Pretty special, isn't it.' Connie glanced around. Just about every guest was down on the beach, along with most of the bar staff, a couple of the waitresses serving canapés and Bella and Theo who had just arrived. He made a beeline for them, grabbing a cocktail on the way over.

'Evening all,' he said, his smooth voice revealing his hint of an Australian accent. 'This was worth the wait.'

He knocked his glass against everyone's and when he reached Connie's, he said, 'To last night's adventure.'

'To last night's adventure!' the six of them repeated and sipped their drinks.

Connie met Theo's eyes and smiled.

'Well done,' he said, as the couples started chatting between themselves. 'This is a perfect end to the last couple of days.'

If it hadn't had been completely unprofessional, Connie would have kissed him. Instead, she fought back her longing for him and echoed his sentiment.

'A perfect end.'

She swirled her cocktail. Life felt simple. The emotional complications of the past few months had dropped away and she was living in the moment. She wanted to capture the feeling and bottle it, so as not to ever lose it again, to never feel as low and desperate as she had over recent months.

'We'd better mingle.' Theo leant closer to Connie and touched her hand. 'I'll catch up with you later.'

She watched him walk over and introduce himself to the Norwegian couple she'd welcomed that afternoon. She was looking around deciding who to talk to first when Bella slid her arm around her waist and gently manoeuvred her to a quiet spot close to the ocean.

'You and Theo,' Bella said. 'Something's changed – that spark I saw between the two of you when you first arrived is back again. What happened last night?'

Connie glanced around to make sure no one was in earshot, least of all Theo who was still talking to the Norwegians. 'We talked. That storm and getting stranded miles from here was a blessing in disguise. We cleared the air about a lot of stuff.'

'I think you did a lot more than talk.'

'Bella!' Connie attempted to sound shocked but was unable to hide her smile.

Bella held up her hands. 'You know me; I don't beat about the bush. Connie, love, you're nearly thirty-eight years old…'

'Yeah, thanks for reminding me.'

'You and Theo are consenting adults and I for one would be delighted if you two got together.'

'That's refreshing, most workplaces would have a head fit about their manager sleeping with one of his employees.'

'Well, Mchanga isn't a normal workplace and the best relationships I know are through people working together – unless you come out to Tanzania as part of a couple, how on earth do you think anyone ever finds love out here? Mostly people fall in love with someone at the place they work. Places like Mchanga, where management and lots of the staff spend the majority of their time living as well as working together, romantic relationships happen. It's the norm.'

Connie nodded. 'I'm just glad I didn't completely mess up having a relationship with Theo.'

'Not that you need it, but you and Theo have my blessing

to get up to whatever you want to.' Bella touched Connie's arm and glanced at her over the top of her glasses. 'Providing of course it's in your own private time. No hanky-panky in the managers' office now.'

'Bella, seriously.'

'I'm teasing you.' She held Connie at arm's length. 'I can't tell you how good it is to see you happy again.'

Connie looked out across the moonlit ocean. 'I am happy, and obviously I think that's a lot to do with Theo, not just, you know, the physical stuff, but I'm happy we've cleared the air and I didn't ruin our friendship because of Felix. But I also feel guilty for feeling happy.'

'Why? Why on earth would you feel that way? You, more than anyone I know, deserve to be happy.'

'Mum passed away less than a month ago – I should be mourning her, not getting excited about a relationship with a new man before my divorce has even been finalised.'

'Forget about that – you've been separated from Felix for long enough for it to be absolutely fine to be moving on with someone else – someone, I should add, who will treat you a lot better than your bastard ex.' Bella paused, as if gathering her thoughts and controlling her emotions before she spoke again. 'And as for your mum, yes you rarely saw her, but that doesn't mean that you didn't love her; I think it just means the impact of her passing away is less than if you'd had a relationship where you spoke to each other every day or saw each other a lot. Being out here you're so far removed from your old life that it's easy to put your troubles to the back of your mind. That doesn't mean you don't care or aren't mourning her. It's a coping mechanism. Grief can hit you in different ways or at different times. You might not be ready to grieve yet.'

Connie let Bella's words filter through. The night sky was dark and filled with stars and a crescent moon reflecting on the ocean. 'Is that how you coped when you came back here after having me?' she asked without looking at Bella.

'It's how I attempted to cope, yes.' Bella moved next to Connie and stared out across the ocean, their backs to the guests on the beach. 'I'd made a few friends in Stone Town, I had a place to stay, people to talk to and go out with, but they were all young like me, with grand ideas of travelling the world, escaping boring lives with unadventurous parents back in the UK or US or Italy or wherever else they were from. None of them were in any place in their lives to even comprehend what I was going through. The hormones after having a baby are a bitch – I was hormonal, I was leaking milk, bleeding like I'd never known before, feeling all these powerful maternal instincts and yet I had no baby to mother. Despite knowing deep down that I'd done the best possible thing for you, it nearly killed me. How I got through that first year I have no idea, but I did. Your mum sent me letters and photos of you and I was able to move forward. I grieved for you and there were times when I couldn't comprehend ever being happy again – but I was and I am.' She moved closer to Connie until their arms touched. 'Don't feel guilty for being happy, it doesn't mean you don't care about your mum or aren't grieving for her. Right now, it's time to focus on yourself.'

Connie took Bella's hand in hers. 'Thanks, Bella, for being here for me. Thanks for everything.'

Bella squeezed her hand. 'I always have been here for you, even if it's only been in spirit, thousands of miles away.' Bella glanced behind her. 'We should get back and be sociable...' She trailed off, her hand still clutching Connie's.

'What is it?'

'I spoke to my brother yesterday, and your brother, before the storm happened and you all got stranded down the coast.'

'You did?'

Bella nodded and her fingers tensed. 'It was long overdue. I can't remember the last time I spoke to my brother... to your father.' Connie glanced at Bella, the significance of her words sending a shiver through her. 'We talked and cleared the air and it was good, a huge relief, I think, for both of us. Without your mum he's on his own now, and I am family, even if it hasn't been that way for decades. I talked to Alexander too, to apologise for misleading him. I'm glad I

reached out, I really am.'
  'Oh Bella, I'm glad too.'

Chapter Twenty-Four

'Me, you and Bella on a road trip? Are you serious?' Connie stood in the office with her hands on her hips. Sweat trickled down the side of her face and back despite being beneath the ceiling fan.

'Well, it's kind of a working holiday,' Theo replied, tucking a folder away on the shelf behind him, 'to go and see the progress at Baobab Beach.'

'And Mchanga can spare the three of us for a few days?'

'It can.' Theo took Connie's hand. 'Bella's sorted it all out. It's my two weeks off anyway, and Bella's up for us having our time off together. Asante is covering me as usual, plus Maria's wanted to move on from her current role for a long time and take on more managerial responsibilities, so this is the perfect opportunity for her to help Asante and prove she's the right person for the job.'

'It also nicely coincides with my birthday.'

'Funny that,' Theo replied with a grin.

'When are we leaving?'

Theo glanced at his watch. 'In a couple of hours.'

It was mid-November and sweltering – one of those days where the air was still and there was little respite without the usual breeze floating in from off the ocean. The thought of travelling in this heat filled Connie with little joy – in fact doing anything was a struggle and she envied the guests being able to do little more than lounge beneath the shade of an umbrella on the beach or have a refreshing dip in the pool.

She was still acclimatising. Bella, Theo, Maria and all the other staff, particularly the locals, didn't seem bothered by the stifling heat, so Connie soldiered on, the thought of an air-conditioned room never far from her thoughts.

It had been almost a month since the storm and Connie and Theo had relaxed into a rhythm of working together alongside being together. The rumour that they were a couple had spread like wildfire amongst the staff and Connie was pretty sure that Bella had enjoyed spreading the gossip. She was okay with that – in fact it was a relief to not have to hide their relationship or feel worried that someone had seen them holding hands or kissing while they had a drink together after the guests had gone to bed. Connie had spent most nights in Theo's villa and she still felt a thrill at waking up at dawn to the sound of birdsong and the ocean, and the sight of Theo next to her.

The last four weeks had been the longest stretch of time that she'd spent at Mchanga, the first two months interrupted by her visits to Selous, Baobab Beach and then back to the UK. The days had flown by and she relished making the guests' experience unforgettable. As Connie struggled up the hill to her cottage she realised she was looking forward to going to Baobab Beach again and seeing what had been done to the place in the weeks since she'd been there.

She'd nearly reached the top of the hill when she caught sight of Maria on her way down. Connie waved and stopped, attempting to catch her breath while she waited for Maria to reach her.

'It's a killer this hill on a day with no breeze,' Maria said, laughing.

'You… don't… look like you've… broken a sweat,' Connie puffed.

Maria smiled and tapped the side of her nose. 'Don't tell anyone, but I had to have a lie down after walking up here earlier.'

'Okay… good to know it's not just me… who's unfit.'

'Are you excited about going away?'

Connie nodded. 'It's a surprise. And I'm pleased… you're

getting the chance to help run the place while Bella and Theo are away.'

'The opportunity is amazing.'

'You're going to be fabulous.'

'Well, I'd better let you go. I guess I'll see you in a few days.' She started walking, then faltered and turned back to Connie. 'Everything's all fine now between you and Theo? I mean, I know you're together...' she said, her face flushing. 'I don't mean to pry, it's just that situation with your ex-husband and what I heard...'

'My ex is very much in the past and yes, thank you, everything is fine and cleared up with Theo.'

'I thought so, I just wanted to hear it from you. Theo deserves to be happy, and so do you.' She put her hand on Connie's hot shoulder. 'Have fun at Baobab Beach.'

Travelling to Dar es Salaam to catch a plane over to Zanzibar made for a long, hot and bumpy journey, particularly when followed by a wait in Stone Town to hire a car – which turned out to be a massive jeep – before setting off to Baobab Beach on the other side of the island. Theo drove while Bella and Connie sat behind, rocking from side to side as they bumped along.

The closer they got to Baobab Beach, the more notice Connie took of their surroundings, until she recognised the stretch of forest and the curve in the road with the pull-in area and the gates to the beach. Theo pulled up outside and Connie jumped out of the jeep. The old sign with its peeling paint had been removed and a new sign had been put in its place to one side of the gate. On a beautiful sand and ocean background, 'The Baobab Beach Retreat' had been painted across it in a deep blue. Connie pushed open the gates, jumped back into the jeep and they set off down the track. Connie didn't realise she was holding her breath until the hotel came into view, its whitewashed walls freshly painted and gleaming in the sunlight behind the baobab tree that soared upwards from the grassy mound by the entrance to the hotel.

'Wow.' Theo pulled the jeep into the space for vehicles alongside a border filled with palms, plants and flowers.

Bella beamed. 'That was my reaction the first time I saw this place, and that's before you've seen the view on the other side.'

The engine stilled and they stepped from the jeep to the sound of silence. The peacefulness was not lost on Connie – even at Mchanga the sound of the waves crashing on the shore filled the air. Here, with the road far enough away and the ocean on the other side of the building almost as still as a pond, the only sound was their feet crunching across gravel to the dark and cool hotel entrance.

With Bella leading, they walked through the hotel reception and straight out to the open-air bar. Connie didn't take her eyes off Theo. A rush of warmth flooded through her as he stopped on the deck of the bar, pushed his sunglasses into his hair and gazed out, mouth open, to the palm trees, beach and achingly clear and turquoise ocean beyond.

Connie sidled up to him and hooked her arm in his. 'Pretty special, huh?'

He nodded. 'That's an understatement.'

'Come on, you two,' Bella called from the top of the steps that led down to a path through the trees to the beach. 'There's lots to see before it gets dark.'

Holding hands, they followed Bella down the steps from the restaurant and bar, along the sandy path that curved beneath the palm trees and on to the powder-soft beach. In the late afternoon sunlight, long shadows from the palm trees and thatched umbrellas fell across the perfect crescent of sand. The tide was in and the shallow aquamarine water gently lapped the shore.

At the far end of the beach, Connie could see the familiar dirty-white cottages that ruined the beauty of the place, but the central ones had already been taken down, and as they left the cluster of palm trees by the restaurant and walked a little further on to the beach, Connie stopped and gasped.

Where the first few cottages had been, six open-fronted beach villas now stood in their place, an almost exact replica of the design Connie had sketched on a piece of paper only weeks before.

'What do you think?' Bella walked up the beach backwards so she could see their expressions.

'Are you kidding me, Bella?'

'Your idea was perfect – simple, natural, luxurious and making the most of that view.'

Timber-clad with roofs made from woven palm leaves, the villas now blended into the tree-lined backdrop of the beach, instead of standing out like the old whitewashed cottages did. They were more spacious than they had been and there were less of them, allowing more privacy. A baobab tree had been hand painted on to the side of each of the finished villas. Bulbous trunks reached up to slender branches that crept out like roots across the natural wood finish.

Connie walked up on to the deck, much larger than it had previously been, with a comfortable seating area and a plunge pool to one side, the front of the villa completely open to take in the view and what ocean breeze there was. Bella sat down on the cushioned seating and smiled.

'Are all six finished?' Theo asked, brushing past Connie and heading inside.

'The first four are all done, bathrooms fitted, water and electricity connected,' Bella said, as Connie followed Theo into the villa. 'The other two need to be fitted out with furnishings.'

The dark wood of the veranda continued into the villa. Large wooden-slatted bifold doors opened right to the edges of the villa allowing the whole front to open. The same as at Mchanga, the bed was in the centre facing the ocean view with see-through drapes hanging from the canopy. The walls were plastered and painted a natural honey-colour, cushions and lamps the only decoration. The bathroom was in a separate room off to the side, and rather than being the airless and windowless room it had been, it now had a polished stone floor, a screened off toilet, a his and hers sink and a sunken bath next to a shuttered window, with views over the plunge pool to the Indian Ocean beyond.

'Make yourselves at home,' Bella said, leaning against the open door into the villa. 'This is yours for the next few days.'

'I don't know what to say, Bella – you've done an amazing job,' Theo said.

'Oh don't thank me – the look is down to Connie, the hard work to the craftsmen around here who are insanely talented, and Geoff with his connections in Stone Town to get things moving. I'm just the money. You two settle in – I'm going to check out my villa next door – how about we meet for dinner in the restaurant in an hour?'

'Sounds perfect.' Connie went over to Bella and kissed her on the cheek. She watched her pad back across the deck and down on to the sand until she disappeared from sight.

Connie turned back to Theo. 'This is the epitome of a honeymoon destination, don't you think?'

'Totally,' he replied, sinking back on to the bed and clasping his hands behind his head. 'Come and look at this.'

Connie slid on to the bed and lay down next to him, her head propped up on the pillows. All she could see was the azure ocean meeting the deep blue sky. 'Oh, I could get used to this life.' She turned on her side to face Theo and tucked her arm beneath her pillow. 'Do you miss working at a safari camp or are you happy being by the ocean?'

Theo continued to look towards the beach and smoothed his hand down the sides of his face to his beard. 'They're so different you can't really compare. Working in the wilds of Kenya or Tanzania is magical, being that close to nature and so far removed from populated places has its perks, but as with everything there are downsides too. I love the wildness of the ocean at Mchanga, but here…' He turned on his side to face her and brushed his fingers against her cheek. 'It'd be a good life working somewhere like here. It's always hard work running a place and looking after guests who've paid a fortune, but a place like this is happiness personified.'

Chapter Twenty-Five

Connie woke, kept her eyes closed and listened. Nothing, not even the sound of Theo breathing. Her eyes flew open to find the bed empty and Theo nowhere to be seen. The slatted doors to the villa were still wide open but the view from the evening before had completely changed. Connie rubbed her eyes, swung herself out of bed and padded across the wooden floor to the deck. The air was still and already hot, the hammocks hanging in the shade of palm trees inviting. The ocean had seemingly disappeared – the beach stretched endlessly, soft powdery sand becoming more compact and decorated with ridges caused by the tide.

'Happy birthday!' Bella called across from the deck of the adjacent villa.

Connie turned to see Bella sitting on the cushioned seat with her feet curled up beneath her.

'Thank you!' Connie called back. 'Do you know where Theo is?'

'He's popped out to pick up a birthday surprise.'

'Oh has he now!' she called back. She was about to ask Bella if she knew when he'd be back when her heart felt like it momentarily stilled with the realisation that she'd never actually spent her birthday with Bella.

Still in the vest and thin cotton shorts she'd worn to bed, she stepped down from the deck and on to the sand, the cool grains in the shade warming up as she walked into the sun towards Bella's villa.

'Can I join you?'

'Of course,' Bella said, smiling.

Connie sat on the low cushioned sofa next to Bella's. 'Do you realise this is the first birthday of mine we've spent together. I've been trying to think – even my twenty-first when we had that big party in Cheltenham you weren't at, were you?'

Bella shook her head. 'No, love, I wasn't.'

'I think you always had a reason for not coming over, but you made it to my wedding.' Connie reached across and took Bella's warm hand in hers. 'It was too difficult, wasn't it, to see me on my birthday and keep up the pretence of being my aunt.'

A tear rolled down Bella's make-up free cheek. 'Every other day of the year – even Christmas – I could get on with life, but each year on your birthday I relived the emotional pain of giving birth to you and then giving you up, of not ever hearing you call me mummy or for you to know just how much I love you. I was always invited – my brother and your mother were wonderful like that – but I just couldn't... It didn't seem right or fair to anyone me being there. So yes, I made excuses and stayed away.'

'And yet here we are together on my thirty-eighth birthday.' The lump in Connie's throat stopped her from saying anything else; the enormity of the moment needed no further explanation.

They sat quietly, their hands clasped together and looked out over the beach – the peace and stillness the perfect antidote to Connie's emotions.

'Well,' Bella said after a while, slipping her hand from Connie's and wiping away her tears. 'This is no good, crying on your birthday. Let's make the most of finally being together.' She stood up and held out her hand. Connie took it and they walked down on to the sand. 'Have you got beach shoes with you?'

Connie covered the short distance to her villa, slipped her feet into her dark blue beach shoes and set off with Bella to where the ocean had lapped the sand only the evening before. The darker, damp sand showed where the ocean had been but the tide was so far out Connie could only see pale sand stretching to a line of turquoise on the horizon. Their feet squelched into the wet sand and they left a trail of footprints as they walked. A good distance from the beach, pools of water had formed over the coral stones, with tiny fish darting in and out of fronds of seaweed.

'Look here.' Bella pointed next to her feet where a sea urchin, black and spiky with red and purple lines crisscrossing it, was only just submerged in water. 'What I love about this place, and it's the same at Mchanga, is there's so much more to it than simply lounging on the beach – although that's wonderful too.'

Even early in the morning, Connie felt the intense heat building, the sun beating down on her shoulders. Without walking far enough to reach the ocean, they turned around and began to head back, their feet sinking into squelchy pools of water, crabs scuttling out of their way as they went.

They showered, got dressed and made filter coffee behind the bar, taking their mugs of coffee back down on to the beach to sit on the deck of Connie and Theo's villa.

'What do you want to do for the rest of the day?' Bella asked once they were settled.

'What we're doing right now suits me just fine – I could stay looking at this view forever.'

'We can barbeque later, take a table down on to the beach and eat there.' Bella blew on her steaming coffee. 'You've not seen the pool since you were last here – it's been cleaned and refilled so we can have a swim if you like.'

'Bella, seriously, thank you so much for organising this, I can't think of a birthday where I've been anywhere more beautiful or perfect.'

'It's my pleasure,' Bella replied. 'As I've got older I've realised more and more how important it is to take time out for yourself – to recuperate and recharge the batteries.' Bella glanced at Connie. 'I see that look.' She held her hands up. 'I know, I know, in the past I've been a total workaholic and never took time out, but without having put the effort in then,

I would never have got to the point I'm at now, where I feel like I *can* relax and enjoy what I've worked hard for. The best thing I did was employ Theo and take a step back from running Mchanga.' She rested back. 'I think I like semi-retirement.'

'You of all people deserve to take it easy.' Connie tucked a stray strand of hair behind her ear. 'And you know what, I'm glad you employed Theo too.'

Bella placed her coffee on the table and clapped her hands. 'I can't tell you how wonderful it is to see you two together – to see you finally looking so happy and Theo looking happy. He really likes you, you know. *Really* likes you.'

'I really like him too.' Connie glanced away.

'What is it, love?' Bella reached forward and put her hand on Connie's bare knee.

'It's silly really. I'm still worrying about being this happy so soon after hitting rock bottom. I mean, a year ago I'd discovered Felix was having an affair and now I'm divorced from him and with Theo in Tanzania. My life couldn't be more different.'

'No it couldn't, but you do realise it's okay to be happy again. My God, it's long overdue after what you've been through. I felt guilt for a very long time after giving you up and leaving you in England. Every time I caught myself laughing it would be followed by a stab of guilt. I chose that path; you didn't choose for your husband to betray you, to lose two babies, to have your life turned upside down; so, Connie, trust me when I say it's absolutely fine for you to have moved on and to be enjoying life again.'

'You're right, I have no idea why I keep wanting to punish myself.'

'Of course I'm right.' Bella laughed. She blew on her coffee again. 'We should have made iced coffees.'

'What we need is bar staff here to make us a cocktail.'

'What at ten in the morning?'

'Too early?'

'You think?' Bella laughed again.

'Hello, hello, hello?' A man's voice called out, carrying

across the beach from the direction of the restaurant.

'Over here!' Bella called back, putting down her coffee and grinning.

Connie frowned, the voice being so familiar and yet completely out of place.

'Alexander?' Open mouthed, Connie watched as her brother appeared on the beach and walked towards her, looking unfamiliar in shorts and a T-shirt rather than his usual shirt and smart trousers. Behind him Rachel followed with Tobin on her hip and holding Francesca's hand.

Connie and Bella stepped down from the veranda and on to the sand. Alexander reached them, a huge grin plastered across his face and Connie threw her arms around him.

'What on earth are you all doing out here?'

Alexander pulled away from her. 'Bella asked us a few weeks ago, and there was no reason to refuse – Francesca will be going to school next year so we thought why not. It's been long overdue coming out here. Bella's asked before, I just never made the time to visit.'

'And work was okay with you taking time off?'

'I put in more hours for them than I care to think about – they were in no position to say no.'

'Hello, Connie,' Rachel said, kissing her cheek.

Connie kissed Tobin, leant down and managed to kiss the side of Francesca's forehead before she curled herself in to her mum's leg. Connie stood up to see Bella a few steps away standing next to her brother.

It took a moment for Connie to register the sight of her father, usually so smart and austere in a suit and tie, but instead looking relaxed for once in a white linen short sleeved shirt and knee-length dark-blue shorts, his usually pale face flushed from the heat.

'Dad... what on earth?'

'Bella invited us and it made sense to finally come and visit the place and country she's called home for so many years.'

'I'm speechless.' Connie paced the short distance across the sand and took her father's hand in hers and kissed him on the cheek.

Her father grunted. 'Damned hot though.'

Connie laughed. The grumpy father she was used to briefly appearing, despite his radically different exterior.

'Let's get out of the sun.' Bella ushered everyone back towards the shade of the bar with its large thatched roof and open sides screened by trees.

Connie was the last one to take the steps up to the bar and she stopped when she reached Theo smiling from the deck.

'You knew about this?' Connie asked, waving her hand towards her family who were heading across the bar.

'I might have done.' He caught her around her waist and pulled her to him.

'Ah, so this was my birthday surprise you were 'picking' up.'

'They arrived yesterday, stayed at The House of Stone last night and I thought it would be better to pick them up this morning instead of them getting taxis over.'

Connie squeezed Theo. 'Thank you so much.'

With their arms curled around each other's waists, Connie gazed across the bar to her family. They gathered by the comfortable seating area that overlooked the pool and the distant ocean beyond. While Bella was busy behind the bar pouring drinks, Rachel had sat down on one of the sofas to breastfeed a squirmy Tobin, and Francesca sat cross-legged next to her playing with her well-worn toy rabbit. Alexander and their father stood with their arms folded looking out at the view, quietly chatting together. A shiver went through her at the realisation that her mum was absent and always would be. Perhaps she was here in spirit, smiling down at the family tableau that Connie never thought she'd see. This was her family – her messed up family: an aunt who was actually her mum, a father who was her uncle and a brother who was her cousin. At the end of the day none of that mattered. However complicated her family was, they were still her family and she loved them.

She rested her head against the crook of Theo's neck.

He kissed the top of her head. 'Happy?'

Connie nodded, unable to say anything for fear of releasing a floodgate of tears.

'Come on.' Theo took her hand and led her across the bar as Bella carried a tray of drinks over to the seating area.

They sat down and Bella passed around tall glasses of cloudy lemonade.

'Cheers,' Bella said, raising her glass.

'Cheers,' everyone said. Even Francesca joined in with the clink of glasses with her cup of pineapple juice.

'And happy birthday, Connie,' Alexander said.

'Thank you,' Connie replied as 'happy birthday' echoed around the group and she caught the slightest of looks pass between her dad and Bella.

'I can't tell you how good it is seeing you all out here.' Connie sipped her lemonade and relished the refreshing fizz as it slid down her throat. 'And how much of a surprise it is! Well done, Bella, for keeping the secret.'

'It was worth it to see your face when they walked on to the beach.'

Connie smiled and sat back in her seat holding Theo's hand, sipping lemonade and listening to Rachel and Alexander chat about the journey and their stay in Stone Town.

'Let me show you the plans,' Bella said to her brother once everyone had finished their drinks. They crossed to the other side of the bar with Theo and Alexander. Francesca sat on the floor with an old Jenga game Bella had found in one of the cupboards, stacking the wooden blocks on top of each other, trying to get them as high as she could before they came crashing down.

Rachel stood up and went over to the edge of the bar, holding Tobin's hand as he toddled next to her. She shaded her eyes from the sun with her other hand. 'This place is incredible,' she said, turning back to Connie. 'To say I'm jealous of you getting to live and work out here would be an understatement.'

'To be honest,' Connie said, standing up and joining Rachel. 'I can't quite believe it either, particularly when I think back to what my life was like just a year ago. It doesn't even compare.'

Rachel placed her free hand on Connie's shoulder. 'I'm so glad you've come out the other side.'

'Me too.' Connie patted Rachel's hand.

'I'm going to go and unpack and get the kids settled in the villa so I'll see you later.'

Connie watched Rachel take the path down to the beach with Tobin stumbling next to her and Francesca racing ahead. A familiar pain struck the centre of her chest. The thought that she might never have the joy of holding her own son or daughter to her flitted through her mind. The loss was still with her but she acknowledged the pain was duller and the fact that she could be in their company without wanting to burst into tears was progress.

'How are you, Connie?' Alexander joined her by the edge of the bar.

'I'm okay,' she said slowly. 'Actually, I'm really good. I finally feel like I'm moving on from all that's happened.' She turned to him. 'How are you? How's Dad doing?'

'Dad's surprisingly okay.' He leant on the wooden rail that overlooked the swimming pool. 'I mean, considering losing Mum and everything. He soldiers on, always has done, although I don't think he's really grieved yet.'

Connie glanced behind them to see where their father was, but only Theo and Bella were still standing at one of the tables where the plans for Baobab Beach were spread out. 'He might need more time to fully register what's happened. He's going to be okay out here though? I mean he's completely out of his comfort zone.'

'It's only for a week, and honestly, Connie, it's exactly what he needs – a reconciliation between Dad and Bella is long overdue. It's just a shame it couldn't have happened while Mum was alive.'

'I know. But it's only because of Mum that this is even happening. I mean, if she hadn't told me what she did that night, I probably would never have found out the truth – neither of us would have. Did you honestly not have a clue

216

that I wasn't your sister?'

Alexander shook his head. 'None. But why would I? And anyway, we are related, it's not that there aren't similarities between you and me and you and Dad for either of us to have ever questioned it.'

'Growing up I always had this niggling feeling that I didn't quite fit in, that I was different to you and Mum and Dad, so I wondered if you'd ever felt the same?'

'Hey, Connie.' Alexander took her arm and held on to it. 'You'll always be my sister, you know that, right? It doesn't matter if Bella's actually your birth mother. You're my crazy, unpredictable, passionate, creative younger sister. Always have been and always will be.'

Connie laughed and put her arms around him. 'You know what, despite all the sadness of the last year, the positives that have come out of everything that's happened are what I'm going to focus on. We're closer than we've ever been and Bella and Dad are talking again. My God, Dad's in Tanzania, I never thought that would ever happen.' Connie pulled away from her brother and glanced along the beach to where their dad stood in the shade of a palm tree in front of his villa, a large straw hat on his head, looking so far removed in shorts and a T-shirt from his usual smart trousers and a shirt combo that Connie barely recognised him. She turned back to Alexander. 'You're the best brother a sister could ask for.'

'Now you're just getting soppy.'

Once Alexander and his family and Connie's dad were settled in the remaining two finished villas, the day passed by in a happy flurry of activity. Connie, Theo, Alexander and Rachel took the children to explore the sandy pools looking for crabs and starfish before the tide began to head back in, while Bella showed her brother the old beach cottages and the plans for the remaining as yet to be built beach villas. When the sun got too hot in the middle of the day, they retreated to their villas to relax before having drinks and nibbles in the bar. It was late afternoon, and the palm trees were casting long shadows across the sand, when Theo dragged a half-drum barbeque down on to the beach and set it up in the shade of a cluster of palms close to the restaurant.

Soon it was lit, smoke spiralling into the air, Theo stoking the coals, waiting for them to catch hold and turn white with heat. Connie didn't think she could remember a time in her life when she'd felt more content. She was happy and in Tanzania with her family, something that she never thought possible only a few months ago.

Kneeling down in the sand, with the sound of the ocean behind her as she rolled a ball to Francesca, she smiled.

'Hello, everyone!' A deep voice boomed from up on the deck of the restaurant.

Connie turned to see Geoff and Jamil, each carrying a cool box, walking down the path from the restaurant and on to the beach. Connie's heart stilled momentarily at the sight of Jamil and her memory of what had happened the last time they were here.

'Just in time!' Bella greeted them.

'We have meat, fish and drinks.' Geoff kissed Bella on the cheek and headed straight for Connie, placing the cool box he was carrying down in the sand next to Theo and the barbeque filled with smoking coal.

He pulled Connie into a bear hug. 'Happy birthday. Who'd have thought it, thirty-eight. You're looking good, kid.'

Geoff went round the group introducing himself and Jamil to Connie's family, shaking their hands.

'Good to see you again, Theo,' he said, clamping his hand on Theo's shoulder. 'You've never met my son Jamil, have you?'

Connie watched as Theo and Jamil shook hands, the two men who'd been such a major and confusing part of her life since she'd arrived in Tanzania. A shiver crept down her spine with the realisation Theo knew nothing about her and Jamil's ill-fated liaison.

Bella hooked her arm in Connie's. 'It didn't seem right to not invite them, considering this place is the fruits of their labour too – and money. I hope you don't mind?'

'No, I don't mind.' Connie squeezed Bella's arm. 'Now it's

a proper party.'

Bella leant closer and lowered her voice. 'It won't be too awkward between you and Jamil?'

'Of course not,' Connie said, her cheeks flushing. 'Anyway, enough about me, are you two...?' Connie nodded towards Geoff.

'God no.' Bella shook her head. 'We'll never be a couple again, of that I'm certain, but friends... well, we always have been in our own way. Even though he often drives me mad, I do still think of him as family, and these few days are all about my family. I think I'm going soft in my old age.' She unhooked her arm from Connie's and paced towards the barbeque. 'Right, let's get some meat cooking. Did you pick up the salads?'

'We sure did,' Geoff replied, opening the cool boxes.

As the sun dipped lower in the sky, the mouth-watering smell of steaks sizzling over the coals rose into the air. Sunloungers had been dragged on to the beach along with chairs and a couple of tables. Rachel played on the sand with Francesca and Tobin, Alexander and their father chatted with Geoff and Jamil, each with a bottle of beer in their hands, and Connie helped Bella put the salads out on the tables.

'I get why you're with him,' Jamil said, sidling up to Connie as she came back down on the sand from the bar with a bottle of chilled white wine. Jamil pointed towards Theo turning meat on the barbeque. 'That rugged handsomeness, hint of an Australian accent – seems a pretty decent guy too.'

'You mean not a pretty boy like you.'

Jamil fluttered his long dark eyelashes at her. 'I'll take that as a compliment rather than an affront.'

Connie reached out and squeezed Jamil's muscly arm, a sudden image of the two of them semi-naked and kissing on the daybed briefly flashing through her mind. 'Decent is exactly what I need – not that you aren't decent, Jamil, it's just you're not Theo.'

He patted Connie's hand. 'Hey, I get it, I really do. I'm just pleased you're happy and finally getting some action.'

'Jamil!' Connie burst out laughing and whacked his arm.

She shook her head and they stifled their giggles as the others glanced towards them. Theo caught her eye and smiled. Connie returned his smile before leaning in to Jamil and saying, 'Do you realise, the fact that Bella is actually my birth mum and was married to your dad – that makes us ex-step brother and sister?'

'Eeuow.' Jamil playfully pushed her away. 'I so need to rid my head of thoughts of twenty-one-year-old you in that bikini.'

'Yes, please do. Even if you were trying to get into my knickers a lot of the time, thanks for being a good friend too. I appreciate it. I needed a friend and someone to talk to who made me feel better about myself, and you did that perfectly.'

Jamil lifted his beer and took a sip. 'My pleasure, Connie Stone.'

He drifted back over to where Geoff, Alexander and her dad were still talking and Connie smiled to herself as she joined Theo behind the barbeque. His tanned face was flushed and his cream T-shirt stuck to his chest with sweat from the heat of the coals.

'It smells so good.' She realised just how hungry she was at the sight of the grilled steaks and giant prawns.

'Jamil likes you,' Theo said, draping his arm across her shoulders. 'Anything I should be worried about?'

'Nope, not a thing. He's had a crush on me since I was here sixteen years ago. He was twelve at the time.'

'Say no more, I get it.'

'He's already tried his best to seduce me – we kissed, but that's it.'

'So you two haven't... you know?' He raised his eyebrows.

'No, nothing more than a drunken kiss and a fumble.'

'It's just I know his reputation.'

'We're friends, nothing more.' Connie took Theo's hands in hers. 'I'm with you.'

'I know, I'm teasing you.' He kissed the top of her head and flipped over one of the steaks. 'If everyone wants to sit down,' he called. 'Food's ready.'

~

The sun had almost disappeared by the time they'd finished devouring grilled steaks and prawns and only the empty bowls of *kachumbari* and cucumber salad were left on the table. With the lamps hanging from the roof of the thatched restaurant, there was enough light spilling across the sand and on to the tables for them to see, along with lemongrass candles to keep mosquitos away. Rachel had gone back to hers and Alexander's villa to feed Tobin in peace and attempt to get Francesca to sleep, while everyone else remained around the tables on the beach, chatting and drinking.

'I have to say this has been one of the loveliest birthdays.' Connie raised her glass. 'Thank you, everyone.'

'I imagine plenty more people will celebrate birthdays here once you get this place open,' Alexander said.

'That and anniversaries and honeymoons.' Bella gestured towards the ocean, which was visible in the glow of the moonlight. The surf bubbled on to the beach, the sea urchins and clams were once more submerged on the ocean floor until the morning when the retreating water would again reveal its secrets. 'I hope The Baobab Beach Retreat will become synonymous with celebrating.'

'How have you found your first time in Tanzania, Edward?' Geoff directed his gaze across the table to his ex-brother-in-law.

Connie held her breath, waiting for her father's answer, sensing that everyone else around the table, particularly Alexander and Bella, were intrigued by what his reply would be.

Connie's father cleared his throat. 'Hot, tiring, unfamiliar, but apart from all that, I like it.' He looked at Bella. 'You've put care and attention to detail into this place and at your hotel in Stone Town and that's impressive.'

Connie fought back tears at her father's words, at his open praise for what Bella had achieved. As if sensing her emotion, Theo took hold of her hand beneath the table, his thumb smoothing up and down hers.

'Thank you,' Bella said, her voice wobbly. 'That means so

much. You're right about it being damn hot though!' She wafted her hands in front of her face as everyone laughed.

'So,' Alexander said, looking between Bella and Geoff. 'Once this place is up and running, are the two of you going to manage it together?'

'Goodness no.' Bella leant back in her chair and folded her arms. 'Apart from the fact that we'd kill each other working in the same place for any length of time, it's far too much work. Anyway, Geoff has his hands full in Selous and my heart will always be at Mchanga, that's my home.' She shook her head. 'No, it needs to be youngsters running this place, with vision and ideas to develop and grow Baobab Beach like I've done with Mchanga.'

'Do you have anyone in mind?' Alexander asked.

Geoff snorted with laughter, waving his hand in front of him and wiping beer from off his chin. 'Sorry,' he said. 'You go ahead and tell them, Bella.'

'As a matter of fact I do have the perfect couple in mind.' She unfolded her arms, leant forward and looked across the table in the dusky light. 'Connie, Theo, how do you two feel about taking on The Baobab Beach Retreat?'

Chapter Twenty-Six

'Are you ready?'

'As ready as I'll ever be.' Connie turned to face Theo. He was watching her intently, his back to the ocean. 'How long have we got until the first guests arrive?'

'An hour.'

Connie breathed out slowly, put her hands on her hips and tipped her head upwards towards the sun, closing her eyes as she did.

The Baobab Beach Retreat was more than ready to welcome guests, Connie was sure of that, she just wasn't sure that she was. She opened her eyes and looked along the beach where all twelve villas were finished, the space between them landscaped with trees and flowers. The beach was as pristine as when she'd first set eyes on it, but was now completed with new hammocks slung between shady palm trees. Connie looked towards the restaurant and bar with its repaired roof finished with the same palm leaves as the villas, the path leading between the restaurant and beach cleared of stones and debris. The main building that housed reception, the managers' office, the kitchen, a guest library, computer room and upstairs staff accommodation had been rejuvenated from sorry-looking whitewashed walls to wood-clad, the same as the villas, so the building blended in with its surroundings.

Theo slipped his arm around Connie's shoulders. 'Do you remember sitting over there on your birthday.' He pointed to the patch of sand by a cluster of palm trees. 'And Bella asking us if we'd take on this place together.'

'How could I forget?' Connie wrapped her arms around Theo's waist and they began walking back across the beach. 'I knew instantly that I wanted to stay here and that I wasn't going to go back to the UK. That moment changed my life.'

'Mine too.'

They took the sandy path that wound through the trees and up to the restaurant. There were lots of people about keeping themselves busy, but all staff and no guests. The bar staff were wiping down an already spotless surface and waved when they saw Connie and Theo; the chefs and kitchen staff were making final preparations for dinner that night and then meals for the next two days when the majority of the guests would arrive. The villas were all ready and Connie and Theo had given the maids from the local village the day off to start afresh in the morning.

'I can't believe it's been only seven months since that night.' Connie adjusted the position of a candle on one of the tables and stood back, surveying the restaurant.

'Not when you think how much hard work has gone into turning this place from a tired beach resort to a luxury retreat.'

Connie paced over to the sideboard at the back of the restaurant by the wall of the main building and fiddled with the flowers in a vase.

Theo took her arm and steered her away, back across the restaurant towards the open double doors to the main building. 'We – and by that I mean you – need to relax. We have an hour to go and nothing left to do. Nothing. We're ready.'

He walked her through the light and airy reception, now painted a warm and welcoming saffron yellow instead of a tired grey. Neema, the guest liaison and host was behind the front desk.

'Can you let us know when the car pulls up, please?' Theo asked.

'Of course,' she replied.

'By the way, go get yourself a drink – they need something to do in the bar besides cleaning the same surface over and over again. Make the most of the peace and quiet. I promise you, by tomorrow we'll be run off our feet.'

With Theo holding her hand and leading the way, Connie followed him out of the side door and along the path that ran along the back of the pool, and up through a tree-clad hillside that overlooked the pool and the adjoining undeveloped bay. Blending into the hillside among trees and undergrowth stood a villa, wood-clad like everything else at Baobab Beach. Although it was not much bigger than the guest beach villas, it housed an open-plan kitchen, dining and living area with a separate bathroom to the rear and two bedrooms off to the side, and it was the place that Connie and Theo now called home.

'I don't like not having anything to do,' Connie said as they walked across the small veranda and through the slatted doors into their living area. 'It makes me nervous and I think too much.'

'About what?' Theo poured them each a glass of cold water from the fridge and sat down on the sofa. 'We're prepared, there's nothing left to do. We're ready.'

'No, it's not about this place.' Connie went into the bathroom and leant on the sink and stared into the mirror. 'I don't know, it's silly really.'

Her face was properly tanned, a few freckles speckled her cheeks, and her dark hair framed her face in waves, her fringe grown out. She glanced behind her in the mirror to where Theo was leaning against the bathroom door.

'What's silly?'

Connie turned and looked at him. 'I don't know, the past couple of days, since I've had a bit more time on my hands, I keep thinking how much my life has changed… This time two years ago I was pregnant for the first time.'

Theo didn't say anything, his blue eyes not straying from her face.

Connie stepped across the tiled floor. 'It's because I'm happy that I'm thinking about it.' She took Theo's hands in hers. 'I know that doesn't make much sense but when I'm happy I get nervous about feeling happy.'

'You've never really talked to me about being pregnant.'

'That's because it's in the past.'

'But it was a major part of your life, even if short lived.'

'It reminds me of life with Felix and quite frankly I don't want to have to ever think about him again.'

'I'm okay with you talking to me about anything, even if it has to do with Felix, you know that, right?'

'Of course I do.' Connie squeezed his hands. 'Being pregnant was the most amazing thing ever – I can't help but remember the dates, it's like they're tattooed on to my brain. Two years ago today was the first scan, when I heard my baby's heartbeat for the first and last time. Even here, so far removed from my old life and somewhere I'm so crazy happy to be, I can't help but remember.'

'Oh Connie,' Theo said, hugging her to him. 'I'm so sorry you had to go through all that.'

Connie squeezed him tight and then pulled away. 'I needed to get that out of my system, let you know what's been going on in my head.' She took his hand and led him out of the bathroom. 'Come on, let's head back and have a drink with everyone before the hard work begins.'

'We just couldn't resist being your first guests,' Hilary said, kissing Connie on both cheeks and holding her at arm's length. 'My you look healthy. The Tanzanian air and sunshine is quite the tonic.'

'Well, I'm delighted you've managed to come back to Tanzania earlier than usual.'

'It's actually wonderful – just three months' difference and it's so much fresher yet beautifully sunny, plus we get to spend September back home with the grandkids and I do think that can be the best month weather wise in the UK.'

'So, a few days here and then another few at Mchanga,' Theo said, shaking David's hand.

Neema handed Hilary and David a cool towel and Connie noticed Raymond, who'd picked them up from the airport, silently cross reception with Hilary and David's bags, heading down the staff corridor that led directly to the beach.

'We couldn't not visit Bella and Mchanga, we love it there

226

but this place is something special.' David patted the sides of his face with the towel and placed it back on the tray Neema was holding.

Connie breathed a quiet sigh of relief that all their preparation was falling into place.

'No safari this time?'

Hilary shook her head. 'Not this time, no. We fancied two weeks of complete and utter relaxation, didn't we, love?'

'We did indeed,' David replied, adjusting his straw hat.

'Well,' Connie said with a smile, easing into her role of host and leading the way from reception and down the wide corridor that led out on to the restaurant deck. 'Let's show you around. You are literally the first to arrive, but we have three more couples joining us this afternoon and then another three tomorrow. By the end of the week, we'll be full.'

She stepped on to the restaurant deck and heard the footsteps behind, stop. She turned round to see Theo grinning from where he stood behind Hilary and David, both of whom had their hands shading their eyes as they looked across the restaurant towards the palm trees and beach and ocean beyond.

'I didn't think anything could possibly beat Mchanga's view, but wow, just wow.' Hilary pushed her sunglasses into her short silvery-blonde hair.

'I definitely haven't taken this view for granted,' Connie said, 'and I don't think I ever will, but I forgot what an impact and how magical the first sight is.'

'Let's show you to your villa.' Theo led the way down the restaurant steps and along the path to the beach.

Room six, otherwise known as 'Sita' had arguably one of the best positions in the middle of Baobab Beach. The four of them walked across the sand and up on to the deck in silence. A tray had been placed on the coffee table by the outdoor seating containing two cocktails and bowls of nibbles.

'For once in my life,' Hilary said, picking up her cocktail and holding it up so its yellow and red colours glinted in the sunlight, 'I'm speechless.'

'And that,' said David, knocking his cocktail glass against

his wife's, 'is quite an achievement.'

Connie laughed. 'We'll leave you to settle in. Feel free to do whatever you wish – if you'd like some lunch come up to the restaurant whenever you're ready, have a drink, swim in the pool. Dinner is served from six.'

The day was as perfect as the weather – cloudless deep blue sky, warm sunshine, a light breeze. Connie had lived and worked through the hot and humid months, followed by the season with the long rains when Mchanga and safari places like Mtazamo closed for two months. Work had carried on at Baobab Beach in both torrential rain and sticky heat. Now, she relished the warm dry days and cooler nights.

Three more couples arrived in the afternoon, their stunned reactions on first sight of the beach and ocean view from the restaurant similar to Hilary and David's. Connie realised the satisfaction she felt at seeing the guests' faces light up was the same as she'd felt in her old career when she'd witness the reaction to an engagement ring she'd lovingly created. Even though the retreat was far from full, there was underlying excitement amongst the staff at finally seeing the pool being used, cocktails poured, and the villas occupied.

Just before dinner, Connie organised sundowners on the beach and encouraged staff who were free to mingle with the guests. While chatting to a young honeymooning couple from Amsterdam, Connie caught sight of Theo talking with Hilary and David. It took her back to her first few weeks at Mchanga, only less than a year before where she'd catch sight of Theo and he'd give her a wink and she'd look forward to having a late-night drink with him. Fast forward nearly ten months and she was still looking forward to late-night drinks with him, except they could head to bed together without having to hide their relationship from anyone.

'What is there to do besides relax on the beach?' the Dutch woman asked.

'Where do I start!' Connie replied. 'Have a swim in the pool, take a walk to the local village or go on a day trip to Jozani Forest to see the red colobus monkeys. And the best thing, when the tide's out,' Connie cast her eyes towards the ocean shimmering in the softening light, 'you can walk right out and find crabs, clams and starfish in the pools left by the ocean. It's pretty amazing.'

Dinner was a quiet affair. Four couples at candlelit tables were served three courses, while the chefs and kitchen staff worked non-stop in the heat of the kitchen to ensure the first dinner at The Baobab Beach Retreat was a hit.

'Tell the chef that was delicious.' Hilary touched Connie's arm as she stopped at their table to see how they had enjoyed it. 'On a par with Mchanga – you're going to give Bella some real competition with this place.'

'That is the idea.' Connie smiled. 'Are you going to stay for a drink?'

Hilary glanced at David. 'I think we're going to head back to our villa for an early night – you've made them far too comfortable and luxurious for me to want to stay away from it for long. A decaf coffee on our deck would be lovely though.'

It was late evening by the time the last couple headed back, hand in hand across the moonlit beach to their villa. The staff finished clearing away with most taking the route back to the village along the beach and around the rocky outcrop at the end. A couple of international staff lived on site and so headed into the main building and upstairs to the staff accommodation.

'Alone at last.' Theo took hold of Connie's hand where she stood in the middle of the empty restaurant.

'What an evening. What a first day,' she said, grinning.

'And we start all over again in the morning. Do you want to have a drink before we head back?'

Connie shook her head. 'Let's just get to bed.'

The walk to their villa was shorter and not as steep as the hike to the staff cottages at Mchanga. Bella had said it had always been a part of the plans for the retreat to have a villa for whoever managed the place, but Connie suspected Bella had spent more money and had created such a wonderful place simply because it was her and Theo who would be living there.

They reached their veranda and Connie kicked off her flip-flops and padded barefoot across the wooden deck, throwing open the doors to the living space. The tension she'd felt earlier that day, thinking back to her past had lifted from her shoulders. She went into the bathroom, brushed her teeth, splashed water on her face and went into their bedroom.

Theo sat cross-legged on the bed, facing the open door that led on to the veranda. Dressed in a knee length skirt and cotton short sleeved blouse, Connie felt comfortably cool as she slid on to the bed next to him and rested her shoulder against his. From their bed, all she could see was ocean, and there wasn't a better feeling in the world than waking up in the morning to Theo next to her and the sound of waves lapping the shore.

'You know, I can just imagine a toddler running riot around here, barefoot in the sand, charming the guests…' Theo said, his shoulder tensing. 'I've been thinking all day about what you said this morning, how two years ago you were pregnant… I don't know if a baby's something you'd want while living out here, but if it happened and it was what *you* wanted, then I couldn't think of anything better than starting a family with you.'

Connie breathed in deeply, unable to meet his gaze, feeling tears prick her eyes as she stared out at the ocean glimmering in the moonlight. 'Theo, of course it's something I want – I can't tell you how much I want that with you, it's just I don't think it's something that will ever happen, however much I want it to.'

'It wasn't you with the fertility problem, Connie.'

'No, it wasn't, but I couldn't hold on to either of my pregnancies, keep my babies safe…'

Theo wrapped his arms around her, pulling her close to his chest. 'That doesn't mean you can't go on and have a healthy pregnancy.'

Connie buried her head into his chest, her tears soaking into his T-shirt. 'I know. I think it just scares me to start trying, to not know what the future holds.' She took his hands in hers and held them in her lap. 'Life with you is so good. I mean, our life here is incredible and I don't want to risk losing that. And what if I do get pregnant – I honestly don't think I could cope losing another baby.'

Theo kissed her, his hands caressing her back. 'I don't want you to go through that again either, but I don't want you to regret not trying or to look back and think, "what if".'

'Do you know, part of me wonders if I'd have been truly happy if my second pregnancy had continued. Would I have still left Felix? Would I have coped as a single mother? A baby would have tied me to him. I mourn for the two babies I lost, but I got free of a toxic relationship and a man who put his desires over his family.' Connie lifted her head up, tears streaking her face as she looked into Theo's eyes. Their faces were lit only by the light from the two lamps on the narrow shelf behind the bed. 'If none of that had happened, I wouldn't have met you.'

She paused for a moment, closing her eyes and resting back against Theo. Maybe he sensed that she had more to say because he remained quiet. Connie focused on the sound of their breathing with the more distant roll of the waves on to the beach as she thought things through. 'Whether I get pregnant or not, whether we have a baby together or not, being with you is enough for me. That longing for a baby that for years tore me apart, it's still there, but it's not all consuming like it used to be, like it was when I was with Felix – and maybe that was because having a baby was more important to me than my relationship with him. Who knows what it was. But if it happens for us, well life couldn't get any sweeter.' She smiled and pushed him down on to the bed until they were lying side by side and face to face, their legs entwined together. Connie ran her hand down the side of his face and kissed him. 'You know what, right now, here with you, I've never been so happy or hopeful about the future.'

ACKNOWLEDGEMENTS

As always, lots of fabulous people have helped me turn *The Baobab Beach Retreat* from a sketchy idea into a full blown novel. Firstly, it helps immensely that my cheeky, energetic and early-rising (I'm talking before dawn early) three-year-old son Leo is in pre-school twice a week and is looked after by my wonderful parents on Tuesday afternoons, so I actually have some quality time to write and do all the millions of other things that are involved in being an indie author.

My six beta readers, Judith van Dijkhuizen, AnnMarie Wyncoll, Elaine Jeremiah, Katharine Smith, Donna Witchard and Julie Brinker were the perfect mix of writers and readers and were encouraging, thoughtful and honest with their comments on an early draft, helping me immensely to polish, re-think and refine the story. Thank you all so very much. A special thanks must go to Judith whose insightful comments were invaluable – my manuscript came back with pencil marks all over it, but without a doubt *Baobab Beach* is a far better novel because of the suggested cuts and amendments – amongst which included lots of 'snaking'…

My editor, Helen Baggott, did another fine job editing and proofreading the book at two different stages, flagging up repeated words and phrases, finding full stops where there should have been commas, a potential plot issue, and helping to shape it into a polished novel ready for publication.

Getting Jessica Bell to revamp the cover of *The Baobab Beach Retreat*, is a decision I don't regret. The original cover didn't entice readers the same way as the new one does, revealing the warmth and beauty of the Tanzania and Zanzibar location mixed with the romance and emotion within its pages. Jessica Bell worked her magic once again with a cover I love and one that's more fitting for a romance story.

The Baobab Beach Retreat was a huge amount of fun to write and I hope that comes across when reading it. Like many of my novels, the initial idea for the book was inspired by a place – in this instance the two weeks I'd spent in Tanzania and Zanzibar while on honeymoon back in 2009. Mchanga,

Mtazamo, The House of Stone and The Baobab Beach Retreat are all fictional, yet they were inspired by real places. It was the glorious Siwandu (then the Selous Safari Camp) and Ras Kutani we stayed at for our safari and beach retreat back in 2009, and Lyndsey Fair, Anita Powell and Festus Njgoro from the Selous Safari Company were equally wonderful and helpful in answering the questions I had about running a luxury beach retreat in Tanzania.

Last but not least, without the support of my ever encouraging husband Nik, writing, creating and publishing books would not be possible – so thank you. This book really is dedicated just to you.

ABOUT THE AUTHOR

Kate Frost is the author of contemporary women's fiction and children's fiction. Her women's fiction, which includes *The Butterfly Storm*, *Beneath the Apple Blossom* and *The Baobab Beach Retreat*, often tackles serious subjects such as infertility, broken families and infidelity, often with a romantic element running through them. The long-awaited sequel to *The Butterfly Storm*, Kate's most popular book, is called *The Birdsong Promise* and was released in autumn 2018.

Kate Frost's children's books couldn't be more different – *Time Shifters* is a time travel adventure series for 9 – 12 year-olds. *Time Shifters: Into the Past* was published in autumn 2016 and the second book in the trilogy, *Time Shifters: A Long Way From Home* followed in 2018. The final book, *Time Shifters: Out of Time* completes the adventure.

Bristol, in the south west of England is home, which Kate shares with her husband, young son and their Cavalier King Charles Spaniel. Bristol is a vibrant and creative city offering plenty of opportunities for writers. Kate's been involved in the Bristol Festival of Literature, and she's the Director of Children's and Teen Events at the Hawkesbury Upton Literature Festival, which takes places in a village to the north of the city.

If you'd like to keep up to date with Kate Frost's book news please join her Readers' Club. To sign up simply go to www.kate-frost.co.uk/minetokeep and enter your email address. Subscribers not only receive a free ebook on sign up, but occasional news about Kate's writing, new books and special offers.

If you liked *The Baobab Beach Retreat* please consider leaving a review on Amazon and/or Goodreads, or recommending it to friends. It will be much appreciated! Reader reviews are essential for authors to gain visibility and entice new readers.

You can find out more about Kate Frost and her writing at www.kate-frost.co.uk, or follow her on Twitter @Kactus77, or search for Kate Frost - Author on Facebook.

A ROMANTIC ESCAPE

The Baobab Beach Retreat is the first book in a series of foreign-set romances, celebrating life and love in exotic or beautiful places.

Probable locations for future books include, Amsterdam, The Maldives, Greece, Morocco, Cornwall and Italy.

To be the first to hear about future releases, join my Readers' Club at www.kate-frost.co.uk/minetokeep.

Manufactured by Amazon.ca
Bolton, ON